THE
SEVEN
OF
DIAMONDS

Also by Max Brand
in Thorndike Large Print

The False Rider
Dead or Alive
Fightin' Fool
Trouble Trail
Speedy

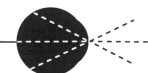

**This Large Print Book carries the
Seal of Approval of N.A.V.H.**

THE SEVEN OF DIAMONDS

MAX BRAND

Thorndike Press • Thorndike, Maine

Library of Congress Cataloging in Publication Data:

Brand, Max, 1892-1944.
The seven of diamonds / Max Brand.
    p. cm.
ISBN 1-56054-076-1 (alk. paper : lg. print)
1. Large type books. I. Title. II. Title: 7 of
diamonds.
[PS3511.A87S36   1990]   90-11278
813'.52—dc20   CIP

Thorndike Press Large Print edition published in 1990
by arrangement with G. P. Putnam's Sons.

Cover design by James B. Murray.

The tree indicium is a trademark of Thorndike Press.

This book is printed on acid-free, high opacity paper.

THE
SEVEN
OF
DIAMONDS

Chapter One

It was not the end of the desert; it was better than that; it was the point where despair ended and hope became a certainty. Through the dusty air the eye still held on a round distance to the mountains and the shadows of their gorges, but that distance was as nothing compared with the marches which lay behind his back! He halted his horse, which was trembling and feverish with desire to get at the water, and looked back to the dimly dissolving horizon, sketched not by pencil or pen, but by a brush dipped into misty colors, and running as flat as the palm of the hand. It looked like infinity.

It was, in fact, the greatest dimension which the eye of man can carry to his brain. Even a ship at sea travels in the midst of a comparatively petty circle of its own; but the eye of the traveler constantly lunges forward upon the desert and sees no end and no hope of the end.

Tirrel felt suddenly old, in the knowledge that he had come out of that vast distance.

Then he had mercy on his horse — and on himself — and let the mustang go down to the water. It was the last halting place, above surface, of a little arrowy stream out of the mountains. It ran so fast and such a short distance that it had no time to grow befouled in the desert sands, or to drink itself dark with the desert dust. Instead, it entered the head of the pool with a rush and a gurgling, and only slowly the noise and the motion disappeared toward the foot of the pool, where, indeed, the endless inflow of water was endlessly absorbed. Somewhere in that region the current was soaked into a vein of porous rock which conducted it to sightless channels of darkness and the cool beneath the surface of the earth.

The mustang was far gone. They had traveled without a taste of food, without a taste of moisture of any kind, since the night before, and it was now the most dreadful hour of the mid-afternoon. The eyes of the little horse were filmed with red and crusted around the lashes with gritty dust, so that it was a painful thing to see the balls roll in his head. He was weak, so that when he went down the slope, his forelegs trembled and shook.

He would have driven belly deep into the water, but Tirrel would not allow that. Instead, he threw the reins and dismounted a step or two from the water's edge and paused there an instant — not altogether in cruelty, but as a man willing to test again the state of perfect obedience to which he had reduced this dumb beast. And the mustang slavered but dared not move a step nearer to salvation while the master's eye was upon it.

After that, Tirrel permitted it to come a little closer, but, at first, he would not let it more than sip the water, taking small mouthfuls. When a few of those were down, he sluiced water from his hands over the legs and the belly of the horse, and dashed quantities of it straight into its face. Either because the coolness was divine, or because it was a game he understood, the mustang thrust its head forward to meet these blinding showers and cocked its ears forward and out, like the ears of a mule.

Only when he had finished ten minutes' work over the horse and had led it further up the bank to a point where the water grew more crystal clear, did Tirrel permit himself to drink. And then he drank with a stern repression of his desire, limiting himself, as he had limited his horse, to a few small swallows in the beginning, faintly smiling with a sort of iron joy as the heat and the grit and the taste of the desert was washed from his throat and his mouth. Then he bathed his face and plunged in his arms to the bared elbows —

powerful forearms they were, very lean, with the lines of muscle unbeautifully distinct and tangled and twisted into masses of strength.

After that, he permitted the horse to drink again, this time deeply, after which he picked out a pleasant spot among the willows where he could stretch out and rest and where the mustang could devour the rare treasure — green grass! He was not only thirsty, he was hungry, but when he looked around and saw neither bird nor beast near him, he blessed his belly for its fullness and banished the thought of food from his mind.

He had something else to think of. First, how soon he could resume the march to Los Cavallos. And after a careful study of his horse, and the bending of its front knees, he determined that it would be best not to go on until the cool of the evening — that is to say, not until the sun was within half an hour of setting. It meant some weary hours of starvation and pause, but again he closed a door in his mind which would contain that subject and those sensations until he chose to open it again.

Secondly, luck threw into his path another thing of interest, and that was a blur of dust across the sands. He was so excited, watching it, that he stood up, his lean face tightening with curiosity.

"Wild hosses!" Then, correcting himself, "*A* wild hoss."

He had to alter that decision, too, for presently he could make out the line of the horse below and the rider above. But this increased his wonder still more, for what species of horse was this which, bestrode by a man, was able to canter along so freely even after crossing the terrors of that desert?

It came to the water's edge with a rush, and as it came nearer, Tirrel made out a chestnut, powdered with the dust of the desert to a dirty cream color. A very tired horse was this, and spent with thirst, and with hunger, and with labor, but still it could canter with head high and with eye undimmed. It was tucked up with famine. A handful of starvation had been hollowed out of either flank, but still the bearing of the mare was queenly; and, since men see more the spirit than the flesh, if they are wise, Tirrel stood up straight beside his tree and admired with all his heart.

He was, as it chanced, perfectly screened from the view of the stranger; and the mustang, also, was grazing just from sight beyond a hummock, so that Tirrel was able to observe the newcomer and all his actions.

Those actions, he was pleased to note, were practically identical with his own. In the same manner the stranger checked his mare at the

11

edge of the water, and in the same manner gave her gradually to drink. But with him, the operation was far more condensed, as though he knew that his animal was of a temper which could not be spoiled by a little over indulgence. Indeed, there was a certain daintiness about her manner, even when she first thrust her muzzle into the stream; and, after the first draught, she jerked her head high and stared straight across the water toward Tirrel. Her master, noticing this, like a hunter whose dog has pointed out game, actually drew a six-shooter — one of a pair which hung low down on his thighs — and looked in the same direction. But Tirrel said nothing, did not stir. He was excited more and more by the beauty and by the intelligence of the mare.

"It's all right, Molly," said her master. "Go ahead and drink your belly full."

But Molly was of another mind. She would not taste the water again, but with large, starry eyes, she stared fixedly toward the spot where the stranger was hidden. Her eye could hardly have seen him, but she might have seen a stir of the foliage of the willow; or else scent or the seventh sense with which some horses are gifted had pointed out the danger mark to her. At any rate Tirrel, his heart beating fast, said to himself that never before had he seen such a companion for a man, whether for mountain or for desert. Her leanness exhibited all the more clearly the perfection of her beauty. She was not covered with sleek lines of fat, obscuring her powers, but the great length of her muscles and the lines of her bones and the neat manner in which her head was fitted onto her neck were all exhibited to Tirrel's wise eye.

He gave the master a similar regard. He was himself of the true desert breed, and this stranger was just such another, tall, spare, strong as a cat, with a face the color of mahogany, and with bushy eyebrows, sun-faded until they were almost white. He was equipped in all respects like one who knows his own value and will not fit himself out with poor tools. His spurs, for instance, had the proper spoon-handle curve and glimmered like spots of fire. Golden spurs! And his saddle, the make and fit of the pack behind it, the polished metal work on the bridle, the fashion of the long, slant holster which contained his Winchester were all to the exact taste of Tirrel. He told himself that he never yet had seen a better appointed cavalier of the desert!

The mare, in the meantime, not only refused to taste the water again — though she was starving for it! — but now stamped, as though to enforce upon her master the fact that his attention was needed for yonder willows. And the stranger did not hesitate. He abandoned her and, circling the little pool, went straight up toward the spot where Tirrel was hidden. The latter chuckled in his leafy screen.

"That's not true Injun style, partner," said Tirrel from his place of concealment.

The other halted, but he answered, unconcerned:

"They don't usually take scalps in this neck of the woods."

Tirrel stepped out into the open — as ragged and unkempt a figure as the other was trim — and submitted himself to the gaze of the stranger.

"It's all right, Molly," said the latter, and Molly dipped her head to the water again.

"She's something extra," observed Tirrel.

"You like her, eh?"

"I like her."

"So do I," said the other. He added with a faint smile: "I reckon that we ain't the only two, either."

"I reckon," replied Tirrel gravely. Then he added: "Set down and rest your feet. Make yourself at home. But I can't offer you any chuck."

"Nor me, neither," was the reply.

"I seen that your belt was up two notches. At that, two notches is better than three."

14

The other nodded, returned to his horse, stripped the saddle from her, and turned her free to graze. Tired as she must have been, she celebrated her freedom by frolicking for a moment with high flung heels. Then she dashed into the water and swam straight across, coming out on the shore again a blindingly bright copper horse. After that she went to grazing.

"She's blue grass," suggested Tirrel. "Dust ain't to her taste!"

Chapter Two

During this time the two men had been watching each other with a great deal of care and with the manner of two connoisseurs; and each thought that never in his life had he had the pleasure of looking upon a more manly figure or one better fitted to all the problems and the trials of desert or mountain life.

They sat down together in the shade and rolled cigarettes instead of cooking a dinner. The last remark of Tirrel had caused the eye of the other to kindle.

"You know hosses," he declared.

Tirrel indicated his own lump-headed mustang with a smile.

"See for yourself," said he.

The other gave a fleeting glance. He replied gravely that it was one thing to take a machine like Molly across the desert, and it was another to bring such a caricature as the mustang through.

"He's only one pack to carry, though," explained Tirrel. "He ain't got any extra freight in the way of ideas to pack along with him."

The stranger smiled — a faint, quickly vanishing smile like that of Tirrel himself.

"Molly has her own ideas," he agreed, "and mostly they're good ones. She knows the smell of an Indian or a greaser as well as I know the sight of 'em. I'd rather trust her by night than trust the best scout that ever wore moccasins. How long were you coming across?"

"Five days. And you?"

"Four."

"Ay," sighed Tirrel, "the chestnut could do it!"

He lapsed into a silence, and, since the other was by no means over talkative, fully ten minutes went drifting past them, unregarded. Emboldened by that silence, a great buck jack rabbit appeared from among the trees and went down toward the edge of the water. He was not a type of the plains rabbit, which usually is a set of four strong feet, a fluff of thin hair, and a scanty stringing of leathery muscles. This fellow was fat with good living and little running. And now he had been tempted from his place, as it appeared, to feed on certain pale green weeds crisp as lettuce at the verge of the water.

He barely had tasted them when the two watchers were sitting erect, each with a revolver in his hand. "You take him!" said Tirrel with a gesture. The other did not wait for a second invitation; but, as though he realized that this was not so much an invitation as a challenge, he did not pause to take careful aim but tried a snapshot. The distance was over twenty paces, and it was no wonder that he missed. However, his bullet knocked up the dirt beneath the belly of the rabbit and sent it whirling about and darting back for cover with a faint shriek of fear and haste. It had the briefest of margins to cover, and a jack rabbit, as desert dwellers know, is a little faster than chain lightning.

But Tirrel was not in haste. He, also, did not take aim but allowed the muzzle of his Colt to swing with the progress of the rabbit for as much as half a second. Then he fired, and the rabbit leaped into a bush and hung there.

The front end of his head had been blown away, they found; and straightway they set about cleaning that rabbit and preparing the fire which was to receive him in due course. Tirrel managed the rabbit; the stranger took care of the fire in masterly fashion, building it small but hot of little dry twigs which he selected with care. The smoke from that blaze would hardly be visible half a mile away, and even then only to a practiced eye that knew what to look for. Tirrel took good note of that.

He noted, also, that the manner of the other had grown a trifle thoughtful, and he understood very well why. It was the same reason that had banished from his own mind all envy of the owner of good clothes, fine saddle, perfect weapons, glorious horse. For what were all these properties compared with the ability to shoot swiftly and to shoot straight? A hard man and a strong man was this master of the mare, but just a significant trifle harder and stronger, perhaps, was Tirrel himself. They could have passed, so like were they, for brothers, or cousins at least; but Tirrel, let us say, was the elder brother, the senior of that blood. Not that he would have showed the slightest sign of superiority, for that was not his way, and, moreover, the fortunes of the marksman are bound to vary. Nevertheless, it had been a significant straw, telling how the wind blew, and for that reason he was quietly warm about the heart and could more easily restrain his appetite until the rabbit was properly roasted.

Each man took his half of the prey, cut it up in an identical manner, and then toasted the bits on splinters. And neither of them hurried. Tirrel, covertly critical, waited expectantly for the other to bury his teeth in the meat while it was half raw, but he noted with increasing admiration that the stranger did not touch it until it was thoroughly roasted to the bone, and crusted over with appetizing brown. Indeed, at the very moment when Tirrel raised his first portion to his lips, he observed that the stranger was swallowing his own first morsel.

Neither did they eat with too great speed, but carefully, almost daintily, picking each bone in its turn. For, after all, though the rabbit was a big and fat one, their fast had been long, and a bolted meal is not half so sustaining as a leisurely one.

So the rabbit was ended. They rose with one accord and washed their hands in the water. They returned, sat down, and at one instant finished rolling their smokes, at one instant lighted them, at one instant leaned back with sighs of satisfaction. Undoubtedly there was a peculiar harmony between their natures.

"You bound for the mines above Cavallos?" asked the stranger.

"I dunno," said Tirrel. "I'm just up to see the town."

"You never been there before?"

"No. Have you?"

"Oh, I been there."

"How does a gent steer there?"

"Wilson runs a square faro game, if that's what you buck."

"Faro ain't my speed. Chuck-a-luck or poker suits my turn."

"Chuck-a-luck is fast enough. You can get that at Wilson's too. But the best poker is Strangham's dive."

"Square, too?"

"About as square as you ever get it. There's a cold pack now and then."

"Ay," sighed Tirrel, "there's always a cold pack being rung in." He explained his gloom quietly: "Gambling is my fun; it ain't my business."

The other nodded.

"We could play a few hands for fun," said he, "with matches for chips. We got a long distance to sundown, and I don't aim to bring Molly under the saddle again till the cool of the day."

He produced a small-sized pack of cards as he spoke, and, Tirrel agreeing with a good deal of pleasure, they began to play on a saddle blanket, sitting cross-legged. The matches at once began to pass into the possession of the stranger.

"I'll have to be borrowing a light from you before we start for Los Cavallos," said Tirrel.

"If mining ain't your game," advised the other, "you ain't gunna find any very soft bunk in Los Cavallos. The greasers have got most of the work on the range."

Tirrel paused, shuffling the cards.

"It ain't so much work that I'm after," he confessed, "I'm looking for a gent, up there."

"What sort of a frame does he set in?" asked the other. "I know some of the gents around Los Cavallos."

"My kid brother," said Tirrel, "was floating around in Los Cavallos with a wad of money that he'd picked up working out a claim in the mountains north of the town. And a gent picked him up and trimmed him. At poker."

"Trimmed him?"

"It was one of them cold packs you was speaking about."

"And?"

"Aw, the kid is game," said Tirrel. "There never stepped a gamer one. But he's been more interested in his chippin' hammer and his single jack than in handling guns. This gent beat him to the draw."

The other waited.

"Bullet sliced along the bone of his right forearm," said Tirrel. "I dunno how good his arm will ever be agin. Neither does the doctor."

"How long ago?"

"Ten days today."

"And what become of the kid?"

"Why, what could he do with a slug through his arm? He tried a pass at this gent with his left hand, but the crook was cool and quick. He could of shot the kid dead, but he didn't. He just slapped him alongside the head with the barrel of his six-shooter and laid him out cold. The kid woke up broke, with a bad arm and a cracked head. Somebody gathered him up and put him in a bunk. He wrote me a letter by dictation."

"Hard luck," commented the stranger, "but a damn sight harder to of got a slug through his head or his heart, eh?"

"I figger it that way," said Tirrel mildly. "I ain't too hot about it. Only, I'm sort of curious. I'd sort of like to meet up with that gent. I suppose that I'd have to start in by thankin' him, but after that I'd have to branch out a mite and ask him a few little questions."

At this, the other smiled, his faint, disappearing smile.

"What manner of a lookin' man was the crook?" he inquired with a good deal of interest.

"Why, easy to spot, I'd say. A broadish built kind of a gent and good lookin', and rangy built, and with a nick chopped out of the center of his chin, as though somebody's knife had made a pass at him there and clipped him down to the bone."

At this, the stranger looked quickly down. It seemed to Tirrel that there was a slight

23

glimmer in his eye which he wished to cover, but, for that matter, it might have been merely the first intensity of thought. However, the suspicions of Tirrel were sufficiently aroused to make him eye the other with the most wolfish care.

"You ever hear of that fellow?" he asked.

"I gotta think," said the other, and looked not ahead toward Los Cavallos, but back across the tainted air of the endless desert.

Chapter Three

It was very hot. It was the very hottest part of the mid-afternoon. East and south the desert was an intolerable glare, except for one dull streak of greasewood; and from the north a range of porphyry hills, misty red, stood down toward the level plain. Over this hot wilderness, tempered and shaded by the yellowish desert air, the stranger now stared with a fixed gaze, as of one who searches through his mind, anxiously, and cannot quite find what he wants.

"It sounds sort of familiar," said he. "It sounds like I'd met up with just such a man, some time or other, but I gotta think."

"Take your time," urged Tirrel. "Don't go feedin' your memory the whip and the spur, because that's the best way to make your wits balk. Play another hand and let the thing drop. First thing you know, you'll remember. You'll see his face and his name come poppin' around the corner!"

The other nodded.

"A brain is a funny damn thing," he agreed.

And he gathered up his hand from the blanket.

He drew two cards and chucked them down.

"The book says draw to an inside straight, but I never got any fat on my ribs that way," he declared, "have you?"

"No, never. Book sense ain't much card sense."

"I can't place that gent yet," said the other. "But maybe I will later. And maybe I never did know such a man. I tell you what: They's a lot of things that we think that we can remember that we never knowed at all!"

"That's too damn true to be funny. Take the desert, for instance!"

"Ay, take the desert."

They looked at each other and sighed in unison once more.

"I've ate my share of sand," said Tirrel.

"I've breathed my ton of dust," said the stranger. "Gimme the cards! Let's make it stud."

That was a lucky deal for Tirrel. It seemed that the cards could not serve him a bad turn. Aces and pairs of face cards fell regularly to his portion, and the pile of matches shifted gradually, then rapidly, to his side of the blanket.

The other, who had played with the most

perfect good humor up to this point, now showed growing signs of irritation.

"A poor loser!" said Tirrel to himself, and instantly two-thirds of his respect for the other disappeared.

"Look here," said the stranger suddenly, some of his irritation getting into his voice in spite of himself, "suppose we make it a real game? I'm tired of the damn matches!"

"I've got four dollars and a quarter," said Tirrel coldly.

"Well," exclaimed the other, "for that matter, you could walk to Los Cavallos, couldn't you?"

Tirrel hesitated. Then he nodded suddenly. "Make it a go," said he. And the money play began.

But the tide of luck on which he had ridden into this game continued. Two rounds of stud put him two hundred dollars in pocket, and the irritation of the stranger was trebled.

"That's all the money I got," he said, "but I'll stake my clothes. They're worth at least a hundred and fifty."

They played the hand, and the stranger won; but immediately afterwards, when he doubled the stake, declaring that his luck was in, he lost. He stripped off the clothes at once and put on those which Tirrel discarded.

"I hate this business," declared Tirrel.

"But you've insisted on it. Doggone me if I wanted to do it. I suppose that you're satisfied now?"

"Hold on," said the gambler and he took a slip of paper out of his pocket. "I got a diamond stick pin hocked in Los Cavallos. Look here — there's a pair of big diamonds in it. That pin is worth fifteen hundred if it's worth a penny. I hocked it for five hundred. That shows you what it's really worth! Well, I'll put that pin and my guns and saddle against everything that you've won!"

"Clothes and all?"

"Clothes and all."

Tirrel hesitated.

"Partner," he said persuasively, "it looks like my luck is in and your luck is out. It's about time to start on for the town. What I say is that we ought to call this game off now."

"I don't like to say that you want to quit because you're winning!" was the reply, and Tirrel flushed.

"All right," said he. "And I wish you luck. Nothing I'd like better than to get clear of all of this stuff of yours. By God, stranger, I don't think I ever won as much as twenty dollars before today!"

They played straight poker, and Tirrel, holding a pair of treys, miraculously drew two more. The stranger threw down the cards with an oath.

"Such damned luck I never seen in my whole life," he said, and studied the other seriously.

"It has me beat," said Tirrel. "I don't understand it at all. Is that the end of it, partner?"

He stared at Tirrel, he looked across the desert, and then slowly his face flushed, then he grew pale.

He said in a trembling voice: "There's Molly Malone!"

Tirrel gaped.

"You ain't meaning the mare, man?" he answered with a touch of romantic reverence.

"Molly!" called the owner.

She came like a dog to his voice and sniffed fearlessly at the hand which he held out to her.

"What about her?" he asked.

"I dunno," breathed Tirrel. "I dunno what to think. Man," he burst out, "if I had a hoss like that there ain't cards printed that would be good enough for me to gamble for her. Not agin a million dollars!"

"There's other hosses," said the other.

He said it sullenly, as though admitting the temptation grudgingly into his mind. Tirrel argued bitterly with himself. It would be, he felt, a simple thing to urge this fellow on to the game. And, if God gave him the chance to have the fine mare once between his knees —

But though Michael Tirrel had not gone through his life with hands altogether clean, he was at heart an honest man. And honesty conquered him now.

He stood up and laid his hand on the shoulder of the mare. Perfectly made, at a little distance she looked smaller. Perhaps it was because of the depth of her body at the girth and the comparative shortness of her forelegs. But now he saw that she was at least sixteen hands or an inch more.

"She could carry a ton," thought Tirrel aloud.

"And never stumble," said her owner.

She turned her head to his voice. Then she looked back at Tirrel and nipped at the sleeve of his newly acquired coat, as though she were trying to pick from him this borrowed plumage.

"How old is she?"

"She's goin' onto six."

"She's in her prime!"

"She is that. She's comin' into her prime."

"Man, man," cried Tirrel, "where would you get another like her?"

"Why, there's other hosses in the world!" said her owner, flushing again.

He began to snap his fingers nervously and Tirrel said: "I'll tell you what: There's other hosses. There's mustang, and there's race hoss. But a mustang can't run; and a race hoss can't stay — not on thistles! She? She's come through the desert like a daisy. Four days did you say?"

"Four days even."

"She'd get fat on sawdust and sand," declared Tirrel, his heart warming. "Man, man, you're a fool if you risk her!"

The other began to snap his fingers, nervously.

"I'll split her in four parts. We'll play it off. The sky's the limit."

"I've warned you!" said Tirrel harshly.

"Damn your warnings. Your luck can't last forever!"

They split up the chips and the game began again — the mare against all the holdings of Tirrel. "And damn cheap at that!" said her owner.

The very first hand he won. His delight was limitless. He won the second, also, with a pair of kings over a pair of jacks in which Tirrel had invested a hundred dollars.

After that, his confidence increased enormously, and Tirrel settled himself for a long and losing game. He could not say no. At that very moment, however, his losses ended.

Three fours were dealt to him on the very next hand and the betting went to five hundred dollars. The stranger, being called, laid down a pair of queens. Tirrel stared at him.

"You got your nerve!" said he.

The other eyed the ground with a curse.

"I thought my luck was in at last!" said he.

He dealt, flicking out the cards with a fluid ease, and so swiftly that each was merely a spinning disk of color as it flashed from the tips of his fingers. Such dealing Tirrel had known before — in professional gambling houses.

His own pick up, on this occasion, was a lonely pair of nines, and the other instantly bet fifty dollars before the draw. He hesitated. The two nines were not worth it, but he felt that it was his sporting duty to play as the other would. So he bet his fifty and drew three — with a nine among them!

"Five hundred!" said Tirrel quietly.

There was a strange quality about the other man. No matter what emotion he might show before or after a hand, during the playing of it his face was a mask, and with a calm glance he would lay his bets. Now, however, a strange gleam passed into his eye — a keen and devilish look, as it seemed to Tirrel.

"Five hundred?" he queried. "Let's see what stuff you're made of, partner!" And he pushed into the center of the blanket the remainder of his matches. They did not represent money; to Tirrel they meant something more; they meant Molly Malone, who stood near by, grazing, and now and again lifting her head and looking upon them and their game with understanding gentleness, until it almost seemed that she pitied these poor mortals and their absorption in such a triviality as this! She pitied them, but she was fond of them, and Tirrel breathed deeply as he looked at the lovely chestnut. Equal beauty he had seen before, perhaps, but never had there been such an electric speaking to his very heart.

He looked back at the cards. Three nines were very strong, and the dealer had drawn three cards. Three nines were very strong indeed. It was easy to remember what three fours had done not long before!

And then, setting his teeth, he began to count out matches. It enormously depleted his stock but he called the dealer, and the latter burst into a loud, ironic laughter.

"My lucky hand. They can't lose for me," he cried. "No, by God, they can't lose for me. Look at 'em, my boy! Three beauties! Three little ol' sevens — "

He laid them on the blanket and Tirrel bowed his head above them for an instant. Now that such good fortune had declared for him, he hardly could believe in it. He had won, and Molly Malone was his.

He put his three nines on the blanket and looked the other steadily in the face. One never could tell. Guns were handy, and one bullet, in such circumstances, will wipe out the largest of debts.

"It ain't possible!" said the stranger.

A puff of wind came and they hastily covered the cards, but it snatched at the dealer's discard, which he had tossed a bit to one side, and rattled them off through the willows and away in the arms of the air.

However, the cards that counted remained — the three sevens of the stranger, and the winner's nines. The former glared at Tirrel with a wolfish curling of his lip, but almost instantly he mastered this cold fit of rage and jumped to his feet.

"I'll have to borrow a gun from you, old son," said he, "because I'll hate to ride into Los Cavallos all alone!"

Chapter Four

It was high time to make the start. The sun was now a broad red image on the horizon line, with cheeks puffed out foolishly; as Michael Tirrel stood at the side of Molly Malone.

"Are you riding in with me?" he asked.

"On that humpbacked son of nothin?" asked the other, pointing in disgust at the bronco.

In fact, the mustang had not recovered so quickly as might have been hoped from the violence of the labor which he had performed, and now he stood with a slumped shoulder, a pendent lip, and a half closed eye, like the very picture of exhaustion and depression.

"He'll go it, well enough," said Tirrel. "I know him. He's a mean devil. Too mean to ever get as tired as all that! He'll take you in in fine shape!"

"Son," said the other sharply, "you're a bright kid, and you know a whole lot about everything, includin' hosses. But lemme foller my own ways, will you? I'm gunna wait until the night wind wakes up, and the cool of it'll blow us back toward Los Cavallos!"

To this speech, Tirrel returned no answer, but mounted Molly Malone and urged her forward. She went willingly enough until she was a little distance beyond the willows, but then she paused, her head turned back toward her deserted master. Tirrel spoke to her gently, and with a shake of the head, as though trying to dismiss a wonder which she could not understand, the mare went on again. Almost immediately her ears were pricking eagerly forward on the trail, and Tirrel smiled, with a very light heart indeed.

He had lived a life which had taught him the peculiar value of a fine animal, and the very first flash of the mare showed a character as perfect as her conformation. It was as though he had gained the use of wings, in having her. Moreover, she was a companion on the way.

He was a good half mile from the willows when the wind, of which there had been a taste and a puff during the card game, whistled over the sands again and blew up before Tirrel a pair of the very cards which had blown away — the discard of the other.

He smiled at them, twinkling in the air, and now high above his head. They fluttered, failed in the air, were caught up again and spun far off. Tirrel followed them at a brisk canter, for he was naturally curious to see them. They dallied in the current of the wind, rose, fell, and flicked away again as though possessed with life; and Tirrel, beginning to laugh at this odd game, cantered the mare on.

She was as keen as a hunting dog. Instantly she realized what he was after, and she followed the cards without touch of the reins, dodging as they dodged, truly tracking them. Tirrel, his heart touched with pleasure, patted her neck, and a moment later, as the wind fell, he actually caught one of the two cards out of the air. It was the seven of diamonds.

He looked at it again. He turned it to make sure that the pattern of its back actually was the same as that of the pack which the stranger had dealt. There was no doubt that it was identical.

It simply meant that the other, discarding from a pair of sevens, had cast away sevens, had cast away a third. And since he had picked another from the pack, his real power should have been four sevens; and of course a ridiculously simple win over three nines!

It has been said that Tirrel was an honest man, and he was on the point of turning back to the willows and telling the gambler that a strange devil had blinded him to one of his cards, but then he knew, by the first after thought, that this could not have been the case. Men do not readily overlook cards in such a manner as this, and above all that quietly collected gamester was not apt to have thrown away a chance.

However, if it were considered that he had done the thing on purpose, it was the act of a madman.

And yet here again, it seemed to Tirrel that this wanderer over the face of the desert was as far from a mentally unsound man as any person he ever had met. He could not have conceived a more matter-of-fact and keen minded fellow.

If it was not carelessness or madness, then what was the impulse which had caused the other to lose deliberately.

With Molly Malone at a halt, sweat pouring down his face, Michael Tirrel turned the matter back and forth through his mind, deeply at a loss.

As he looked back over the rest of the game, he could see a certain oddity in the manner in which he had won so rapidly from the very beginning. Wealth suddenly had flowed into his pockets. Suppose, then, that the smooth dealing of the stranger had been something more than an elegant accomplishment and really was the token of an expert who was handling the cards expressly so that he might lose?

The idea maddened Tirrel, for the reason that he could not possibly fathom the significance of the action. The longer he thought of it, the surer he became. The owner of Molly Malone deliberately had lost to him first his money, then his watch and clothes, and, last of all, the priceless mare herself!

He turned her head, ready to sweep back toward the willows and confront the other with questions, but he could have answered for the stranger before hand. Oaths and violent protestations and huge damnings would be the reply.

So he sent Molly Malone on for Los Cavallos again, shaking his head, and bitterly in doubt.

It seemed perfectly clear that, if the other had lost all these things of price on purpose, he had some gravely sinister purpose in mind. But what?

Moreover, why should he choose Tirrel for a victim?

The latter, looking through the years of his life, tried to recall a meeting in the past with this same man. But he could not. To be sure, the stranger, like Tirrel himself, belonged to a class most common upon the desert, where one fellow in three, at least, is apt to be tall, lean, wide-shouldered, sun-blackened, and with sun-faded eyebrows. However, there is a touch of quality about some men which speaks with a peculiar strength, and the man of the case, as Tirrel felt, was an excellent type of the exceptional. Once met, it would not be very easy to forget him.

No, they never had met in the past. They had met in the desert casually and naturally enough. And yet, as he glanced back upon the affair, it was almost as though he had been pursued and overtaken on purpose by the stranger, who wished to endow him with horse, saddle, and clothes and send him on his way.

Again, what could the purpose be?

But the marvel of the adventure and the light step of Molly Malone beneath him both helped, now, to banish all care from his mind. He rode gaily on, and began to take note of what lay around him. He was drawing fast toward the hills among which Los Cavallos lay.

Chapter Five

He rode through the beauty of the evening and under the desert stars into the hills themselves, following up a narrow cañon which, in time, widened into a comfortable valley, and this rose to a tumble of hills. He went to the top of one of these and saw the lights of Los Cavallos for the first time. Molly Malone saw them, also, and kept well up on the bridle from that moment forward. Half an hour later they were in the town.

It was very old and very Spanish. It had been built in a time when defense against the Indians was a great item in the selection of a town site, in those days before breech-loading rifles, when clumsy muskets and pikes had to be used against the shower of Indian arrows. So Los Cavallos was built upon a broad-backed hill, and a wall was drawn about it. That wall, long useless, was still intact, still kept white with a new coat of wash every year, so that, even in the starlight, Los Cavallos appeared first to Tirrel as a pleasant village surrounded by a shining girdle.

He entered narrow, winding streets, with a medieval aspect of charming irregularity. Once he could have stretched out his arms and touched a wall on either side. These walls, without exception, were built of adobe, which time had settled so that there were few sharp edges left; but the whole place had rather a battered and hand-made appearance.

It made Tirrel feel greatly at home, for he spoke Spanish like a native, and the odor of Mexican cookery which drifted out to him from open doors and windows made his mouth water. He was glad when an elbow-turning of the street brought him sharply before a hotel. He did not wait to ask if this were the best. The line of horses tethered at the hitching rack answered his question before it could be spoken, and there was a stir of comfortable life about the place.

So he entered into the court around which the old building was distributed. A waiting *mozo* would have taken the mare to the stable, but this he would not allow. He would rather have let a stranger clean his guns for him, when a battle was in prospect!

So he was allowed to conduct Molly back to the stable, and there he found for her, luckily, a fine roomy box stall with two high-laced windows which would give her plenty of air without a draft. He looked narrowly into the quality of the hay that was pitched from the mow into her manger, but it was good, clean wild-oat hay and excellent barley was poured into her feed box. Then, as she ate, her new master rubbed her down thoroughly.

He wanted to let her have a two- or three-day period of utter rest, for that, he felt, would restore to her her former strength. As for her spirit, it could not have been improved upon, and when he left the stall, hungry as she was, she turned from her food and whinnied softly after him.

He, delighted, hung in the doorway, brooding fondly over her. He had had his ups and his downs of fortune, but never had he possessed such a treasure as this one.

The Mexican boy lingered near by, also. Through the windows came just enough glooming light to enable a keen eye to make out the lines of the mare, and the boy murmured in admiration:

"*That* is a queen, señor."

"That," agreed he with emphasis, "is a queen."

"And is she of the señor's raising?"

"She's of my finding," said he with a grim little chuckle.

He went back into the courtyard and paused there for a moment. He was very hungry. His portion of rabbit, that day, had done no more than emphasize the famine that was in him. But there were other things than food to enjoy in this town and in this courtyard. There was, in the first place, the sound of water, for the hotel was blessed with a natural spring which bubbled up in the center of the court and trickled away with a soft murmuring through a paved bed.

The lights of the hotel gleamed upon that moving stream; the air was cooled by the very sound of it; and all the earth was so moistened by its seepage that, no doubt, this explained the great size of the wisteria vine which grew up the side of the old building. It was a vast tree, rather than a mere vine. Its huge and twisted trunks clambered up almost to the top of the second and highest story before they began to pour forth foliage, but, once begun, this leafage was extraordinarily profuse. It climbed totally across two sides of the court and poured down a constant shower of bright yellow green, so that tendrils were constantly waving back and forth across the windows.

Such vegetation and the delicious sound of water, entering the soul of the wanderer from the desert, marched deep within him; he enjoyed it deliberately and slowly before he entered the building.

It was just such a place as he had imagined

from the outside. The walls were so thick that every window seemed set in an alcove; and the heat of the day had been excluded so success- fully that already there was an evening cool- ness through the hotel. An old Mexican with a white goat's-beard officiated as host, took his name upon the register, and led him up to a pleasant room. There his pack was brought and he was in the midst of the washing-up process when his host returned in some haste, profoundly apologetic. It appeared that this room had been reserved for another guest, but Tirrel could be accommodated even better in another room.

The new room to which Tirrel went was, in fact, twice as commodious as the former. It was planned for more than one guest, a big double bed standing in one corner and a single bed opposite. And the only criticism might be that, instead of a view of the plaza of Los Cavallos, it looked out upon an adjoining roof from its window. However, Tirrel had had enough of large prospects on the desert and he was very glad to settle into such spacious com- fort as this.

Having finished his washing, he tried the double bed with his fist. His very bones ached expectantly at its deep softness, and he went down to dinner loosening his belt in prepara- tion for a feast.

It was such a meal as he had dreamed of. He was late; there was only one other table in the big dining room occupied, and that by a single man. So, undisturbed, he loosed his fancies and ordered soup, a green salad, roast chicken, a steak with three eggs on top of it, French fried potatoes, enchiladas, Spanish beans, hotter than fire, apple pie — two vast wedges — and four large cups of blackest coffee.

When he rose from that prodigious meal, it was quite late. He was stuffed like an anaconda, and he was rather surprised to see that the second guest was still at his meal, eating fruit and drinking Mexican wine. A blond fellow was this, but something in the cut of his mustaches and above all in the whites of his eyes made Tirrel know that the man was a Mexican. He felt the head of the Mexican rise, as he went by, and the curious, steady eyes look after him.

So greatly and thoroughly was Tirrel sufficed by his food that he paid little heed; only, at the door, he turned enough to cast another glance back, and then he was aware of the eyes of the stranger looking after him — eyes of pale, clouded blue, like agate.

He went out into the plaza. The band of Los Cavallos was playing in the center of it, the music straying out through a bower of greenery; and around the square, true Mexi-

46

can style, strolled the people, the women keeping to one path and the young men to another, running around in opposite directions, so that at every round of the plaza expectant lovers could have one keen, fervent glance at one another.

Tirrel did not want to walk. He stretched himself at ease upon a comfortable bench and lighted a cigarette; then he began to smoke with a deliberate enjoyment. He could have remained there for half a day, in that humor, and it would have been impossible to repeat all the things that drifted into his mind. His thoughts came slowly and in a constant succession, each blowing softly up above the horizon of his mind and slowly traversing his thoughts, to be followed by another, and another. Mere physical sensations occupied a vast proportion of his attention. Sometimes it was only the cool showering of the plaza fountain that he observed, noting that at times it was a far off whispering, and again it bubbled and rattled musically at his very ear. And as the fountain loomed in his mind, he would take heed of the lights from the surrounding houses which were entangled in the falling web of spray, sometimes a sharp ray, passing through like a knife, and sometimes a dispersed radiance, dissolved to a moonlight nothingness.

So it was with the crowd. Now he would be aware of the whole movement, and of the colors, and of the black mantillas, and of the gait and rhythm of the mass. Again he would open his eyes to the individual faces, photographing them in a happy haze of content. The burn of the desert was still in his skin, and only gradually a healing coolness possessed him; it seemed to him that these happy idlers never could have felt the sun!

Indeed, to Tirrel, all was flowerlike and charming about Los Cavallos. Most Western towns in the States are so young that they carry their raw, overweening aspirations with them; they intrude their ideas upon the mind, like newly graduated college boys: but Los Cavallos was more gently subdued, for she had seen many generations and, like middle age, she knew her limitations and was willing to make the most of them and give what she could of pleasure, and take what she could of enjoyment.

One could not say that there was nothing but the hum of sleepy voices and the cool showering of the fountain, however. Now and then Tirrel heard an angry voice raised in dispute, and now up the walk which led past him he saw two caballeros who were evidently a little too filled with tequila. They were arguing with sullen anger. Just opposite to Tirrel they paused and their voices were raised, so that several faces turned toward them with a flash of eyes and teeth, from the current of pedestrians. The blow came unexpectedly, however. He who was nearest to Tirrel received it and staggered far back, while the aggressor, following with a tigerish lunge, struck again. This time it was not with an empty hand, and Tirrel saw the wink of the knife as it cut through a meager ray of lamplight.

Now most of us are so accustomed to turning all our ideas into words that we gasp first, speak afterward, and only in the third place act; but Tirrel had been long in the wilderness, in the years of his life, and therefore the flash of the knife made his hand react with an instinctive speed — as the smell of cat makes a dog show its teeth. So into Tirrel's fingers came his six-shooter and at the same time he saw the knife miss its victim and drive straight down at his own throat.

He could have pulled the trigger, but instead he threw up the gun, and the long, heavy barrel struck the knife hand at the wrist and unlocked the fingers and allowed the knife itself to fall with a light tingle to the ground.

He sat, then, with his foot on the knife, and his gun on his knee, unalarmed, but watchful, while from the crowd came voices of alarm and the frightened cry of a girl like the peal of a little silver bell.

The two Mexicans were equally apologetic, as though they had, in that instant, realized the dreadful crime which was almost committed.

"It is nothing, *amigos*," said Tirrel. "The knife of a friend has no edge!"

They bowed to him. They took off their hats and bowed again. A policeman appeared, but no one had a charge to make, and the pair went off together, elbow by elbow.

Tirrel, looking after them, wondered at the steady straightness with which they walked, but then the shock of danger is often like a clean wind to blow away the clouds of alcohol and show the mind the true world again. He waited until the little crowd which had gathered dispersed, and then he leaned and picked up the knife which was under his foot.

Chapter Six

With the knife inside his belt, he returned to the hotel and went to his room at once. The night was still cool and pleasant in the plaza, but he was ready to sleep, he felt. He locked his door, smiling a little when he thought of the unguarded nights he had spent so often in the wilderness. But prowling wolves and bears are not like prowling men!

He laid the captured knife upon his table beneath the circle of the lamplight and examined it. It was rather like a stiletto than a hunting knife. The blade was sharpened upon both sides, to be sure, and was fully six inches long, but the steel was straight, and the bottom of the handle was guarded by a small button of metal. A fighting knife, he took it for granted, and a very deadly one. A great portion of the good humor with which he had regarded the drunken knife wielder disappeared that instant, and he would have welcomed a second meeting. That knife had too much of a professional appearance.

However, as one in the habit of dismissing the most serious matters, he put this behind him and turned promptly into bed. In one instant he was asleep and passed into a profound dream of a most singular nature. It appeared to him that he was sitting again on the bench in the plaza when the two drunkards fought before him, and that once more he saw the knife flicker past the shoulder of the staggered man. Now, staring in his vision, it appeared to Tirrel that he could see the course of the knife suspended and slowed almost to nothing in mid-air, and gradually the deadly point swerved until it was aimed at his own throat. Again, in his sleep, he threw up his revolver to ward off the stroke, but this time the gun missed its target, and the knife descended —

He wakened, sweating, hot, breathing hard, and heard a little tinkle on the floor of his room, near the door. Somehow, he could guess what had made that sound. The key had fallen!

But keys do not ordinarily fall from doors. Perhaps he had placed it in the lock inaccurately, but even then it would have required an earthquake to shake it completely loose, he thought. He slipped from his bed and went noiselessly to investigate, picking his steps one by one as he crossed the floor. Even so, the board squeaked a little beneath his weight.

He found the key at once; it had, in fact,

fallen from the lock, and he went back to sit on the edge of his bed and wonder. He returned to the door, gun in hand, unlocked it, and looked up and down the corridor outside. There was no stirring soul. It was one o'clock by his watch. All of Los Cavallos slept heartily, in appearance, and yet he had fairly complete proof that someone had tampered with his door.

He went back to the bedroom and locked the door again, again leaving the key in the lock. Two possibilities occurred to him. Men who come to town from the desert often are marked down by thieves who visit them in the night. Or again, might it not be that the worthy who had lost his knife, remembering after the confusion of the moment where it had been knocked from his hand, now had come again to trace it and put his hand upon it if he could?

At this thought, Tirrel peered upward in thought, striving to remember the face of the wielder of the knife, but he could not, in spite of himself. All he could recall was swarthiness, flashing teeth, smoky eyes. These features might be true of a hundred Mexicans.

Then, with characteristic philosophy, he went back to bed and willed himself to sleep.

When he wakened again, he found it pleasant to see the clear sunlight streaming into the room. He rose, bathed, dressed, and went down at once, in the freshness of the day, to see the chestnut mare.

She greeted him like an old friend, whinnying and pawing as though she wished to express her willingness to take the out trail once more. He smiled at her with a deep, quiet pleasure. The stable boy hung at his shoulder.

"There's been a dozen to see her, already," said he.

"Who knew her?" asked Tirrel.

"You can't hide a horse like that," said the boy, "not even in a box stall! People will hear about her and come to look! Don Pedro came out."

"Who is Don Pedro?"

"Señor!" exclaimed the boy in surprise. "Of course he is the owner of the hotel. He told me that I must take good care of the mare because she is worth many thousands of dollars. But I didn't need that telling. I have eyes in my head!"

He laughed cheerfully as he said it, and the incident slipped out of the mind of Tirrel. He saw to the feeding and cleaning of the horse, noted with pleasure that she drank well and had cleaned out her manger, and then returned to the hotel for his own breakfast. The room was well filled and with all manner of men, from wealthy mine operators to flashy

54

gamblers and roughly dressed laborers. He looked them over with satisfaction; it was the sort of world with which he was most familiar. After breakfast, he went into the patio for his cigarette and sat down on a bench beneath the trailing frail arms of the wisteria vine. The patio was a place of bustle, now — overnight guests preparing for departure, freshly saddled horses being led out, buckboards rattling off across the paving stones, and brisk, cheerful voices of farewell shouting here and there.

For his own part, he was staying on, and he relished the thought. There was the man of the clipped chin to find, but there was no hurry about that. There was his brother to see. But there was no hurry about that, either. He could go out before noon and talk everything over with the lad and learn far more than he had gathered from the letter. There was also the pawn shop to visit and the diamonds to recover — if indeed they appeared to be worth more than the five hundred dollars which the former owner of the mare said he had received for them. There was that owner in person to find again. It seemed odd to Tirrel that he had not learned the name of the stranger; but, for that matter, neither had the stranger learned his! Undoubtedly he must have arrived in the town by midnight, even mounted on the tired mustang!

While he revolved these thoughts and plans in his mind, he became aware of a stranger who had walked slowly past him, twice, and who now, catching Tirrel's eye, grinned, nodded, and sat down upon the bench, as though invited.

He was a sturdy barrel of a fellow, bandy legged, bull-necked, with his shirt open at the throat and even part of a hairy chest showing. He wore overalls, a sun-faded brown coat with heavily stuffed pockets, and a battered felt hat. He would have been taken for a vagrant in any other part of the country, but here he might well be a millionaire mine owner, about to set out on another prospecting tour. He had a very red face and keen, quick eyes. A stubble of two days flourished darkly upon his cheeks.

He rolled a cigarette, nodding and grinning companionably at Tirrel again.

"You just in?" he said.

"Yeah."

"Long trip?"

"Tolerable," said Tirrel, not inviting idle gossip.

"I seen the chestnut," said the other.

Tirrel waited for further comment.

"She looks fit," said the stranger, "but it appears to me like she's done some work. You take one of her kind, you gotta grind 'em pretty hard before they lose their guts like she's done."

"You know her, eh?" asked Tirrel curiously.

"Why," said the other, "anybody that's been raised on the range is pretty sure to know her. One look's enough to tell what she is!"

"Besides," said Tirrel, "she's been here before."

"She has," said the stranger, "I suppose she's been a good many other places, too!"

And he laughed, with an air oddly full of meaning.

Tirrel made his second cigarette and lighted it in silence. He was not attracted by his companion who, leaning closer, mumbled: "What's the name?"

Tirrel eyed him with open disapproval.

"It's all right. Tirrel, ain't it?" said the stranger. "It's all right. *I* don't talk!"

He nodded again, more confidential than ever.

"I see you don't make me out," said he.

"I don't," said Tirrel.

"I'll cut it short, then. I'm Ormond!" said he.

Chapter Seven

He said this in such a manner, rather as one who delivers a blow than one introducing himself, that sheer politeness would have forced Tirrel at least to say: "Ah?"

So he said it, and raised his brows in pretended surprise.

Ormond leaned back on the bench comfortably, at once at home.

"You wouldn't of thought it, I guess?"

"No, I wouldn't."

"You wouldn't of took it to be me, either?"

"I can't say that I would."

"You see how it is," said Ormond. "When I done that stretch, they put more on me than they took off!"

He laughed, his fat sides shaking.

"I oughta be able to live two weeks on my hump, if I was a camel," said Ormond. "But under the fat, I'm the same gent as always," he added, with a little touch of savagery in his tone and in his air.

"I can see that," said Tirrel.

He was not fumbling altogether in the dark, now. Ormond was a man who, at least in his own eyes and probably in the eyes of some others, was a fellow of importance. Among other things, he had recently been in the penitentiary, where he had grown fat. It was odd that he seemed to expect that Tirrel should know so much about him; his whole manner of talk was odd. But Tirrel waited, willing to postpone deductions.

Said Ormond: "You're up here for quite a spell, or passing through?"

"I dunno. I'm looking around."

"For what?"

Tirrel stared at him.

"Aw, it's all right," said Ormond, raising a hand of protest. "*I* don't want you to talk. All that I say is: If you ain't busy, I got a job on."

"What sort?"

"What would my sort be?" demanded Ormond.

Again Tirrel chose to be silent.

"Something fat, old-timer!" insisted Ormond.

Suddenly Tirrel touched his arm.

"Are you sure you know me?" he asked and looked straight into the face of the other.

Doubt whirled like a cloud in the eyes of his companion, for a moment. Then he drew a little away.

59

"Look here," said he, "I dunno that you get me. I ain't tryin' to butt in. If you ain't known up here, you ain't known; and if my talkin' to you bothers you, I'm done. I got the name, all right. Tirrel, wasn't it?"

It was perfectly plain that he mistook Tirrel for some other identity, merely wearing a new name. It would probably be difficult to dissuade him of the conception.

"You don't bother me," said Tirrel.

"The job I spoke about is fat *and* sweet," said Ormond. "But I need another hand. I need somebody with guts. You see how it is? I see you; of course I'd like to have you with me!"

"Thanks," said Tirrel, more and more amused, though he felt that he might be walking on dangerous ground.

"And what you feel about it? I can tell you what we got a chance of cleaning up. I'll give you the low down on — "

"Hold on," said Tirrel, raising his hand against a secret of which he could not take advantage. "Fact is, I'm busy, up here."

"Ah?" sighed the other.

"Yeah."

"You couldn't catch on — just for a couple a days?"

"I got my hands full, I think," said Tirrel.

"You're sure?"

"Yeah."

"Well — there's the end of *that* rope. And damn my luck, anyway! When I seen you, I thought I as good as had fifty thousand in my pocket!"

He paused an instant, to see if this fat bait might make the other rise, but it failed. Tirrel shook his head decisively.

"Let her go, then," said Ormond. "But maybe we can tie up on some other deal, one day. You got nothing agin me, old-timer?"

"Nothing in the world!"

"I'm glad of that. I'll just sashay out and grab another partner, if I can."

He nodded at Tirrel and left him. The latter, having finished his smoke, went slowly on to the stable and saddled the mare, not to give her a ride of any distance, but merely for a bit of exercise. Then he went into Los Cavallos to the pawn shop, with the golden moons above the door.

In the shop, he was met by a heavily spectacled old Mexican with the softest of husky voices who took the ticket and turned it once or twice in his hands, as though uncertain whether to read it right side up or upside down.

Then he adjusted his glasses and looked through them earnestly at Tirrel. Those glasses were so very thick and the light fell so upon them from the side that it was almost as

61

though Tirrel were looking at a human being without eyes except those heavy lenses; it gave the proprietor of the shop a peculiarly owlish aspect. The first emotion of Tirrel had been sympathy and pity, such as we always feel for the aged who live in a sort of fumbling quiet, forgotten by the world. But now, instead, he was conscious of a sense of fear; the quiet of the pawnbroker was the quiet of a mousing owl!

From a drawer behind him, the old man produced a stick pin and placed it on the counter. Tirrel at once put five hundred dollars beside it, for, at the first glance, he knew that the three diamonds with which it was set were worth four times the price which had been borrowed on this security.

But, even with the money on the counter, the proprietor hesitated. He picked up the pin and turned it a little so that the light trembled like a point of fire upon the jewels.

"You've come to take this away, then?" said he.

"Yes," said Tirrel. "There's the money and — "

"But suppose that I would buy it?"

"For what price?"

"If you want to buy anything in this shop," said the other, "I can make you a price. I can make you a price to bargain on and a price to sell on. What do you want for this pin, señor?"

"I haven't decided to sell it."

"Do you love jewels, then?"

"I ain't saying that."

"Old men are apt to grow foolish," said the broker. "I see that time is creeping on me. Now, for this diamond I would pay a great deal more than it is worth, because the stones have a good color. They are not very fine and they are not very large, but their color pleases me. I take them out and look at them in the day!"

"Suppose that I put a price on — well, three thousand dollars, say?"

He suggested the figure almost with a blush, but well prepared to accept a smaller sum. Behind the thick lenses of the broker hot indignation burned up. For a moment his face fairly glowed and made him seem more softly, subtly predatory than before. He began to comb his beard with a hand like a claw.

"Three thousand dollars!" said the broker.

Then he laughed, and his laughter was the most disagreeable sound that Tirrel ever had heard.

"Three thousand dollars!" repeated the broker.

He clutched the edge of the counter and again his eyes burned at Tirrel.

"Where have you learned the prices of stones, my friend?"

"Why, I've seen some sparklers, here and there."

As he said this, Tirrel picked up the pin from the hand of the broker and dropped it into his pocket.

"One moment, señor!" said the old man.

Now the shop was divided into two portions. One, which contained the glass-topped exhibition counter, held all the small objects of value, and even in the dimness of the shop it sparkled with many gems. The other was reserved for larger articles, such as saddles and all sorts of horse wear, and guns, and household furniture which was piled in a great confusion and shut off from the smaller and busier portion of the shop by a long calico curtain. Up to this time, the shop had been very quiet, but now Tirrel thought that something stirred behind the curtain. He could not be sure. It was a mere suspicion; it was a hint of sound and movement, but he was freshly from the wilderness, where the ears are extra senses of danger.

So he had picked up the pin and stepped back toward the door. But at this moment the pawnbroker cried: "Hold on! You *do* know fine gems, señor! Why not three thousand dollars, then?"

Tirrel looked at him, and the old fellow was

64

looking in turn rather askance. It might well be that he was wrong about it, but it strongly appeared to Tirrel that the other had again that owlish fire behind his spectacles.

"The pin ain't for sale, now," said Tirrel. "So long!"

He pulled open the street door and this time he was perfectly sure that he heard a sound behind the curtain — or perhaps it was only the noise of the draft which, at that moment, poured in through the door and set a paper flapping and rustling at the rear of the shop.

"Thirty-five hundred — four thousand dollars!" said the pawnbroker.

He was trembling with emotion. Tirrel merely closed the door behind him as he stepped onto the street, but he felt a shuddering sense of relief and, to get quickly from the vicinity of the shop, he crossed the street at once with a chill settled in the small of his back!

He mounted the mare and turned down the winding alley. It was high time that he should see his brother and hear from him all of the details of the shooting scrape and the man with the nicked chin.

So he took the road from Los Cavallos into the southwestern hills, and he was instantly among groves of cool trees. He became like a boy, and he laughed to himself as he rode on.

Chapter Eight

Tirrel, passing through sunlight and shadow, let his thoughts drift in waves, before him and behind — before him to his brother as he might find him, and behind him to the other days. For Jimmy was always a burden to everyone, and to no one, naturally, as much of a burden as to his brother. Tirrel was a year over thirty and looked four years older. Jimmy was twenty-five and looked four years younger. It was not that he had not moved about in the world, but as though he had moved too fast for any time or place or person to make a legible mark upon him.

As a youngster, he had begun falling into troubles of all kinds, and Michael Tirrel was constantly at work dragging him out of the scrapes. There were infinite good intentions in Jimmy. He was kind, gentle, winning, affectionate. He was brave, too, and strong, and skilful on a trail, or with his weapons. He had many talents tucked into his brain. He could have made an excellent mathematician. He

66

knew how to tell a story. He was liked by everyone.

But, as a fly in the ointment, more than he liked anything, and more than he hated anything, he dreaded pain. Not physical pain. That he could endure most heroically, but pain of the soul he could not bear. In short, he was like a magnificent race horse, perfect in blood lines, magnificent to see, perfectly capable of walking away from nearly all other horses, but unable to stand training.

Such a horse is worthless. And Jimmy Tirrel was worthless.

Blinded though he was by a semi-paternal affection, still Michael had been the first to discover this failing in his brother. By the primitive curse, labor is pain; and because he hated pain, Jimmy Tirrel could not work; and he who will not work is damned, no matter what the size of his bank account.

Jimmy, however, had no bank account, and so he lived by drifting here and there across the face of the range. He was always finding new friends, always making new starts in life, always piling up good resolutions, always about to turn the corner to fortune. For years Michael had believed in him; gradually he had been disillusioned. But no matter how much he distrusted Jimmy, he could not lose his affection for him.

Out of those thoughts he came almost suddenly on the place to which he had secured directions in Los Cavallos. It was a log cabin, set off from the main trail on a bridle path, with a clearing around it, and the young second-growth forest scattered about it. As Tirrel came up this winding way among the trees, he saw his brother walking before the cabin, his right arm supported in a large sling.

There was a shout of greeting, a shout of welcome. In a trice their hands were gripped and Tirrel looked anxiously into the face of his younger brother. Two years had not altered him. Time had no meaning to Jimmy; he never paused for it to catch up with him. There was little to find fault with in his appearance. He had the jaw and the eye of a fighter, like his older brother. He had more ample power, too, in his wide shoulders; but perhaps there was a touch of weakness about the mouth, and the eyes were a shade too closely set.

"You've struck it rich and never let me know!" said Jimmy. "Where in the name of God did you get that mare?"

"I found her in a pack of cards," said Michael.

"You? You never won a fat pot in your life!"

"This one was a crooked deal," said Tirrel.

"What!" cried Jimmy, more astonished than ever. "Have you been learning the deck?"

"The other gent did the crooked dealing. It's too long to explain, now. Where can I put her up? Then I want to hear your yarn, Jimmy."

They put the mare in the shed behind the house. Then into the cabin they went. It contained only one room, with corners reserved for cooking, sleeping, living. Several guns were propped in a gun rack. Saddles, rusted traps, battered old clothes hung on the walls, and a picture of Lincoln with a yellow water stain obscuring half of it.

They sat down on home-made stools.

"Somebody framed the cards for you to get the mare?" said Jimmy, persistently turning back to the subject.

"Let that go. I want to know about you."

"The arm, you mean?"

"That and anything else that's worth knowing."

"Well," said the boy, "roll me a cigarette and prop your ears wide open. You've got something to listen to."

This request was complied with, and when the cigarette was lighted, Jimmy tilted hack against the wall.

"You might start with the fellow who owns this shack," said Tirrel.

69

"That's Dutch Methuen. He took me in. Kind old gent, with a heart of gold."

"Old friend of yours?"

"I'd hardly met him before I was plugged. You don't have to know Dutch a long time. He makes up his mind on the spot."

"I'd like to meet him."

"You will. He's off looking at some traps he's got sprinkled through the woods."

"What does he bag up here?"

"Nothing worth a damn. He gets a coyote now and then and collects the bounty. He gets a painter, too, once in a long time. Then there's squirrels and rabbits that clog up the traps a good deal, and a bob cat now and again. That's about all. Days and days and nothing in the trap."

"How does he live, then?"

"Why, he don't need much. You see how things stand here. And he don't care whether he's got venison to eat with his corn pone, or just the soggy pone without the meat. That's the way that he is!"

"Let Dutch rest for a while. Now tell me about this job that was put up on you."

"I dropped fifteen hundred in that game," sighed Jimmy.

"You!"

"It sounds pretty big, don't it? Fifteen hundred for me to have in my pocket?"

"It sounds damned big!"

"Well, I didn't steal it."

"Go on, then, and tell me where you got it. Somebody gave it to you for luck, maybe?"

"You look half sore and half scared," said the boy. "I didn't swipe it, either. I found it!"

"Found it!"

"Yep. I picked up a red leather wallet."

"With fifteen hundred bucks in it?"

"There was."

"You couldn't find an owner?"

Jimmy frowned.

"Look here," said he, "you always have carried honesty around the corner. Doggone it, Mike, when you pick up a wallet like that on the open range — "

"All the more reason for wanting to find the owner of it!"

"I knew who the owner was!"

Michael flushed.

"And you didn't take it to him?"

"I didn't."

"I don't follow that," said Michael, sternly.

"Well, there's a pretty good reason. When I picked up the wallet I knew that it belonged to Bramber!"

"Bramber? The same man that shot you up?"

"The same man. I knew it was his. And why should he get back fifteen hundred?"

"And why not? He has a right to his own property, I guess."

"Look here," exclaimed the boy angrily, "you know who this here Bramber is?"

"I never heard of him before."

"What!" cried Jimmy.

"Never."

Jimmy stared.

"Well," he said, "you'll hear plenty about him before you've been up here for long! When you meet up with old Dutch Methuen, for instance, he can give you an ear full!"

"Is he a crook?"

"Is he a crook? He is! Is Bramber a crook!" echoed Jimmy to himself.

"All right. Bramber is a crook. What next?"

"Why, Mike, the next thing is to tell you that in that wallet there was something more valuable than money."

"Jewels, eh?" said Tirrel, fumbling in his pocket, where the pin lay secure.

"Jewels? Something more valuable than them, either."

"What could be? More than diamonds?"

"More than diamonds, too."

"More than this?" smiled Tirrel, and held out the pin.

The first glance of Jimmy turned into an amazed gaping.

"Great guns!" he breathed.

"What would you say that's worth?" asked Tirrel.

Jimmy stood up.

"You're in it, too!" he said. "You're part of it, too, eh?"

"Part of what?" asked Michael.

"Bah!" said the boy, suddenly bitter. "Do you think that you can fool me, too? I see where you got your mare, now. I see all about it. You'll get more than fine hosses, too, I guess, before you're through!"

"I don't know what you mean," said Tirrel.

The boy stepped closer to him. His face was white and tense, and his eyes met those of Michael with a sort of angry scorn.

"I've been a worthless hound," said he, "but I never done anything like that!"

"Like what, I ask you? What the devil are you talkin' about, kid?"

Jimmy snapped his fingers, and sneered.

Then he came still closer, and he whispered so that his brother hardly could hear:

"I told you that I found something in the red wallet that meant more than money."

"You said that. What d'you mean by it?"

"Ain't it clear?" asked Jimmy, suddenly fierce again. "Ain't it clear what I mean?"

And he pointed at the diamond stick pin with a sort of savage air of triumph!

Chapter Nine

The stick pin was regarded by Tirrel with equal interest. He said at last: "I don't know what the devil you mean by this, Jimmy."

"Of course you don't, Mike," said the younger brother. "You couldn't. It wouldn't be the regular or the right thing for you to know anything about it. But — aw, let it drop. Doggone me if I ain't surprised!"

He looked his surprise, as the saying is, from every pore. And he shook his head again, as he watched his older brother.

As for Tirrel, he could not make head or tail of this thing. It began to appear as though the stick pin had a mysterious meaning, not only for his brother, but for the pawnbroker — and perhaps for other people as well.

He said bluntly: "What do you make out of this pin, Jimmy? Come out with it! I want to know!"

Jimmy started to speak, as though in angry impatience, but he checked himself at once.

"I ain't a mind reader," he declared sullenly. "Only, it shows me that there's no use talking to you about what I really wanted to say to you."

"Jim," said Tirrel, "you talk like a young fool. I've just got this pin out of a pawn shop with a pawn ticket. Ain't that straight enough to explain how I got it into my hands?"

"A pawn shop!" exclaimed the other.

"Yes, right out of a pawn shop."

"Where?"

"Here in Los Cavallos."

Jimmy laughed harshly.

"It's likely that I believe that kind of junk, ain't it?" he asked.

"I'm telling you the truth. I don't lie, kid. And most of all, I don't lie to you!"

Jimmy regarded him darkly, in doubt.

"I've gone a long time without knowing you, Mike," he declared at last, "and I'm damned sorry that the time had to come when I couldn't keep my old ideas about you."

"Look here," said Michael. "You connect up this pin with something that I don't know anything about. You think that I'm lying to you and hiding a lot of the truth. I'm not. I'm telling you the straight."

"Where'd you get the pawn ticket?" asked Jimmy.

"I got it from the same man that I got the mare out of."

"Ay," said Jim Tirrel fiercely. "I can believe that. You got it from the same gent. I suppose that it's a kind of a compliment to you that they'd rate your services that high. Hell, Mike, why don't you come out in the open and talk to me straight?"

"It's no use," said Tirrel gloomily. "You can't see that I mean what I say."

"I'm going to tell you something," said the boy. "And maybe it will loosen you up a little and show you that you don't risk anything with me. I told you about finding the red wallet."

"Yes."

"Well, in that wallet I said that there was something that was more valuable than money, didn't I?"

"Yes, you did."

"Can't you guess what that was, then?"

"No."

"Not even after all of the leads that I've given to you?"

"I got no idea at all!"

"Well," said the boy sternly, "I'll tell you this: Inside of that wallet there was enough to tell me everything that that pin means!"

He stiffened a little, as though to meet the shock of a violent passion from his older brother, but Tirrel merely examined him from beneath dark brows.

"If you know what the pin means," he said,

"tell me. Because I got an idea that it may snake me into a whole pile of trouble!"

Jimmy laughed, and his laughter was short and hard.

"It *might?*" said he. "Well, I guess that it might. And it would surprise you a good deal, I guess? You wouldn't talk back to me with a gun, maybe?"

As though half frightened, while still sneering, he watched his brother's face, and Tirrel said gently: "You're pretty sore at me, Jim. You think that I'm mixed up in some dirty business, but I'm not. I want to know what you know, that's all."

"Sure you want to know," said the boy. "And still, God help me if I should tell. Ain't that the case?"

This continual avoidance of the issue and beating about the bush, as the older brother felt it to be, annoyed Tirrel greatly. He said at last:

"We'd better switch the subject. You've found a red leather wallet. I've found a stick pin. You don't like what I've done, and I don't like what you've done. And there you are!"

He could not help exclaiming: "A damned fine reward this is to me for the care I've tried to take of you, Jimmy, always!"

"Are you chucking in my face the money

77

that you've loaned to me?" said Jimmy.

"I'm not."

"You are. Wait a minute. I want to show you something."

He took some paper and a pen and sat at the central table, frowning in thought.

"It'll take three weeks for this arm to be fit again. After that, it ought to be finished up in a month at the outside. Look here, Mike!"

Clumsily he scratched on the paper with his pen held in the left hand, and at last he showed the writing to Michael, who made out, with some difficulty:

"Two months from date, I promise to pay twenty-five hundred dollars to — "

Here he had paused and now he asked: "What name do you want me to put down there, Mike? Are you still wearing your old name in your new business?"

Tirrel picked up the paper and crumpled it into a tight wad. This he threw across the room angrily.

"This is a damned funny business, Jimmy," said he. "Are you trying to insult me? What the devil do I care about the money? And how would *you* ever raise that much cash — except with a gun?"

The eyes of Jimmy blazed with light.

"I'll tell you what," he said confidentially, "I may have to use a gun to get this coin, but

78

when I get it, it'll be honestly mine! And when I get it, I pay you back and retire. I put down twenty-five hundred. Why, it's not half of what I'm going to give to you, Mike, old fellow. You've wanted a ranch all your life. I'm gunna buy you a ranch, and I'm gunna stock it with prize cows. I'm gunna set you up! I'm gunna make you rich, because I'll be able to afford it!"

Mike Tirrel looked on his brother with a sort of affectionate amusement and contempt. And Jimmy flushed.

"You think that I'm talking through my hat. But I'm not. I know where the stuff is. I've *seen* it!"

"And why didn't you get it?" asked Michael.

"Because my gun jammed. That's why!"

"This is an honest business, you've been telling me."

"Is it dishonest to plunder a robber?" asked the boy.

"Robber?"

"Mike, don't ask me any more. The fact is that it ain't right for you to know, being what you are now."

"You young fool," said Mike Tirrel, "you seem to have it planted in your brain that I'm a crook, now. I'm not."

"You'd shake hands on that, and swear it

79

on your word of honor, I s'pose?" said the younger brother with a sneer.

"I would. And here's my hand and — "

"Great God!" breathed the boy. "Is that right?"

"Of course it's right."

"Then I can tell you the whole yarn!"

"I'd like to hear it, of course. It's taken you long enough to warm up to it!"

"Then here goes!"

A loud stamping and trampling broke out in the horse shed, and Tirrel, fearing lest something were alarming the mare, hastened out to have a look.

When he came into the stall, he found Molly Malone back at the end of her halter rope and half crouched, trembling with terror. A rustling in the manger attracted him; and there working through the hay he found a large garter snake. He took out the snake and threw it from the barn; he was not foolish enough to kill the most efficient of all rat catchers. He stepped back to examine the manger more closely, and as he came into the stall, Molly Malone crowded over against him, apparently very glad of his company.

He scraped the hay from the manger and was amazed to find that it was a perfectly tight box, through which a snake could not possibly have crawled. He looked above, since it must have fallen from above if it had not come up through the bottom of the manger, and there he saw nothing but the projecting front of the hay in the mow.

It was very hard indeed to see how such a snake could have remained in that hay as long as it had been in the barn. This little problem worried Tirrel enough to make him pause for a minute or so, in thought, but at length he left the shed and returned to the house.

There he found that his younger brother was still on the stool, slumped back against the wall, with his head fallen upon his breast in the most profound thought.

Was he changing his mind, perhaps, about telling the secret?

"Well, Jimmy?" he asked.

Jimmy refused to raise his head.

"Are you asleep," called Michael.

But Jimmy did not answer.

Michael stepped suddenly to him and raised the head of the boy.

The half closed eyes were dead. No, at that moment a wistful flicker of life returned to them.

"Three white birch an' —black rock — "

There his face tightened in a single convulsion of death. He spilled loosely into the arms of Tirrel, who lowered the lifeless body to the floor of the shack.

Chapter Ten

A small spot of blood showed on the breast of Jim Tirrel's coat, and as his brother hastily opened coat and shirt, he saw a narrow puncture that seemed to be just over the heart. There the blow had been delivered with a knife.

Tirrel stepped back, his brain whirling. As he did so, he heard a footfall outside the cabin and looked out into the face of a gray-bearded man who carried a shotgun slung across the crook of his left arm. He started at the sight of Tirrel.

"Hello, stranger," said he. "Didn't know that they was any — great guns!"

He hurried into the cabin, tossing the gun into a corner, and knelt beside the fallen youngster. One glance was enough to show him what had happened, and he rose and turned a grim face upon Tirrel.

"Stranger," he said, "you're gunna hang for this, as sure as they's a God! You're gunna hang! What harm did the poor kid ever do to you? You come in and take him when his right arm's done for and you murder him like a — "

Tirrel said quietly: "I'm his brother. Don't be a fool. The thing for us to do is to find out who's been here while I was away in the horse shed a minute ago. Help me go over the floor, will you? And then we'll take the ground outside of the house."

"His brother? His brother?" echoed the other.

"You're Dutch Methuen?"

"I am."

"Methuen, it happened inside of two minutes while I was looking after the mare that was raising a ruction in the hoss shed. Whoever done it can't be far. Find his trail, and God help me or him; I'll ride him down!"

Methuen gave one earnest look at the other and then asked no more questions but fell to scanning the floor all about, bending double to bring his keen eyes closer.

Tirrel exclaimed, after a moment, that the dirt floor was as hard as stone and that they would never find satisfactory sign upon it. Therefore they transferred their work to the outside of the shack, and there, beginning one at the front door and one at the back door, they cut for sign in broadening semicircles. For a silent hour they worked, and then, as of one accord, they returned to the shack and stood looking down upon the white, smiling face of the boy.

"A friend done it," said Dutch Methuen suddenly.

"A friend?" asked Tirrel bitterly.

"He's killed from in front. He was killed sitting down, according to you. Who could of finished him off like that without walking straight up to him from in front? Can you tell me that?"

"He was sitting thinking. He may have closed his eyes," said Tirrel.

"No enemy would of dared to take that chance. Instead, he would of tried a shot from the door, most likely. Somebody that knew the kid walked straight into the room and then sank the knife in him. That's as clear as day, I reckon!"

"Who could have come?" asked Tirrel. "What friends did he have who would be apt to walk in on him here?"

"How can I tell?" asked Methuen. "Everybody liked the kid. Me, I never met nobody like him. Allus good-nachered, easy-goin'. Never got excited about nothin'. Allus had a pleasant way of talkin' to everybody! Who could of been his enemy, I'd like to know, unless somebody that he owed money to. I gathered from the kid that he was a pretty strong borrower!"

"Leave the body exactly where it lies," said Tirrel. "That's the best thing. I'm going back to town and get the sheriff, if I can find him. But if it takes me ten years, Methuen, I'm going to get him — I'm going to get the hound who did this!"

He clicked his teeth at the finish of that speech, rather ashamed that he had let himself go as far as that. Then he went hastily to the shed, got the mare, and rode her forth.

As he went, he looked back at old Dutch Methuen, who sat outside the door of his shack in the sun, smoking a pipe as though nothing in the world were the matter on this cheerful day among the woods.

Straight back on the trail toward Los Cavallos went Tirrel, his heart aching, and his mouth, now and again, twitching a little so that it almost seemed that he smiled. But it was the sheer excess of grief as his memory placed young dead Jimmy before him out of the past, when he had been a bright and handsome child and the hope of the family, and, growing older, the humor and the trouble of his first escapades, and the head shaking and the smiles which had surrounded him until, as the years went on, everyone unwillingly had to agree that Jimmy Tirrel was turning out a worthless man.

Now he lay dead, and yet all that had been

he was not dead. And it came home to Tirrel that the living have only the moment, and a vague, uncertain hope for the future, but all the past is dead; and if the living are the sum of memory and the moment, then the dead live and the living are dead. And, in a sense, it was as though the actions of Jimmy Tirrel had been translated into stone or into paint, for they would be sure to live in the minds of those who had seen and known him.

Now, this unhappy philosophizing did, at last, bring a certain comfort home to the cold heart of Tirrel; but underneath all thinking the greatest comfort of all was that he would never rest until he had found the murderer.

The trail crossed the shoulder of a hill and dipped into a little hollow, thick with trees and their shadows. Sweeping down into it at the splendid gallop of Molly Malone, it seemed as though something of the night coolness and damp remained in the air here, undispersed by all the hours of the morning.

Molly, too, seemed to feel it. At least, she grew nervous and tense as coiled springs beneath him, shortening her gallop, raising her head with ears that strained forward, and suddenly she swerved so violently that a lesser rider than Tirrel would have lost his seat. Even he was jerked far to the right side and had to clutch the pommel; while from the opposite side of the road two rifles exploded one after the other, like the double beat of sledge hammers working big iron. He heard the hornet-hum of the bullets jerked past his head — and then he was in the woods, brought there without his volition by the rush of Molly.

Other bullets thudded against tree trunks or crackled briefly through the twigs and leaves. Then suddenly the guns were silent; he heard a beating of hoofs, and knew that the ambush was scattering.

Still he paused for an instant to wait until his heart beat should sink toward normal again, and he stroked the quivering, fear-hardened neck of Molly Malone and murmured comfortingly to her. He could thank God and a crooked gambler for this mare. Perhaps, through a rift in the wind-stirred branches, she had seen a leveled rifle, and even dumb brutes soon learn what that means! But, long before, entering the hollow, she must have smelled danger like a wolf on the trail!

Her rider looked down on her now with a little sense of awe mingling with his gratitude. Then he turned back to the trail to find the sign of the would-be assassins.

Their tracks were clear enough. They must have stood for some minutes close to the road; he counted four cigarette butts — Bull Durham. He passed back to the point where they had tethered their horses, saw where the latter had grazed the surrounding brush, and marked the direction in which they had ridden off. This line of their flight he followed for a few minutes until he made sure that it pointed straight south.

But that proved nothing. In due time, they might swing to the left and come back toward Los Cavallos; they might eventually lounge past him in the streets of the town, looking calmly upon him, promising him death at the first opportunity!

So thought Tirrel, and, coming back into the trail, he pursued his way toward the town, reasonably sure that the pair would not venture to lay another ambuscade on the same trail.

It was the climax of all the strange events which had taken place here in Los Cavallos and its surroundings. If all had gone as planned, both his brother and he would have been ended on this day. This one morning would have seen the finish of them both.

And to what purpose? In what way had they accumulated enemies, and who would gain by the disappearance of a pair of obscure cowpunchers?

If he had allowed himself free rein, he would have gone half mad with the mystery of this affair; but he kept himself well in hand.

The diamond stick pin had something to do with all this. And how much did yonder crooked gambler know about the pin and its significance?

He would very much have enjoyed five minutes of brisk conversation with that skilful poker player!

When he got within the thick white walls of Los Cavallos again, he went straight for the sheriff's office, but found that the sheriff was not there. A hawk-faced youth, however, declared that he was Sam Lowell, the deputy, ready to take the sheriff's place.

To Lowell, therefore, he gave the brief details of how James Tirrel had been murdered that morning by the stroke of a knife in the shanty of old Dutch Methuen. Lowell listened in quiet, his eyes seeming to read the face of the speaker at the same time that he listened. Then he said :

"We'll have a look. The coroner will have to take a glance at things. Know any enemies of James Tirrel?"

"Not one in the whole world!"

The deputy nodded.

"It's not the first time that strange things have happened around Los Cavallos," said he. "Will you go along with me to the coroner's?"

"I'm going back to the hotel to make up my

pack. It may be that we'll hit an out trail on the line of that knifeman; and if we do, I want to be ready to ride."

The deputy agreed to pass the hotel and pick him up before leaving town, so Tirrel returned, and when he asked for his key, it was given to him along with a letter.

He read across the envelope:

"Mr. Daniel Finch."

Chapter Eleven

It was the first impulse of Tirrel to return the envelope with the remark that it was not his name, and that another name, in fact, had been placed by him upon the hotel register; but when he glanced down at the inscription: "Mr. Daniel Finch," it was as though a flash of light passed through the mind of the cowpuncher. Very much, indeed, could be explained if his identity in this town had been mistaken, and if to him had been attributed the name of Finch. Whoever Finch might be, it was probable that he was a person such as Ormond the crook could approach with the greatest ease. Daniel Finch, if it were for him that Ormond had mistaken him, was perhaps a man of some eminence in the illegal profession.

And, since he had been placed in the shoes of Daniel Finch, it was hardly more than fitting that he should see what the letter had to say about that gentleman.

Now, these thoughts leaped in a swift chain

through the mind of Tirrel, and he turned without a perceptible pause away from the hotel desk and went up to his room.

There he opened the envelope and shook out into his hand, first of all, the picture of a very pretty girl. It was a smiling face, and, with all its beauty, there was such an air of frank simplicity about it, such a lack of that mystery of manner which pretty women are so apt to adopt, that Tirrel found himself brooding earnestly upon it, and dropping into such deep thoughts that he had to draw himself from them with a sigh and a great effort of the will.

Then he put the picture to one side, still with his eyes going toward it from time to time, and drew out the letter. It was brief. It came from Glendale, and it was signed "Peter Lawrence." It read:

Dear Dan,

I've just heard that you've come back to Los Cavallos. In that case, I suppose that you'll come over here to pay us a visit. I think that you'd better. Kate is sort of changing her mind about things, and perhaps if you dropped in, you could switch her back to the right line of thought.

I know that you're probably pretty busy, but I think that maybe you'd better come this way to see us before you drift on again.

My own idea is that, no matter how you're pressed, you'd better spend the extra effort and take Kate right along with you. She's getting prettier every day. The boys pay her more and more attention.

Even if she was crazy about you, which you and I know that she ain't, as yet, it would pay you pretty much to take her now. But as it is, with the young gents dropping in every day or so, who can tell what will happen?

Kate's as steady a girl as I ever seen, and as straight and as faithful, but all the same, she's apt to lose her head over some young puncher or something better. Young Hugh Dalrymple, the son of the mining man, was in the last month about seven times, and I'm telling you this just as a sample of the sort of competition that you're up against. I keep putting the best foot forward for you, but all the same, I have to keep working at it. And words from a third party ain't what a young girl likes.

Mind you, I'm going to keep her lined up to her promise as well as I can, but I can't swear that I'll succeed. I'm sending this to you in dead serious warning. You use your own discretion about what to do.

All the time, the best of luck to you from your friend,

PETER LAWRENCE.

This letter he re-read twice over, and rubbed his chin with his hard knuckles, pondering.

He could make out that the above mentioned Daniel Finch had attained some hold over Peter Lawrence and Kate, who was probably his daughter, and through that hold, he had endeavored to win the girl; she, indifferent to him, was being held to her promise by Peter Lawrence.

And then he looked at her picture again!

It was only reassuring himself of what he already knew — that he never before had seen such a face, and that he probably never would see such a one again.

Then he restored photograph and letter to the envelope and sealed it with the greatest care. He had opened it with equal care, and though the inner strip of the paper had adhered to the mucilage in places, still he was able to close the envelope with some degree of success.

Then he assembled his pack, threw it over his shoulder, and went down to the desk.

He paid his bill but left warning that he might return that night. Then he handed in the envelope.

"You gave me that by mistake," said he. "Who's Daniel Finch? My name is Tirrel, you know."

At this, the proprietor nodded gravely.

They made such mistakes, from time to time, said he. So much mail came through in one day! But all the time that he was saying this, Tirrel eyed him closely and he was sure that he saw a sort of fierce content in the face of the other.

Then he went out to the mare and almost immediately found Deputy Sam Lowell riding down upon him. There were four men in the party, and when they came up Tirrel was introduced. He made sure that these were picked specimens of the manhood of Los Cavallos. One was a Mexican; the other three were types of the American range. The coroner was the Mexican, a gloomily proud and reserved man. He bowed to Tirrel without speaking, and in another moment all five were clattering out of the town and toward the house of Methuen, deep in the woods.

They passed the place where Tirrel had been fired upon, and he pointed it out to the deputy and asked what it could mean.

"How should I know?" said Sam Lowell. "I ain't a mind reader, and I can't figure out how many enemies you got in the world, can I?"

"I've never been here in Los Cavallos before," declared Tirrel. "It's damned strange. People look at me in a funny way. I was in a pawn shop this morning and I got an idea that

95

they were planning to tap me over the head!"

"From behind the curtain?" asked Lowell.

"That's the idea! Have they ever done that to anyone?"

"If I knew, I'd have them in jail," answered Lowell. "But I don't know. All I know is that you hear some funny sort of yarns about the pawn shop, and some say that more gents have gone in under the three yellow moons than have come out again! I dunno. Maybe I oughtn't to repeat things that ain't proved. But if nothing was so in this here town except what was proved, it would be the quietest joint in the world, which it ain't!"

He asked, in conclusion, if the other had the slightest idea as to how the assailants could be described.

"A few," admitted Tirrel, and he suggested that one of the horses was very tall indeed, that one had a broken front tooth, and that both the men were of medium size and weight.

"That's a good deal to know about them," said the sheriff. "How did you make that out if you didn't see any of the horses or any of the men?"

"It works out easy enough. I looked over the grass that they'd bitten off. One of them didn't crop the grass smooth. There'd be a little tuft sticking out from every bite he'd made. That seemed to look like a broken front tooth.

Then there was plenty of sign to show how the other horse had spread his front legs a little while grazing. Only a pretty tall hoss, as a rule, has to do that, you know!"

"Sure," said the deputy. "You use both your eyes, I see! You've lived in the desert for a while, I guess!"

"What makes you think that?"

"Because looking through the dust of the desert develops your eyes pretty well. You've described the horses, pretty well, but you haven't described how you come to know that the men were middle sized and middle weight."

"I looked at the marks of their feet, and where they'd walked along, they took shorter steps than I did. But their heels sank in about the same distance as mine. That's why I say that they're probably middle sized and middle weight."

All of this the deputy listened to with a great deal of attention. Then he said: "I'd like to have you alongside of me, in some of the work that we have to do. The trouble is that out West a lot of the talent is used up in the crooks and there ain't much left over for the officers of the law!"

They rode on to the turning in the trail and then passed up the bridle path to Dutch Methuen's house. There sat Dutch in front of the house smoking his pipe, and the greeting he gave to them was affably cool.

After that, the deputy sheriff and the coroner worked quickly and methodically. Plainly it was not the first murder case they had witnessed or handled. They examined Dutch Methuen and then they examined Tirrel; after which they excluded everyone from the house and fell to work examining it to make out what clues they could.

Tirrel, turned from the shack in this fashion, walked beside the little creek which ran behind the house, idling gloomily along.

He had come to the instinctive conclusion that, before he was free from the mysterious tangle in which he now found himself, he would have high cause to remember Los Cavallos and all of its people. From that gloomy thought, he turned his mind to the picture of Kate Lawrence, and he cursed himself for not having kept the snapshot. After all, the real Daniel Finch never would have much chance to complain about the loss of it! It would be cheap to him having the girl herself, and a treasure to Tirrel.

He made a cigarette and scratched a match against the bark of the nearest tree. But it refused to light, the hard sulphur head simply cutting into the very soft bark, for it was a white birch of splendid size, and near it, standing in a natural triangle, there were two

98

other birches of nearly equal size. Having lighted his cigarette, Tirrel sat down on a large black rock at the edge of the creek and watched the spreading of the water into a flat faced pool, hardly stirred by the ripple of the incoming current. Staring down in this fashion, he saw the tall white streaks of the birches, and the black image of the rock. And suddenly he jumped to his feet, for he had remembered.

Chapter Twelve

And indeed, here were the three white birches and the black rock of which his brother must have been thinking when he spoke his dying words. He looked about him keenly, therefore. It would have been folly to imagine that those were random words which had come from the lips of Jimmy Tirrel. Rather, they were the result of the determined and calculated effort in which he had used the very best of his strength to force out: "three white birches, and the black rock!"

There had been no delirium in the face or in the voice of Jimmy, but the dimness of death was there, and a fighting, grim resolve which had been able to postpone the end for only a few seconds.

But now that he was here among the birches, with the black rock beneath him, as it were, what was he to make of it? He stared about him hungrily, casting frantically about for the thing which could have been in the mind of the boy, but finding nothing. So it occurred to him that perhaps the trees and the rock had been part of a complicated direction — they, in relation to something else, would point the way to a secret of prime importance.

He felt that if he took a little distance and stared at the place, something might come to his mind; and, since there were convenient stepping stones over the shallow water, he crossed the creek and turned on the opposite shore.

But nothing of the least importance offered itself to his eye, unless it were the blue rim of a mountain which appeared, cloudlike with distance, beyond the tip of the central birch. This, in fact, might be the very goal which the dying boy had wished to point out. Or again, some one among the trees might be of peculiar interest, or the black rock itself. Then, looking back at the big, ragged stone, he saw a splash of blood-red stain for an instant the edge of the water beneath the stone.

It startled Tirrel. It brought into his mind with a breathless leap the death of the boy, and the blood upon his body. He looked again, but the stain of red no longer appeared, and the water ran as crystal clear as ever, through the narrow shadow that fell from the upper lip of the stone.

However, this was enough to start him investigating. He re-crossed the stream, and, bending down from the stone, he peered at its lower edge, which almost met the water. And, once more, he saw the flash of red, less bright. He craned still more, and then he saw that there was a little hollow scooped in the gravel at the water's line. A small wall of pebbles had been raised to shut it away from view and away from wind or weather, but perhaps a rise of the creek, giving more force to the current, had undermined and caused that slender wall to topple. Now a mere edging of the pebbles shut the water away from the interior, and, in that interior, he saw a wallet of red leather!

He snatched it out hastily and unfolded it. Inside, there was no more than a single sheet of paper which he opened and read as follows:

Dear old man,
It is under the head in line with the tiger at the forking of the dead spruce.
Yours by the old sign.

This sign, scratched down roughly, was of the simplest nature. It was merely a down-stroke of the pen, on either side of the top of which was a dot, a little below them was a cir-cle which the line cut through, and below the circle were two more dots, one on either side.

The heart and the hope of Tirrel, which had risen so high at first, now fell again, suddenly, for it was as though he had come to the wishing gate, and found that it answered only to an unknown language. However, it was patent that this hiding place was what his dying brother had spent his last strength to name. Perhaps it was on account of this that the knife had been buried in his breast!

He scanned the paper again and could make nothing of that odd sentence: "It is under the head in line with the tiger at the forking of the dead spruce."

Perhaps something else was hidden in the wallet. He opened the seams with his knife and searched every corner of the pocketbook, but he found nothing whatever within. There was the paper, and the paper alone.

He would gladly have destroyed this, but he felt that some mysterious import, other than the words, must attach to it — he could not say what, of course!

So he replaced the paper in the wallet and slipped the wallet itself into his coat pocket. Then he wandered back to the little house. The deputy sheriff, the coroner, Dutch Methuen, and the others were all gathered in front of the house now, seated on a fallen log in the shade, smoking and conversing seriously, with a good many shakes of the head.

A new man had joined the party, and it was he of the pale blue eyes, like clouded agate, whom Tirrel had seen the night before at the hotel.

The conclusion of the coroner was, in brief, that the deceased had been murdered by person or persons unknown, by the use of a sharply pointed instrument, probably a slender knife or dagger. When Tirrel heard this decision he said quietly:

"I've no doubt that you fellows have used your wits as well as you can on this job. I've looked around myself, as much as I can, and I haven't found anything worth seeing. But somewhere there's an answer. Jimmy never was the boy to make enemies. He had a thousand friends, and no real enemy. I want to ask you all to keep this thing in mind, and if you come across anything that's likely to point to any trail, don't bother the sheriff with chatter that maybe he'll think amounts to nothing. Just send the word to me, and I'll see that you haven't wasted your time and trouble!"

Said Dutch Methuen with an equal gravity:

"That's the whole thing. There *ain't* any enemies of the kid. Not around here. He ain't been here long enough to make any. Somebody followed him in from the outside and downed him. And there you are!"

Sam Lowell expressed his regret that he had been unable to unravel any part or portion of the mystery, but he vowed that the case was not shelved with him. He would keep it fresh in his mind and perhaps he would be able to make something of it.

Since that was the decision, perhaps it would be as well to dispose of the body at once. It was Dutch Methuen who pointed out the most fitting place for burial.

"The kid," said he, "was always fond of walkin' up the stream and sitting near the creek, where there was some white birches. He used to say that he liked to see the faces of them in the water. We'd better put him there."

The deputy sheriff was a busy man and so was the coroner, but they all helped with the work. They wrapped the rigid body in a blanket and carried it to the place of the three white birches and the black rock. Beside the rock they dug the grave. The soil was a sandy gravel, easily worked, and the grave was sunk rapidly to the proper depth. Tirrel and Dutch Methuen lowered the body into it after Tirrel had removed the boots from the feet. For he said that no Tirrel had died with boots on and been buried in that manner. Then the group paused. Sam Lowell said:

"There oughta be some sort of words spoken, here, but I dunno that there's a Bible handy."

"I'll say something," said Dutch Methuen.

105

"When I first seen the kid, I cottened to him. I took him out here, where we live pretty simple and poor. These here woods was our butcher shop, and sometimes there wasn't much to find in the ice box. He took everything as it come. He never had nothin' but a smile. He done his share of everything that he could do with one hand. He done the cooking pretty good. He could even chop wood. My cabin was a pretty cheerful place while he was there. Now before we shovel the dirt on top of him, and close him up forever, I wanta speak this out, so's them can hear that had oughta hear. This was a man. He died before his prime, but if God don't count dollars and watch only the big city houses, the kid is gunna find his way home, all right. Amen!"

To this, the others joined in with a rumbled "Amen!" and the ceremony was over, except that Tirrel, on one knee at the edge of the grave, checked the shoveling of the earth for an instant so that he could gaze down into the white, upturned face of his brother. He, in silence, sternly registering that vow in his heart, swore that he would never rest until he had brought justice home. Then he stood up, and himself cast in the first shovelful.

When the grave was filled and the mound made, the rest joined in carrying large stones, with which they made a considerable heap,

and on the side of the black stone itself, near by, Dutch Methuen chiseled rapidly:
"Here lies Jim Tirrel, a good bunkie."

Chapter Thirteen

When Tirrel reached Los Cavallos again, it was late in the day. He ate his dinner with a frown on his brow, for his mind was crowded, and by degrees he brought out the problems which obsessed him and laid them in order for his attention.

He wanted to know, as he told himself, first, who was the stranger who had given him, through the card game, the horse and all his possessions, and for what purpose had so much been passed over to him?

Second: Who killed Jim Tirrel?

Third: What was the meaning of the writing he had found in the red wallet?

Fourth: Who was Dan Finch?

Fifth: Who had fired upon him in the woods?

Sixth: What mysterious significance attached to the diamond stick pin?

He had come to pie and coffee when he reached this last item, and, taking the pin from his pocket, he glanced down at it in a careless curiosity, knowing that it could not answer him, for had he not already stared at it a hundred times? But the first glance startled him, now, for he saw between the pin and the sign at the foot of the letter from the wallet a most odd and pointed similarity.

Suppose that the pin itself were to be taken as the straight down stroke, then the two lesser diamonds at the top represented the two dots; and the big diamond — the chief value of the pin — stood in place of circle; and beneath the circle were two much smaller dots here represented, again, by two very small diamond chips.

This resemblance seemed to him, on second thought, so extremely doubtful that he took out the pin and regarded it again, but this time he felt more sure than ever. Once the idea had come into his mind, it would not out again. So, with his blood quickened, he went out into the patio to have his after dinner smoke; his pack had been sent up to his former room.

It seemed to him that his evidence was beginning to form into a chain, at last. At least he was beginning to establish a dim and shadowy continuity between the signer of the note from the red leather wallet, the diamond stick pin, and hence back to the first owner of Molly Malone.

And he prayed for such brains as clever detectives so often show — in books! However, all was a blank before him. Somewhere was the solution, but he was far from it. The more the face of the mystery was shown to him, the more complicated it appeared. But he felt that he was living in the path of a shower of events and eventually the truth might come to him, even though the revelation might be the death of him.

Certainly, common sense bade him get out of the path of trouble as rapidly as the matchless mare would carry him, but, on the other hand, there was the necessity of remaining here to solve the cause of his brother's murder. He could not resist the pull of that cause no matter how much value he placed on his own life. But that he lived in the most imminent peril he could not doubt. The very death of his brother perhaps, pointed indirectly toward him. Beyond that, he had the knife thrust started for him in the plaza the evening before and the shower of bullets which had been poured at him when he was riding through the wood.

Through this haze of thought, he saw Ormond suddenly appear and sit down on the bench beside him again. He looked up. The sky was filmed over with tender sunset colors, the water whispered in the fountain, the music was beginning in the plaza, and the wind stirred softly in the drapery of the great wisteria vine above him. It would have made a setting for a fairy tale, but into it had walked the brutal face and form of the yegg.

"You ain't changed your mind, Danny?"

Tirrel jerked his head up.

"What did you call me?" he asked.

"There ain't a soul in hearing distance," said Ormond sulkily. "What's the reason that I can't call you by your real name, Finch?"

Danny Finch!

The heart of Tirrel beat perceptibly faster, but he maintained a calm gaze, fixed upon the other.

"You're sure that I'm Finch?" he said.

"Why hell, Danny, didn't we recognize each other the other night? And if I hadn't known your face at all — still, wouldn't I of knowed you by the hoss that everybody's talkin' about? I guess that the whole world knows Molly Malone belongs to Dan Finch! Loosen up, Danny. Don't try to dodge me all the time!" He was growing angry.

Tirrel said. "It's all right, Ormond. But I wanted to see if I couldn't pass up here in spite of the mare."

"You can't! Why, the whole town knows who you are!"

"Do they?"

"Well, step around and watch their faces when you go by."

"How much did I ever show myself here before?"

"Far as I know, never, except to pass through on the wing. But that don't matter. The mare is your card!" He added: "You been thinking over what I cracked to you the other night, old son?"

"What's the game?"

"All you gotta do is hold the bag while I pour in the money, as you might say," responded the other.

"Hold the bag between your knees."

"You know what I mean. It's a slick plant and a fine frame. I never saw better prospects. I can open the old safe with a can opener. There don't even have to be any noise about it. Now, what I say is: you come in with me?"

"Why go double when you can pull the wagon in single harness?"

"You know what I mean, Danny."

"Cut out that name, will you?"

"Well, then, you're damned touchy about it! But let that go. The idea is that, if I can have decent luck, nobody's going to disturb me at all. I could do it single handed easy. But if there's gotta be an alarm, and my luck is out, then I'm going to need faster and straighter shootin' than I can do by myself. That's why

I'd figger you in!"

"You like my style of shooting, eh?"

"Who don't?" said the other with a flash of sinister enthusiasm. "Maybe there's others that are fancier shots, old son, but there ain't none that do so well when faces are the targets, and hearts are the bull's-eyes."

"Thanks!" said Tirrel.

"You're hold-offish. You been hearing about the bloomer that I pulled on that Tucson job. But the facts never come out straight about that. It was the Joe in the bank that talked and got me in dutch. I would of had a walkover, if it hadn't been for that sap, there!"

"I don't hold that against you."

"You'll come in? I said fifty thousand the other day. Why, Danny, it's as likely as not to be a hundred grand apiece!"

It seemed to Tirrel that there was no point in offending the other. Perhaps out of Ormond he would be able to learn a great deal more about the identity and the achievements of this Daniel Finch; already he had learned a great deal. He knew, from Ormond, that Finch was a professional gunman, and perhaps a professional yegg as well. It threw much light upon the lean, grim face of the first owner of Molly Malone, and it made more miraculous than ever the truth that such a man should have given up such a mount. If to a law-abiding citizen Molly was a treasure, was she not priceless to him whose life, many times, might depend upon the speed and the wind of his horse?

"Ormond," said he, "I like what you have to say, but I'm busy, just now. I've got a job of my own on my hands."

Ormond groaned with disappointment.

"A big one?"

"Sure. A big one."

"Then why not count me in?"

Tirrel smiled in spite of himself.

"You wouldn't like the style of it," he assured his bench companion.

"Try me! My pockets are full of nothing but holes! I've only ate once a day for ten days, Danny!"

Tirrel drew money from his pocket. In fact, he felt sure that he could have paid much higher for such information as he had been able to extract from this fellow.

"Here's twenty," said he.

"Look here — that's goddam white of you!" said Ormond.

"If you're hungry, you're welcome."

"My belt's up three notches! I've had to drill two new holes into it!" said Ormond.

Then, having softened the heart and perhaps the judgment of the other, Tirrel said, unhurriedly: "You know Bramber?"

The result was equal to the presentation of

a loaded gun. Ormond leaped to his feet; panic was on his face.

"Bramber!" he said. "Good God, what about him?"

"You know him, then?"

Ormond sat down, lowering himself gingerly to the bench and, in the meantime, looking cautiously around the patio, as though he expected that he was being spied upon. Then he turned to Tirrel with an air of curious bewilderment.

"Do I know Bramber?" he asked, amazed more and more. "Man, man, do I know the devil?"

"Have you ever seen the devil face to face."

"Yes, because I've seen Bramber!"

"When for the last time?"

Again Ormond looked curiously at him. A sort of vague doubt was beginning to form in his face, and a light of cunning hesitation in his eyes.

"You ain't spotted him?" said he.

"No," said Tirrel, beginning to wish that he had not entered upon this conversation, or at least that he had not turned it toward Bramber, of all men.

"Well," said Ormond bluntly, "you don't expect that I'm gunna open your eyes for you, do you?"

"You've been talking friend," said Tirrel.

115

Again the look of amazement and cunning hesitation appeared in the face of Ormond.

"Look here," he murmured, "I been talkin' friend, yes. But does that mean that I'm gunna hang myself just to please you?"

"Hang yourself?"

"Well, what's a better way of putting it, if I get in to the way of Bramber? Will you tell me that? I'd as soon clamp a gun to my head and pull the trigger as get that devil after me. Can you show me a better reason?"

"I can't," admitted Tirrel. "Bramber can be dangerous."

Ormond shrugged his shoulders.

"That's one way of puttin' it. I'd say that he's *poison!*" Then, as though his thoughts were running away with his tongue, in spite of himself, he went on: "What could of brought him out here? What could of made him come to a small dump of a town like this here? I thought that Bramber never worked nothing but the big lays no more?"

"So did I," agreed Tirrel, fumbling in the dark to keep up the conversation. "But you never can tell which way he'll jump."

"No, you can't. He's a cat," agreed the yegg heartily. "He's a cat, and he's a wild cat. And damn him!" went on Ormond. "But what could of brought him away out here? I thought that he was gunna work New York and London and such like big game, from now on."

Then he suddenly asked:

"*You* ain't in trouble with Bramber, are you?" He looked at Tirrel as though he asked if he were a leper.

"I haven't said so," said Tirrel.

"No — sure," nodded Ormond. "If you was in trouble with Bramber, you'd be dead, by now, or else you'd be traveling as fast as your hoss could go!"

Chapter Fourteen

When he got rid of Ormond, Tirrel went out for a stroll in the plaza. It was a dreamy, fair-faced night, with the warm wind touching the face like water, but Tirrel was in no dreamy humor, and as he sauntered with the throng around the plaza, with the music of the band hanging heavily above him, he kept a sharp lookout upon all sides. For he knew that he walked, as it were, arm in arm with a mortal peril.

Twice he thought that he was aware of Mexicans following him through the crowd, and, though he could not be sure of this, he soon changed his mind about the evening stroll and went back to his hotel room.

He had determined that he would risk himself no longer in the face of such dangers as were obviously around him, but he would pack and depart. Perhaps he would linger in the woods while he carried on his investigation of the murder of Jimmy. Perhaps he would go straight to the shack of Methuen and live there if he could. But in Los Cavallos the dangers were too great. All the greater, in that he never could tell how they would take form, or who his enemies might be.

However, when he reached his room the bed was a powerful invitation to rest. The fatigue of the desert was not yet out of his bones. He only made sure that his chamber was tolerably secure, first bracing a chair under the knob of the door, then putting his possessions of greatest value under his pillow, together with a revolver. His belt he hung over a headpost. He took off only his coat and boots, and lay down wrapped in a blanket. The red wallet of mystery he slipped into a pocket of his shirt. And so he slept.

Undoubtedly, there is an imp of the unconscious mind which, when properly warned and stationed at his post, will rouse us at need. Tirrel, lying down with the determination to be on his guard, actually was so, although his sleep was very sound and deep. He wakened from it with a start and was instantly thoroughly roused, level-headed, keen.

The door, which he had locked and against which he had braced the chair was now standing several inches ajar, and the movement inward was perceptible. So very softly had the unlocking been done that Tirrel had not been wakened by that. The remainder of the inward movement had been managed very noiselessly,

119

also, but not without bringing a single light scraping sound from the door as it was thrust inward.

Tirrel was, that instant, out of the bed, and his gun belt was clasped around him

A hand, visible in the light which flickered dimly through the window from the lamps of the next building, now slipped around the corner of the door and fumbled at the chair. In continued silence, the chair was found, gripped, and lifted with slow softness away from the door, which was now pushed open again.

There was no surety, by such a light as this. The movement of the hand, for instance, had been no more than a softly stirring shadow among shadows, and similarly it was difficult for Tirrel to make out what happened in the deeper darkness of the hallway. He was only reasonably sure that more than one man waited there.

He had both Colts out, now. His thumbs were on the triggerless hammers; he was ready to pour a terrible tide of leaden destruction down the corridor, but still he could not fire. These fellows could not have come to do him any good, but, to shoot, suddenly, from the midst of darkness, was more than he could manage, and yet if he spoke to challenge them, it would be to direct all their guns straight toward him.

Through the doorway the first of the shadows stepped and paused there. Then, from the hand of the shadow leaped a long ray of light, thin as a needle, incredibly piercing in the silent blackness of the chamber. It fell upon the tumbled clothes of the bed and at the same time it gave enough illumination to the side to show Terril the glistening of a Colt in the other hand of the lantern wielder.

He could not hesitate after that. With his right hand weapon he sent a bullet straight through the lantern. It fell with a great jangling, and the bearer of the light, with a frightened oath in Spanish, tumbled back through the doorway, jerking the door to behind him. There was a minor stampede down the hall and Tirrel did not follow.

He was stepping quickly into his boots and his coat, jamming his hat upon his head. Somehow, he felt more armored against danger, having on him his usual apparel. He even took his pack from the floor and draped it over his shoulder.

This work all required only a few seconds, and during that time Los Cavallos was beginning to wake up. He heard windows slammed open, and excited voices pealed heavily across the night; feet stamped in the room beside his, as though some man were hurriedly

121

jumping into his boots.

In the corridor outside his room, however, there were more significant voices, and distinctly he heard one speaking loudly in Spanish, haranguing the rest, and telling them that they would be rich as devils, every man of them, if they'd go back into that room and finish the killing. And they came, not with a charge, but cursing to keep up their courage.

He did not wait for them. The window of his room was tall and wide. He stood up in it with the greatest of ease and looked to the edge of the roof of the nearest building. It was seven feet away and the gap looked perilously wide at this moment. When his eye dropped, he saw that it would be impossible to descend down the side of the building without seriously risking a broken neck. The narrow alley beneath was paved with cobbles, newly washed down, very dimly glistening with the mountain stars; and a cat walked sedately down the midst.

That way of escape was not for him. He flung the pack from his shoulder and across the narrow gulf. He himself followed with an easy bound, and he was stooping to pick up the pack again when a shadowy form rose from behind a chimney pot, looking gigantic against the northern sky. White Capella burned over the left shoulder of this monster, and red Aldebaran at his right shoulder, and in his hand was a rapidly barking revolver.

The flash of the fire, the cough of the gun, the thud of bullet against the adobe wall behind him half bewildering Tirrel, he stood three shots before he could answer. He had snapped up his gun to reply when he tripped and stumbled heavily to his knees. Doubtless that sudden change of position saved his life. And, shooting upward as he recovered his wits, he saw the giant throw his hands into the heart of the starry heavens with a wild cry. Then he toppled out of sight, crashing noisily down the tiles until he reached the gutter on the farther side of the roof.

Tirrel had climbed swiftly to the ridgepole. He saw the wounded man, no longer gigantic, writhing in the gutter — let him lie! — while into what had recently been his own window of the hotel, appeared a closely packed crowd of men, reaching out with guns and with heads to peer after the fugitive.

But Tirrel was already behind the big chimney pot, and making for the skylight, which he saw open before him.

It opened upon a flight of wooden steps, very narrow and steep, and so he came out of the attic into the upper hallway, where he found the stairs. It seemed a sleeping house to which he had gained admittance, yet he went down as smoothly as possible. After the first disturbance, Los Cavallos had closed its windows and doors securely, once more, and now was prepared to sleep again. It would require more than a few random shots to really arouse that slumbering town!

They had gone back to rest, and to their dreams of other murdered men, no doubt, comfortably sure of hearing another stirring tale of assault and of death with the coming of the next morning.

Tirrel came down to the bottom floor of the house, slipped back the complication of bolts which secured it, like the gate of a fortress, and so issued out into the street.

There he strained his ears, but Los Cavallos was indeed incredibly still. Two or three windows, which had been lighted in the hotel, were now turning dark again, one by one, sure proof that the inhabitants were giving up all hope of hearing scandal or seeing more battle.

To Tirrel this sleepy indifference on the part of Los Cavallos made it appear a far tougher and wilder place than any of the cattle towns, famous for their murders.

He had had enough of it. He had a vague impulse to go into the hotel, secure the person of the proprietor, and pass a Colt halfway down his throat, threatening him with death unless he would tell what he knew of these plots and machinations against the life of a guest in his house. But he knew that this was the most liberal sort of folly, and the best thing for him to do was to get out of the town at once. His instinct of the night before, as he was now assured, had been the proper guide for him.

If they had thought out so complicated an attack upon him, blocking his escape over the roof of the nearest house, then it was reasonably certain that they would not altogether overlook the necessity of blocking his return to his horse. In fact, that might explain the sudden silence among them. Having failed in the first attack, they now were waiting near Molly Malone, ready to bag him there in the security of the stable.

At this, he gritted his teeth and cursed heavily, and he hesitated, so patent and to be expected did all of this seem to him.

Yet he suddenly went on. He was amazed at his own fool-hardiness of course, and yet he felt a most irresistible desire to get to Molly Malone at once. It was worth the imminent peril of death to be on her back, and so ranging forth over the free hills again, far off from the deadly taint of man.

Now, when Tirrel had come to the stable, he heard a pair of voices whispering in the front of the place, and, by the light of the smoky lantern which always burned through the night, there, he made out two stable boys, sitting with shoulder crowded against shoulder, very pictures of midnight terror.

To see fear in others, for some reason, greatly comforted him. He went straight on to the box stall of Molly Malone, entered it — and then heard the door of the stall click behind him.

"I guess you're our man," said a voice from the darkness outside.

Chapter Fifteen

"Who's that? Who's that?" demanded he. "Ain't that Sam Lowell, the deputy sheriff?"

"It is!"

"Why, damned if I ain't glad to have you here! Come in, Lowell, or shall I come out?"

"If you come out, come with your hands in the air. That's all that I have to say to you."

"What in hell do you want with me?"

"I'll tell you when I have you!"

Tirrel hesitated.

"Look here," said he, "this is damn funny!"

"I don't see it that way."

"Well," said Tirrel, "I never was afraid of the law before, and I'm not gunna begin now!" And he stepped through the doorway.

"Hands up!" said the sheriff.

Behind him there were four or five men.

"Are those the skunks who tried to murder me in my room?" asked Tirrel.

"Murder? You?" asked the deputy.

"You heard me talk, Lowell! I won't put my hands up. I'll go with you, if you want, but I won't put my hands up, and I'll keep my guns, because I'm not a-gunna be murdered off hand here in Los Cavallos!"

"You talk like a fool! Whoever heard of an arrest that left the guns on a gent?"

"You can hear of it now!"

"I've got you covered, man!"

"You ain't got me dead, though. Not in this light! You got your free chance, Lowell. Start shooting, and you may drop me, but I'll take you with me, by God!"

Lowell fairly panted with angry impatience.

"What d'you want?" he said.

"I want to go with you wherever you want, while you explain to me what in hell this is all about!"

"Come along, then. You gotta right to know."

In this manner, therefore, it came about that Tirrel was ushered forth from the stable and into the hotel. The commotion, which had died down immediately after the shooting, had now blazed up again, as though a far more important event were taking place. The patio was filled with scurrying, half dressed figures, and everyone was asking questions, everyone making random replies.

Tirrel walked with a gun in either hand, a very grim and ready-looking figure, with the deputy sheriff immediately behind him. He was taken up the steps to the front entrance, and there the proprietor was waiting for them. He was more suave than ever, and bowed them into his own office, a pleasant, large room.

Tirrel, thoroughly roused, walked up to him.

"I think," said he, "that you're the coyote that's underneath all this. The fact is that you've had a hand in the whole affair. You've let in the pack that tried to nab me a while ago. Is that right?"

The proprietor was still nodding and smiling a little, as though the main desire of his life was to understand what his guest desired, but he could not understand the language in which the other spoke.

Lowell broke in: "You've get enough trouble on your own hands now, without trying to make trouble for other people!"

"What sort of trouble?"

"You've murdered Jim Tirrel, and you're going to hang for it, and that's my firm belief, Dan Finch!"

"Finch?" shouted Tirrel. "You blockhead, I ain't Finch!"

"No, you're another Tirrel, I guess?"

The deputy was grimly sarcastic.

"Why, you fool," exclaimed Tirrel, "I can get a thousand men to prove that I'm Tirrel!"

"You can?"

"Yes, of course."

"Where are they?"

"Anywhere from Tucson to San Antone."

The deputy smiled sourly.

"But not here in Los Cavallos?"

"Why, certainly not. How could I know a flock of people up here when it's my first trip here?"

"Your first trip?"

"Yes."

"You don't know anybody?"

"No."

"Then how does it come that so many here in town know you?"

"How the devil should I tell?"

"You can curse, Finch, but it won't do you any good. The law has wanted you for a long time. It's got a long list agin you. Now it's got you cornered. You've murdered a gent who had his gun arm helpless. The tree ain't yet growed high enough to hang that kind of a skunk from!"

The deputy sheriff was young; his wrath possessed the fury of youth. Moreover, behind his speech there was the deep-throated murmur of approval from the men behind him. They kept their ominous faces steadily toward Tirrel, eying him as though he were a wild beast.

"I'd like to know," said Tirrel, "who dares

to say that I'm Dan Finch!"

"Would you?"

"I would."

"Finch," said Lowell, "this is conversation that had oughta be saved up for court, but I got reasons for talkin' this out with you. Suppose that I send every man out of this here room, will you turn your guns over to me and have a quiet chat?"

"I'll do that."

"Let's have the guns, then."

"Let's have the room empty, first."

"You gotta make the first move."

"I'm to trust you?"

"That's the way it'll have to be."

"Since I come to this town," said Tirrel, "I've had a knife drove at my throat; I've been shot at in the woods, and I've had a gang of murderers burst into my room tonight. Now you ask me to trust you or anybody else in this here town!"

"It'll have to be done. Finch, do what I say, it'll be better for you!"

He said this without anger, very seriously.

And Tirrel answered, after a moment's consideration: "There are the guns!"

He laid them upon the table.

Lowell turned instantly on the others.

"We want the room to ourselves," said he.

One of his men protested: "You don't know

Finch. He's as tricky as a fox, and his bite is poison!"

"Do what I tell you," commanded the deputy sheriff. "And bring out my hoss. You better bring out Finch's mare, too. She'll have to be shifted over to the jail stable."

This insistence finally removed the others from the chamber. Tirrel remained alone with Lowell. His guns were in the possession of that young officer of the law — as brave and steady a youngster as ever wore the badge of that dangerous office in the West. And Tirrel knew definitely that his back was crowded against the wall.

The deputy began, when they were alone: "I want to get at one thing first. You say that your room was entered by a gang of gents that was after you, tonight?"

"They were your men, of course?"

"Mine? D'you think I try to do murder at night? What are you talkin' about, Finch?"

"Partner," answered Tirrel, "no matter who you think I may be, don't use that name to me! My name's Tirrel. I'm Michael Tirrel. I've never wore any other name for a minute during my whole life. I've never been in jail. I've never done a crooked job. I can get a thousand men to tell you all about me!"

This assurance, not untouched with anger, had some effect upon the deputy. He said, frowning: "Well, call yourself what you please. I ain't the judge of your case. But I gotta judge you in part. Lemme hear about this raid on your room."

"Last night, I heard the key fall out of my lock. I got up and investigated. There was nobody outside the door. How did the key fall? Well, suppose that somebody was trying to get an impression of the lock?"

"Well?"

"Tonight I lock my door again. I wake up a while ago. The door is open, the chair I propped agin it is being lifted to one side. Gents come in, a ray out of a dark lantern is sifted onto the bed — I see the gleam of a gun in the gent's other hand, and I shoot out the light. They run back into the hall. I take my stuff and get through the window onto the top of the next house. There a gent stands up behind the chimney pot and sends three slugs my way. I drop him. He rolls down the roof and lands in the roof-gutter. I go down through the skylight to the street and find the town quiet again. I don't suppose you heard the guns at all, maybe?"

To this sneer, the young deputy answered calmly: "There ain't any use in talking this way to me, and you know it. Of course I heard the guns. I've heard guns before in Los Cavallos. My job was to get you."

"So you sent up men to murder me in bed, eh?"

"Those weren't my men — if it happened the way you say!"

"No?"

"No, I sent up my boys to see if you were in your room. While they were gone, I watched the hoss, here, thinking you'd come for her if they alarmed you and you got away. And that's the way that it turned out."

"And them that tried to murder me?"

"I'll look into that later. My job now is to save you alive for a decent trial. And it's going to be a hard job. This town is pretty hot about you; the jail is a flimsy shack. If the crowd wants you, they're apt to lynch you. But here's my proposition to you. Write out a confession that you killed young Jim Tirrel, and I'll try to shift you out of Los Cavallos to a safer jail. Otherwise, your life here in Los Cavallos ain't worth a bad nickel!"

Chapter Sixteen

To this odd speech, Tirrel listened with a good deal of composure. He even turned his back on the deputy sheriff and looked out the window. It opened upon the patio of the hotel, and there he saw that a considerable crowd was gathering and each moment growing more dense. In obedience to the orders of the deputy sheriff, his own horse and that of his prisoner had been taken out into the open. Three or four lanterns, also, had been lighted, and the patio was given a very wild effect by the shifting of the lights as they swung in the hands of those who carried them; for the shadows of the people in it sometimes appeared gigantic and sometimes they were dwindling into dwarfs.

There were already twenty or thirty men in that patio, half dressed, some of them, but all fully armed. And the first person he saw was the unmistakable fellow of the clouded agate eyes, who leaned against a corner of the building with a shotgun beside him.

That crowd was rising against him; for that matter, it was not strange that, according to Western ethics, a man who murdered a cripple should be summarily executed by public vengeance, without waiting for the instrumentality of the law's machine. But, as in most cases of mob violence, the danger was simply that they would pick the wrong victim.

He turned from the window back toward his captor, and found Sam Lowell resting a revolver on the back of a chair.

"You're takin' no chances, I see," observed Tirrel, with a cold sneer.

"I can't afford to," said the deputy sheriff. "I've heard a long lot about you for a good many years, Finch, and it's gunna be a grand boost for me if I can bring you up for trial."

"Ay," said Tirrel, "that would make you pretty famous."

"It would," said the boy. "And that's what I want. Fame! Fame! Fame!"

He bent back his head a little as he said it; savage ecstasy was in his face; he even trembled a little. And the older man, watching him, knew at once that either glory or death, or both together, could not be very far removed in the path of this youngster.

"But if the mob takes me away from you and strings me up to a tree, what then? That

136

spoils the party, so far as you're concerned?"

"It does."

"Particular if it's found out that they've hung up the wrong man?"

"Well, that's true," said Lowell, good-natured again and unperturbed.

"It don't bother then — that chance?"

"Not much."

"Would you mind tellin' me what it is that makes you so damn sure that I'm your man?"

"Well, there's the make-up of you. I've looked over a dozen descriptions of you. You see? They all tally, very exact. Man about six feet tall, a hundred and seventy pounds or a little more, lean face, strong shoulders, sandy hair, intelligent looking, pretty brown, hair sunfaded. All of those things fit in with you, Age between thirty and thirty-five. Well, there you are! It's a pretty close fit, ain't it?"

"You know," commented the other, "that there's a thousand men on the range that would fit in with the same picture."

"Maybe there's about a thousand. Well, there's other things, too."

"Such as what, then?"

"There's the hoss. How would you dodge that? Why, I've heard about the mare for a couple of years. I suppose that you'll be telling me that the hoss is just a close copy, too? Or are there a thousand more like her?"

"I hope to God that there ain't!" said he. "But, for all that, ain't it a chance that she could really belong to Finch, and that I could be named Tirrel?"

The deputy sheriff shrugged his shoulders. It was clear that his mind was made up.

"Suppose that I told you, then, that I was coming out of the desert, and at a water hole, on the edge of the hills, there I met up with Finch, and that we played a long game of poker, and that I cleaned him out of everything that he had — down to his skin. I got his clothes and his hoss. He got mine. I had some worn out old rags and a lump-headed mustang. Suppose that I told you that?"

The deputy sheriff raised a finger and pointed.

"Finch," he said sternly, "why d'you keep on bluffing? It's known for a fact that you went to the pawn shop here and that you paid five hundred dollars on a pawn ticket that Finch himself had left here the last time that he sneaked through the town. Don't that link you up with him pretty close?"

Tirrel, listening, saw that the case against him was fairly well closed; it would take direct testimony other than his own to convince this or any other man.

Sam Lowell summed up quietly, and with effect:

138

"These things don't work up by addition. You gotta multiply. First off, suppose that somebody says: 'There goes Finch.' I look and I see a man the same age and general cut and line and weight and look of Finch, why that makes it pretty sure that Finch it is, don't it?"

"Who pointed me out to you and called me Finch?"

"That ain't to be brought up," said the sheriff.

"All right."

"Then comes the fact that you wear jus' the same sort of clothes that he used to wear, down to golden spurs! Well, that ain't making just twice as sure that you're Finch; it makes it ten times as sure. And when on top of that we find out that you got the mare that Finch always used to ride, and that answers her name of Molly the same as a dog would, why, that don't double the proof again, but it multiplies it again, and by a hundred. There simply ain't a chance in a thousand that you ain't Finch! You'd be content with that — no, by God! You even redeem the same pawn ticket that Finch sure was knowed to of left behind him! Well, that makes it one chance in ten thousand or a hundred thousand that you ain't him! And there you are!"

"You'd hang me on that I suppose?"

139

"Old son," said the deputy, "if it was in my hands, and I was judge and jury all combined, I'd string you right up and make no more expense and trouble."

"But you want to get your reputation out of it, of course!"

"You understand me now!"

"And the fact that I'm Finch proves that I murdered my brother — Tirrel, I mean?"

"He was killed by somebody that he knowed — somebody that could walk right in and he not think him an enemy."

"Because he was stabbed from in front?"

"Yes, that's one reason. He never made no outcry, neither. He didn't have the time for that."

"What would my reason be for murderin' him, then?"

"A damn good one. He'd borrowed a lot of money from you. He thought that you'd come to collect. So you had! But you wanted the cash right then, and when he put you off again, it peeved you a good deal. He started to write out a note promisin' to pay you, some time soon. But you wouldn't listen. You got to wranglin'. Then you stabbed him to the heart. He crumpled the paper up in his hand and it fell in a corner when he fell. But there Dutch Methuen found it after all of us left. It was the shaky writin' of a gent writing with his left hand. It was interrupted right in the middle. But there's the case all out agin you! D'you doubt that?"

He could not doubt it. As the deputy spoke, with a swift and a burning conviction, he was himself almost convinced that, in a dream, he must have done as was said of him.

The deputy saw that he had gained much, in this talk, and now he said: "Take another look out the window, will you?"

Tirrel did so, and the crowd had gained another dozen members; a grim lot of faces they presented to the eye. The man of the agate eyes no longer waited at the corner of the building; in fact, at that moment there was a knock at the door, and a voice called through; "Sheriff Lowell!"

"Yes, Mr. Chandos!"

It was the voice of the man with the agate eyes, a soft, deep, rich voice.

"I'm glad to hear you speak, sheriff. I know that's a dangerous man that you have in there with you — a desperate man, sir! I advise you to search his pockets thoroughly, while you have a chance."

"For dyamite?" chuckled the deputy.

"You might see if he has — let us say, a red wallet on his person!"

In spite of himself, Tirrel could not help

starting, and by bad luck, that start was seen by his captor, and the eyes of Lowell instantly narrowed. He called his thanks through the door, and then as the footfall of Chandos departed, he approached his prisoner.

"Even Mr. Chandos knows about you," he observed, "and I see that he touched the quick, that time. I suppose he never makes a mistake!"

"I never heard of Chandos before."

"I suppose you never did," sneered Lowell, "but it appears that he's heard of you. Now, partner, you sort of see how the position sizes up, and that the best thing you can do is to do what I want you to."

"Beginning where?"

"A written confession. On the strength of that I may be able to save your life."

"By getting me out of the town you mean?"

"Yes, to another and a safer jail. I've got a fast hoss. You've got one too. I think that maybe we could beat out the crowd!"

"Thanks," said the older man.

"You won't do it?"

"No!"

"You'll be dead before morning, then."

"I'll have to die, then, and if you're an honest man, you'll curse yourself for this before the week's out!"

"I'll take the chance. But what I want now

is to go through you. Hoist up your hands."

Slowly, Tirrel obeyed, and at the first dip of the sheriff's hand, he drew out the red wallet.

Chapter Seventeen

Now, at the glimpse of the red leather, and the memory that the paper with its strange message was contained within it, Tirrel winced a little, and the deputy sheriff noticed the wincing. He said in a sharp, ugly tone: "You don't like it, eh? I've an idea that you'll like things a lot less before I'm through with you."

Instinctively, and not with malice afore-thought, he emphazised the last remark by jabbing the muzzle of his revolver a little deeper into the ribs of his prisoner. It was the worst thing he could have done. Logically, as a level-headed man, Tirrel saw that he was at the mercy of the other; but every man of pride possesses a last barrier which may not be sur-mounted by another without bringing resis-tance. Defeat can be recognized, but insult will not be endured.

So, without thinking, Tirrel jerked his two fists down and beat them into the face of the deputy. The knuckles of the left hand tore and bruised the flesh over the bridge of the sheriff's nose; but the right hand like a hammer struck on Lowell's temple, and his wits went blank. His forefinger did not curl around the trigger. But he sank limp toward the floor.

Tirrel supported him a little and laid the youngster out on his back. He was limp as a rag; his eyes were a little opened, and looked like death, but dead he was not.

This was the deciding instant. It did not occur to Tirrel to wait until the deputy had recovered, in order to have the law's protection against the crowd. He only made sure that it would be some time before the man of the law recovered his wits. Then he stepped to the window and looked out. The crowd had grown more dense in the patio. There were a hundred men, and every man of the hundred was armed. They were gathering in close, serious groups, here and there, and if ever he had seen a lynching in the air, Tirrel saw it now.

He turned back to the deputy sheriff. He took from him two revolvers, a packed cartridge belt and a Winchester which was leaning against the wall. The sheriff's sombrero, too, by lucky accident fitted him to a T.

As for the rest of his possessions, they were neatly done into a pack which was strapped behind the saddle upon the back of the mare. From the window he had another glance at her and saw her tossing her lovely head and shaking it against the restraint of the bridle. There was a close group surrounding her; no man in the world could rescue her by a sudden dash, and yet it seemed to Tirrel, at the moment, that liberty regained without her was hardly worthy to be called liberty at all!

He heard a groan from Lowell, at this point, and, stepping back to the fallen boy, he quietly and quickly prepared a gag which he fitted between the teeth of the man of the law. Then with Lowell's own irons, he fettered the hands and the feet of the deputy.

By this time, the eyes of the latter were wide. He made no attempt to speak against the gag, but with burning eyes of shame and hatred, he watched the other at work.

Finally Tirrel paused above him.

"Thanks for the hat," said he. "I don't know where we've put mine. As for the rest of it, you've worked your best on me; I don't blame you for having been wrong. So long, Lowell. I wish you luck everywhere else!"

He stepped to the door, unlocked it, and listened a moment. There was no sound in the hall. Quickly he jerked the door wide and peered up and down. The corridor was empty, so he walked on down it toward the front of the hotel, turned down a smaller side passage, and so came, uninterrupted, to the door which opened directly upon the street. It was so little used that it was locked, and the key grated heavily in the lock. But a moment later he stood in the street. Up and down it, he heard voices, he saw people coming like iron filings toward a magnet, and in the plaza the band halted in the midst of a stirring air. The news had come to it, as well, and stopped the music, like a leader's command.

He himself, his sombrero drawn down well over his eyes, walked briskly along toward the gate of the patio, and, as he went, he heard from within the hotel the distinct sound of irons clashing. He remembered, too, that he had foolishly failed to lock the door behind him when he left the deputy.

He reached the mouth of the patio, then, and looked in upon an excited crowd just as a window went screeching up and a voice shouted:

"He's gone! He's fooled Lowell and he's gone!"

Tirrel called loudly: "Molly! Molly!" And he stepped back against the wall, still calling. Molly came with a snort and with rattling hoofs. Out she came, swinging grandly into her stride, and Tirrel leaped at her and struck her side like a wild cat. With all except his left hand he missed, but that caught the pommel of the saddle, and he stretched out to the speed of her gallop like a streamer in the wind.

Then he managed to catch hold with the other hand and drag himself onto her back. He looked back and saw men boiling out from the mouth of the patio. Guns crackled. He turned Molly down the first street on the right.

He was by no means sure of Los Cavallos, but he hoped that he would strike a quick way out. Molly flew through a narrowly winding alley and brought him out, presently, upon a pleasantly wide and straight avenue that pointed fairly for a gate of the town.

Toward that goal he forced her at a wild gallop and saw an ox-cart being maneuvered rapidly into position to block the exit. They kept some watch and ward in Los Cavallos; more than once the sudden closing of their old-fashioned gates had kept mischief out or kept miscreants in to be disciplined for their crimes.

And now the alarm bell was beginning to crash and clamor. It was beaten with such vigor that there was no chance for any note to rise and swell and boom, but the next harsh impulse came crashing at its heels.

In the meantime, the cart, in spite of all his haste, had been deftly backed into place, and the driver now sheltered himself on the far side of his span. One massive panel of the gate itself had been forced home; and the second panel was creakingly started.

That way was stopped, it appeared, and Tirrel looked desperately back across his shoulder. There was no chance to retreat. Two streets converged toward the gate, and both of these were now thronged with hurrying riders. They were not wasting ammunition. They saw that they had their man neatly bagged, and the yelling of their triumph rang in the ears of Tirrel like the shouting of the waves of the sea on a hollow shore.

He gathered the reins of Molly, prepared to swing her around, for he well knew that, with their blood so well worked up, if the crowd had contemplated lynching before, it would now tear him limb from limb. Perhaps if he charged at them, a revolver spitting fire from either hand, he could send some of them to death before him. Perhaps he could even split a lane through them and, twisting through the center of the town, secure another chance to flee. But without Molly Malone — for the gates would be closed agin him, then.

So he reasoned, as he flashed a look across his shoulder at the hurry of the crowd. Then he turned forward again and a sudden hope bloomed in his mind. The cart which partially blocked his way was huge, high, cumbersome, but the span of oxen were not over-large, and they stood close together.

An Indian yell burst from the lips of Tirrel.

In a red fire of enthusiasm he rushed the mare for the pair of silver white oxen, and she acknowledged the work that lay before her by shaking her head, and then pricking her ears, most gallant.

A slight pause in the gallop, an upward tipping, a mighty spring, and she soared above the span as they grunted and swayed their horns in fear beneath her. The driver, with a screech, toppled backward upon the earth, mortally frightened, and Tirrel and the mare shot on through the unclosed panel of the gate.

It was of the heaviest oak; and now, pushed stoutly from behind, it was jammed shut after him, as though to secure his retreat.

He was grateful for that blank spot out of which so many rifles would otherwise have peered after him. The road wound before him across perfectly level meadows; he left it and, riding hard to the left, he was quickly within the safe, dim borders of the woods. And from the moment when he left the gate behind him, not a single shot had been fired at him.

He pulled down the mare to a dog-trot. He wanted to listen well to the forest noises, but there was a light wind blowing, and its continual whispering among the leaves and the voice-like groaning of bough on bough, now and again, would have been sufficient to cover the approach of a hundred careful men.

Moreover, there was two days' rest in Molly, so he let her range on again, he hardly cared where. Wherever he went, from this time forth, he would be a marked and wanted man; and he wondered where the adventure had begun.

It was not when he struck the blow at the deputy sheriff; neither was it the mysterious hand which had struck down his brother and shifted the blame upon his shoulders; neither was it his visit to the pawn shop; not one of these was the beginning, but all had come from the letter of his brother calling on him for help. That letter had begun the trouble, and the chance meeting with Dan Finch at the water hole had given a resistless momentum to it.

Grimly and bitterly he wished to encounter Dan Finch again!

In the meantime, the mare strode on steadily, tirelessly, covering the easy slopes of the road with her smooth pace, until he came out of the woods and found before him, from a hilltop, a scattering of light strewn across a small valley.

In the very next hollow he overtook a teamster whose blacksnake was encouraging eight mules, which tugged in creaking unison at their collars. A big, iron-wheeled wagon rolled behind them.

"What town is that?" asked Tirrel. "That one ahead of us, I mean?"

"That's Glendale," said the other. And the sound went like the music of a bell through the mind of Tirrel. He had heard the name before, and he remembered the face of Kate Lawrence as though she had appeared at that instant, with a candle in her hand.

Chapter Eighteen

The string of mules, at that moment, dragged the wagon to the top of the grade and, without spoken order, they halted, slacked the fifth chain and panted in unison. The teamster looked fondly down upon the scattering of light.

"Yep, there she lies!"

"I've heard of Glendale, somewhere," suggested Tirrel.

"You have, have you? Well, you ain't the first."

"You got some climate here, I reckon," remarked Tirrel.

"You aiming to settle down?"

"I'm tired of the range. Why not a place like this here Glendale?"

"Well, why not?"

"That's orchard land, by the way the trees grow."

"It might be, at that. Nobody does much except wheat and barley. People know cows better than they know ploughs in this part of the world!"

"That's so, too."

"But Jud Fisher, he's got a couple of apple trees in his back yard. They've growed up fine and big, though I can't say that the apples on 'em are very good. You aim to buy a place?"

"I got only a little money. I'd rent, and try to save."

"That's a hell of a long row to hoe. I've tried that myself. I ended up with nothin' but a half interest in these here mules."

"It's a fine string, partner."

"It ain't bad."

"No, you got some weight in these wheelers."

"I got a green near leader, but she's learning. She's got the brain for the job, but she's ornery, damn her heart!"

"You gotta have time to make a near leader."

"There's nothin' truer than that! You skin mules?"

"I've done it. How many people you got in Glendale?"

"Two hundred and fifty by the last census. Some folks estimate it up at around three hundred and fifty now. I reckon maybe that's stretching it some."

"Got some rich people?"

"Bigbee is worth nigh onto half a million, some says. He keeps fine hosses. Always buyin' land. Regular land hog, is Bigbee. Lawrence used to be rich, too, I guess. But he's lost his!"

The heart of Tirrel stirred. His patience, it seemed was about to be rewarded.

"How'd he lose it?"

"He lost it always raising the same crop. Wheat used to be lucky for him, so he thought that it always ought to be lucky. But the ground won't stand it. You can't raise twenty crops of wheat off of no ground, no matter how rich it is."

"You gotta summer fallow it, of course."

"Every other year. And even then you'd ought switch crops now and then. But old man Lawrence, he wouldn't hear no reason. He's busted, now."

"Bankrupt?"

"Sure. He would be, except that young Bigbee hankers after the Lawrence girl and wouldn't let his old man foreclose."

"Bigbee gunna marry her soon?"

"I dunno. You never can tell. You take a girl as pretty as her, and you never can tell what way she'll jump. She might go and pick herself up a millionaire, somewheres, or again she might up and run off with some ornery cowpuncher that ain't got a cent. I better be sashayin' along. I'm late tonight."

Another question came to the lips of Tirrel, but he choked it back. It would hardly do to

155

ask questions too freely, but in this case there was no need. As the teamster drew the black-snake from about his neck, he pointed.

"There's the Lawrence house yonder, on the hill. You can see the top-story lights above the trees."

He called goodby and snapped the black-snake, shouting loudly: "Gee up! Yeah!"

The mules, flattening their ears at the familiar command, leaned forward and stuck grimly to their collars. The wagon groaned, hung in its tracks, and lurched reluctantly forward. So Tirrel waved his hand to the teamster and jogged on into the lead.

The first turn to the left was a narrow country lane pointing straight toward the Lawrence house, and up this he turned his horse. The road dipped twice into shallow hollows, but rising, each time he had a closer view of the Lawrence house, the lights shining more boldly through the surrounding screen of trees. And so at last he came to close range.

He noted that the trees were not merely a little grove planted about the house but apparently an extensive forest, which extended down from the highlands into the valley beyond. Somewhere among the trees he was reasonably sure of finding good quarters for the rest of the night. Or, it might be, he could feed the mare at one of the tall haystacks. For, like many another Western farmer, the poverty of Mr. Lawrence did not prevent him from carrying on his operations on a comparatively large scale.

Tirrel left the mare in the grove at the left of the house and wandered nearer to explore. The grounds of the house itself were set off by a picket fence, very old and broken down; and half a dozen fig trees, very ancient and vast, shadowed the lawn, which was simply an alfalfa field, irrigated by the windmill which ceaselessly spun and clanked in the breezes that blew over this high point. Tirrel went to the mill first and drank deeply of the chilly water which gushed from the spout into a tin trough and so was conducted toward the alfalfa.

He was curiously excited. No matter how he told himself that his halt at this place was purely a matter of accidental convenience, he knew in his heart of hearts that he had come hoping for the first glance at Kate Lawrence in the flesh.

He passed behind the house, circling softly about the creamery. A dog ran out at him with a snarling challenge. He caught the brute by the scruff of the neck and choked it to silence. Then he threw it from him, and it sneaked silently away. He had learned that trick in old days. Granted a certain speed and strength of

157

hand, it never failed to work.

So he came toward the front of the house and the murmur of voices, speaking only occasionally, sounding cool and peaceful in the quiet of the evening. Tirrel slipped through a hedge of rose bushes, and silently drew near.

There were four people on the veranda — a bald-headed man asleep over his newspaper, a gray-haired woman, knitting, another, younger man, indistinguishable in the greater distance and the shadows at the end of the porch, and, close to him, Kate Lawrence.

It was not that Tirrel could see her clearly, but he knew her at a glance, as though she were a creature differing from other women and to be known by her own light. He could see the curve of her cheek, and the highlight which played and died upon her temple as she turned toward her companion.

And Tirrel, on his knees in the brush, watched with the eyes of a wolf.

The woman stuffed her knitting into a bag. "Charlie's sound asleep," said she.

"He has been for a whole hour," said the girl.

"Dear me!" said the other. "Think of that! I wondered why he didn't answer me! I'd better be getting him in to bed, Kate. Charlie!"

A long soft snore was the answer.

"Charlie, it's time to go to bed."

"Ay, Delia."

He stirred; his hand fell from his knee and dangled far toward the floor. His head fell forward.

"Dad!" said the voice of the girl.

He raised his head instantly, blinking.

"He *always* would hear you," complained the wife. "Charlie, do be coming along with me to bed."

"I must of dropped off for a moment" said Lawrence, stretching and yawning.

"Are you coming to bed?"

"Yes, yes. I disremember. We was talking about something important, or was that just a dream?"

"We were talkin'."

"Yes."

"About Kate, I reckon?"

"Ay, about Kate."

"Is there anything settled?"

"Everything!"

"Hold on! I don't recollect — "

"You sat nodding. We thought you were saying yes. Maybe you were only going off to sleep."

"Maybe," said the farmer humbly.

Then he added: "Wait a minute, Delia, will you?"

"You'll be off asleep again in a minute, if I wait for you."

"I want to know what was decided?"

159

"Well, Kate, you had better tell him."

"Dear Dad," said Kate Lawrence, "we all think that it's best to let Dan have his way."

"The devil you all think so!" said Lawrence. "I'm one that don't! "

He struck his hands together, heavily.

"Father!" exclaimed his wife. "Ain't you ashamed of yourself? To talk like this right to Danny's face!"

"Would you a lot rather that I'd say it behind his back?"

"I'd rather that you'd go to bed and be quiet and talk in the morning, if there's any talk to be done!"

"I'll say my say now," said Lawrence. "I got nothin' agin Danny. He's made a lot of money, and he's made it young. That shows that he's got either brains or luck. And I dunno which is the best of the two to have! He allows that he loves Kate. Everybody allows the same thing, for that matter! But I tell you straight, Danny, I got nothing agin you, but I jes' nacherally can't settle myself down to the idea of you bein' the husband of Kate!"

"Charlie!" exclaimed Mrs. Lawrence. "You're gunna ruin everything! I knew you would! Are you gunna try to bust up Kate's happiness?

"Kate!" called her father.

"Yes, Dad."

"D'you love this feller so's you can't live without him?"

She took by the hand the man who sat beside him, and she drew him forward. So Terril saw her fully for the first time, walking hand in hand with Daniel Finch.

"D'you love him so's you gotta have him, Kate?"

"Yes!" said she.

Chapter Nineteen

The father listened to this statement with a frown, but finally he nodded and then shook his head.

"You're old enough to run your own affairs, honey," said he. "You got a right to do as you please. Only I want to say to you that this is a thing where one step forward never can be taken back. You've thought of that, honey?"

"Yes."

"Then I'm gunna go to bed. Good-night. Finch, you're a powerful lucky feller."

He went into the house with a somewhat dragging step. Life had been a heavy burden for Lawrence, and he showed the weight he was carrying. His wife went behind him, pausing at the screen door to smile back hopefully at her daughter and her lover.

"Don't you be stayin' up too long," she warned them. "Tomorrow's a new day, and you can't settle everything in the world in one night!"

So Finch and Kate Lawrence were left

alone, and Tirrel, the eavesdropper, crept closer, without shame.

The moment that the screen door had jangled shut, and the steps of the older people had faded out of hearing into the house, Kate Lawrence turned her back on her lover and walked to the front of the porch.

Dan Finch hesitated a little, doubt and distinct trouble in his face. Then he followed her.

"Shall we take a stroll through the woods, Kate? It's cooler out there."

She turned back to him, but instead of answering, she merely looked him up and down and shrugged her shoulders.

"Look here," said Finch, "if you're going to take it as hard as all this, *I*'m not the gent to drag you into any marriage, Kate."

She said simply: "Well, I've taken the plunge, and the water's pretty chilly!"

Her matter-of-factness was a shock to Tirrel. She was as calm and deliberate as could be. Gentle and lovely as her face was in repose, when she spoke, her eye was as direct and as straight as the eye of any man.

Finch did not attempt to become sentimental. He met her on her own ground.

"Of course it's chilly," said he. "Always is. Every girl cries when she leaves her home, for instance."

"I won't cry. I'm a thousand miles from crying!" said Kate Lawrence.

"Fight, then," chuckled Dan Finch.

"I'd rather fight than cry."

"Mind you, Kate — I'm not putting the whip on you."

"You're not. No. It's only devilish luck that's whipping me."

"In what way? In wishing me on you, you mean?"

"Why couldn't I lose my heart to you, Dan, the way that I've lost my head?"

"If I've got one," said Finch, "I'll get the other before long. I've got a fisherman's patience, Kate!"

"I suppose that you have."

She faced him, frowning, a weight of some decision in her eyes.

"If it don't work," she said, "it will be an awful smash!"

"It's got to work! The way you see it now, Kate, you don't know how I'll work to make a go of things!"

"I think you will," she said. "And, once I'm in harness, I'll pull my share of the load no matter how sore my shoulders get. Still — that doesn't make love!"

"No," he admitted, "but it makes friendship, and that's a lot safer basis to start on, most of the time, than love. That's blindness.

But you're not blind. You have your eyes wide open and you can see the facts about me. If you care a little about me this way, then I'll take my chance to get your love afterward. That's reasonable, I think."

She considered this.

"Yes," she decided. "That's reasonable. But still I hesitate. It's like staking all your money on one race. Because, to my way of thinking, a girl can only be married once."

"I'm glad to hear you say that. And of course I don't wonder that you hesitate, Kate. If I had longer time, you could take as long as you wished."

"You really *have* to go, Dan?"

"I have to. There's nothing for it except to get under way. I should be in London in a couple of weeks at the latest."

"London!" said the girl.

"That'll be a trip for you, Kate!"

She sighed.

Then he added gently: "As for the old folks, everything'll be fixed for them as neat as wax. You can depend on that!"

"There's nothing but kindness in you, Dan!" cried the girl with an impulsive richness in her voice. "Ah, what a God-send you've been to poor Dad! And whatever happened to him would happen to Mother, too!"

"Look here," said Finch, "sometimes I'm

afraid that you're willing to marry me only because I *have* helped out your father!"

She said thoughtfully: "Well, there's something in that. But you know, Dan, that what holds me back most is your own mystery."

"Mystery?" laughed Finch.

"Yes. Exactly that. For instance, who's the man we heard is in Los Cavallos?"

"You mean the fellow they called by my name?"

"Yes."

"Well, there are plenty of men who look like me."

"But there's not another mare like Molly."

"She probably ain't much like Molly. People haven't any close eye for the looks of a hoss."

"But where *is* Molly? You've never come here before, without her!"

"I had to leave her behind to rest up. She can't go forever."

The girl shook her head.

"That's all honest Injun?" said she.

"Of course it is, Kate."

"All right," she answered. "But it worried me, just the same. It kept me worried. Where was Molly Malone? I couldn't get over that, you know! And it still stays a little in the back of my head. Then came this talk about Dan Finch in Los Cavallos — well, it muddled me a good deal!"

166

"How could they really know me over there? I've only made one flying trip through!"

"I've heard that. But there are other things — well, I won't ask questions. I've put my money on the horse, Danny, and there's no use thinking while the ponies go to the post!"

Tirrel had heard enough, and rising from his concealment in the shrubbery, he sauntered forward into the light. He had left his rifle with Molly Malone, but his Colt was conspicuous on his right thigh as he walked into the light. The girl saw him first and cried out a little, surprised.

"Is that you, Billy?"

"My name is Michael," said Tirrel. "My name is Michael Tirrel; excuse me for comin' in so late!"

So saying, he walked slowly and steadily forward, and up the veranda steps, keeping the closest of eyes upon Daniel Finch. The latter, at this unexpected apparition, started, changed color, and then his eyes rolled very wildly. For an instant, Tirrel was sure that a gunplay was coming, and he kept his hand in readiness for the draw.

But perhaps the death of the rabbit at the water hole was in the memory of Dan Finch, at the present moment, and his gun remained in its holster.

The girl, in the meantime, was watching

both men with the most intense interest.

"I've been listening out in the bush," confessed Tirrel. "I've been hearing you all talking together, since your mother and your father went into the house."

She exclaimed:

"That was a fine thing to do!"

"I had a reason for it," said Tirrel. "I wanted to hear this gent talk some more."

He raised his left hand and pointed with deliberate insult at the other, while Dan Finch, grim, silent, waited.

"There's no use talking here," said Finch. "If you've got anything to say to me, Tirrel, we'll step off into the woods and finish it!"

He had made his voice hard, as he spoke, but there was no real confidence in his manner.

Tirrel smiled in his face.

"I want to say some things here before Miss Lawrence. I want her most particular to hear 'em."

Finch turned sharply upon her: "Kate," he said, "you'd better go inside."

She did not hesitate.

"I'll go in," she nodded.

"You'd better stay," said Tirrel.

"I don't listen to blackmail," said she.

"If I say a word that isn't true — why, here I am up against the great Dan Finch, the gunfighter. I'd be afraid to tell a lie about him! Isn't that true?"

She paused at the door.

"Goodnight, Danny!" said she.

Tirrel stamped, impatiently.

"You're playing the part of a fool. Lemme show you that I've got the right to talk. I'm the other Dan Finch. I'm the Dan Finch that your father wrote to in Los Cavallos!"

She closed the door which she had been opening. Then, turning back on the porch, she said crisply: "I think that you ought to do something about this, Danny!"

"I'm gunna do plenty about it," said Dan Finch. "Tirrel, I'm inviting you to step off into the woods with me!"

But Tirrel merely laughed.

"Molly Malone is waiting out there," he said, "but I don't think that she's waiting for you!"

"Molly!" cried the girl.

"Sure," said Tirrel, "I'm the gent that he left Molly with — for a rest!"

Chapter Twenty

At this, and the sneer with which it was said, the girl started. She asked suddenly: "Is there something in this, Dan?"

Finch answered hoarsely: "There's nothing that can't be explained. I — I wanted to cover this up, Kate, I'm willin' to admit that. I met up with Tirrel in the desert, when I was comin' back. We got to gambling, and he cleaned me out of everything, down to my boots and my pocketbook. He got Molly too."

"You gambled Molly away!" she exclaimed again.

"Ay — I'm ashamed of that!" said he.

She shrugged her shoulders.

"I've heard worse things," said she.

"I could tell you a story of four sevens," said Tirrel slowly.

And Finch turned deathly white, and the beads of perspiration stood upon his forehead.

"What's the story?" asked the girl, looking not at Tirrel, but fixedly at Dan.

"Kate," said Finch, "I want to ask you something pretty important."

"What is it?"

"I want to ask you to go inside and leave me alone with Tirrel for a while. In the morning there'll be a chance to make everything straight with you."

"I'll not be here in the morning," said Tirrel. "I'm being hunted as Dan Finch — I'm wanted for murder — I'm wanted for the murder of my own brother!"

Dan Finch said with a desperate eagerness: "Tirrel, I know everything that you've got in your mind to say. You've got some reason behind it, too. But I'm going to ask you to spend one hour with me. We'll leave the house and come back to it inside an hour. Kate will still be up and awake. We can finish the argument with her, then!"

"You're making a pretty big mystery out of this," said Kate Lawrence. "D'you think that that's wise?"

"I don't suppose that it is," said Finch. "But where there *is* a mystery, I've got to face it. Tirrel, I ask you for God's sake to do what I say!"

This he said with such entreaty in his voice and with such almost panting earnestness that Tirrel paused and then weakened.

"I'll go with you, Finch," he said. "I'm a

fool to do it, but I'll go along — and head myself into a trap, I suppose!"

"You'll go — that's all that I want!" said Finch. "Kate, we'll be back inside of an hour."

She nodded. And she looked at Dan Finch with what appeared to Tirrel to be a mixture of contempt, and pity, and surprise.

Finch led the way down the steps of the veranda. Tirrel walked close behind him. As soon as they were among the trees, he drew a revolver and carried it openly in his hand, and he warned Finch that he was watchful, and certainly that he would be merciless.

"You're a fool to be afraid of me now," said Finch. "Don't you see? I've got to bring you back to her and put myself straight with her again through some yarn you'll tell. I've got to convince her that I'm O.K."

"Man," answered Tirrel, "you'll never do that in a thousand years!"

Finch stopped short, fumbled blindly, and finally leaned his hand against a tree.

"D'you think that?" he said in a shaken voice. "D'you think that she's as savage against me as all of that?"

"I think that she is. I know that she is. I watched her face when she was talking to you."

Finch groaned.

"It's a damn miserable business. She believes that I was up to some crooked work against you."

"Well, Finch, you sent me up to Los Cavallos to be murdered. You know you did."

"Who said so?"

"A knife that barely missed my throat, and bullets that barely missed my head. Are those pretty good reasons?"

Finch said: "What have I to do with that? I ain't been near Los Cavallos since I seen you last."

"Of course you haven't. You sent me there to eat lead in your place. I dunno all about it, but I know that much, and I'm gunna let the girl know, too!"

"Are you?"

"I am."

Finch laughed, both with savagery and with triumph.

"You wait and see!" said he. "You're gunna do nothin' of the kind. You're gunna march on with me and see something that'll change your mind!" And he strode ahead.

He said, as he walked: "It's got to go through. I've worked it too far. I can't break down now!"

He was arguing with himself, and he added to Tirrel: "I'll convince her again through you. I'll make her think through you that

173

this was all right!"

He laughed again, as he said this. And even in the darkness, Tirrel could see that the man was nodding his head as he walked along.

For his own part, Tirrel had not the slightest idea of what could be lying before him. He could not conceive anything but a bullet through the head that would make him change his mind; and, as Finch already had explained, he would be ruined with the girl unless he brought Tirrel back alive and well at the end of the hour.

They had walked straight on into the woods, keeping up a brisk pace. The forest grew more and more dense. It was a second-growth wood, with a tangle of cowpaths worked through it in all directions, a perfect labyrinth through which Tirrel's guide seemed to hold the thread, for he never faltered.

The terrain was now greatly broken. The trees thinned out; huge boulders thrust up everywhere, lying on their sides or angled awkwardly upon corners and edges. It was a dark, very hard rock, yet it had been weathered here and there into poor soil, and everywhere lines and plumes of brush grew out upon the big rocks.

They already had been walking for twenty or twenty-five minutes when Finch turned into a veritable grove of stone, intermixed

174

with lodgepole pine. He took a lantern out of his pocket and cast the small ray of a bull's-eye before him, now and then probing the dark with it, and then proceeding confidently, as though these pencil strokes of illumination recalled the whole text of his surroundings to him.

Tirrel had to more or less flounder in the rear, making great efforts, but constantly stumbling.

Suddenly Finch paused.

"Suppose that I wanted to get rid of you?"

"Well?"

"Would it be hard for me to side-step around one of these rocks — and then to hunt you down like a cat hunting down a mouse?"

"Maybe," agreed Tirrel. "There's something in that."

In fact, there was everything in it, and he saw that he had practically disarmed himself in permitting himself to be led into such surroundings.

However, he followed on still until Finch suddenly leaned over and laid hands upon a rock. With a heave and a grunt he pried up a two hundred pound slab and rolled it back. It opened upon a deep, narrow well of darkness, into the mouth of which Finch sent the prying ray from his lantern.

"We go down there," said he, and immediately he descended, going down by jerks, as though using irregular steps. Tirrel paused for a moment on the verge. He told himself that he was, very likely, entering his own grave. But then he nerved himself again and, fumbling inside, he found the first step and gradually fumbled downward.

The dimensions of the tunnel increased every moment. First, he could stand erect, and second, he no longer touched wall upon either side. And, as he began to breathe more deeply of the cool, damp, confined air of that underground region, he was suddenly met by a blinding torrent of light.

It dazzled him but it did not keep him from action. His Colt glittered instantly in his hands, but the light went out, and the voice of Finch was laughing.

"You see what I could of made happen to you, Tirrel, if I'd been of a mind?"

"Try one more trick like that," said Tirrel, "and you'll be tagged with lead. Now, what's all of this here damned foolishness about?"

"I'm gunna tell you a story, old son," said Finch. "But first I want you to look at this here."

He sent the beam of his lantern upon what appeared to be a great rock coffer. It lay in the center of the cave, which made a room of some size, the entrance tunnel narrowing and rising like an awkward flight of steps to the side of it.

"You see?"

"I see," said Tirrel, his heart suddenly leaping.

"Well, I gotta tell you a story about what's in it. In the old days, they used to have sea pirates, and they used to have land pirates, y'understand? And the birds that cruised around on shore used to get pretty fat, what with Spanish gold and silver, and with crosses from the churches, all with emeralds, and pearls, and rubies, and all kinds of things. They had the jewels that they'd whittled here and there off of the robes of the priests. And they lived pretty gay on those things, if they wanted to spend money as they went. But some of the best of 'em at the sea-pirate business, they never spent much on this side of the water. They wanted to get back to their own old country — maybe Spain herself, or to England, or to France, most likely. They wanted to spend that money where the spending would bring in the wine! Y'understand?"

"Yes, yes!"

"Well, one of those gents that had been mighty successful, and that had stowed away a whole load of stuff out of churches and church treasuries, the gent, he up and dropped his collection here, and probably got croaked before he could come back for it.

"Later on, another gent of our own times, he had a good reason for finding a hiding place — and he happened to stumble upon this, and this is what he saw!"

As he spoke, he thrust aside the covering rock and revealed the interior of the great stone casket, entirely empty!

Chapter Twenty-One

Out of the throat of Finch came a strangled cry. He dropped upon his knees and thrust his hands blindly into the cavity. He stood up, staggering, and with the lantern fully unveiled, he threw the light here and there across the floor of the cavern. Something glistened. He leaped at it and raised in the palm of his hand a large pearl, such as might have made a pendant.

"They've got away with the whole body; they've left only one drop of the blood behind. But you can tell by this, Tirrel. I was gunna split the whole thing with you, half and half! I would have paid you fair and square to keep away from Kate Lawrence with your talk. I would of paid you up to the hilt to go back there and undo the harm that you've done me with her already! And now I been cleaned out!"

"Who could have done it?"

"The rest of 'em did it. I'd made fools of 'em. I had it all to myself. And they've trailed me down — God knows how! How could they ever of found *this* place? I found it myself only by a freak of chance, but they've found it after me!"

He beat a fist into his face.

"I'll be after them again, like a bloodhound!" declared Finch. "Tirrel, come with me. Here's the proof of what it is. Look here! I'll give you this thing. It's worth a couple of thousands, anyway. I'll give you that to begin with. Here, take it, will you?"

But Tirrel drew back.

"To help you trail those others?"

"Yes."

"Who are they?"

"Throw in with me, and I'll tell you everything. I'd want no better partner in the world than you if there was a fight at the end of the trail!"

"Thanks," smiled Tirrel.

"You'll do it, eh? Of course you will."

"What makes you think that I will?"

"Because there's a million apiece in it! It ain't the banknotes so much, though there's over half of a — "

He paused.

"Tirrel, will you throw in with me? Will you be with me in this deal?"

"I wouldn't be with you," said Tirrel, "for the sake of ten millions. I want none of your dirty game."

"Hold on!" muttered the other. "Lemme think for a minute. I'll give you reasons enough, in a minute, Tirrel."

He walked slowly away, and paced back and forth.

"It's no good," Tirrel told him. "I came out here with you because I was curious; not because I ever intended to take anything from you."

"And why should you be so dead set agin me, will you tell me that?"

"That seems queer to you, does it?"

"It does."

"Because you've been wanting me murdered, Finch, in your place at Los Cavallos. You sent me up to the town for that end. You even gave up the mare, so's you could let them fill me full of lead. What answer have you got for that, Finch?"

"I'll answer the whole thing in a way that'll surprise you," said Daniel Finch. "Just gimme a chance to think it over, will you?"

"Take as long as you want. You'll be explaining away knives and bullets, Finch! A damn fine talk you'll have to make!"

"I'll explain! I'll explain!" said the other.

With head bowed, he disappeared into the darkness of the cave as he spoke; and for a moment he did not return. The next that Tirrel knew, there was a loud crash of falling rock at the mouth of the cave, and he saw with what childish ease he had been tricked and trapped.

Stifled with distance, and more than that by the small aperture through which he was calling, came the voice of Finch:

"There's the explanation. May it satisfy you while you lie there and rot in the dark, Tirrel! You've changed your mind. When I wanted you to show down, you backed out. You've run off, and even left Molly Malone behind you, you were so keen to get away from me. That oughta satisfy the girl, eh? And it oughta satisfy you, Tirrel, and may you be damned for a fool!"

There was another heavier fall of rock, and a sensible settling of that which covered the cave mouth. Earth, loosened inside the tunnel, fell with a rattling shower. And dull echoes traveled slowly back and forth.

Tirrel, like a wise man, sat down in the center of the cave and gathered his thoughts. The dampness and the staleness of the air, hardly noticed before, now became chokingly important. He lighted a match to look about him and the flame burned small and blue.

It was so small a circuit of the walls that that match alone enabled him to make it, constantly looking up toward the corners of the walls in the hope of spotting some crevice.

But he saw nothing except a surface of ragged and apparently solid rock. No doubt, in the meantime Finch was watching for a little, rifle in readiness!

From the main body of the cave two branches extended, perhaps the course of the subterranean stream which, in past ages, had dug this passage through the earth. On the right hand side, the passage dipped sharply down beneath a solid wall of rock and disappeared as into a well of darkness. To the left, it was equally blocked by a sheer wall of earth and pebbles.

But it was the one possible solution to Tirrel. Rock he could not work with his bare hands, and he knew well enough that the mouth of the cave was now buried under a mass of those big rocks which he had seen hanging near by, already staggering upon a precarious balance. There remained this one possible place. He fell to work upon it, not in hope, but simply because to sit idle would bring madness on.

With the butt of a revolver he struck at the gravel and sand wall which choked the passage. It crumbled rapidly. Once the surface crust was broken, he was able to scrape it away with his bare hands, and presently, after a scant half hour of work, he thrust his arm straight through a hole. A few seconds widened that aperture so that he could wriggle through. Lying on his side, he scratched a match and held it before him. He could see nothing but rough edges of the rocky tunnel until, as the flame of the match died, he thought that he saw above him a faint gleam, like a highlight in the eye of a wild animal.

The red cinder of the match died; and now he saw not one gleam, but many, high and far. The stars.

In ten seconds he was out of that weak trap and standing up, breathing deeply, thanking God, it is to be feared, without much profound feeling, for already his mind was reaching forward to his return.

How should he meet Daniel Finch again, and could he prevent that clever fellow from finding the mare which was tethered in the woods? Perhaps if he so much as called to her, she would answer, whinneying. So the search of Finch would not have to be long!

In the meantime, he had the tangled labyrinth of the trees to thread. He closed his eyes and mapped the direction as well as he could. Then he took note of the trees, slightly mossed on the northern face of the bark, and thereby giving him all the points of the compass.

So he set his course and worked patiently along the line which he had set for himself, often checked, often blundering, but, as nearly as he could, staying to a northeasterly direction. In this manner he came, at last, out of the trees and the rocks and into the more open country, and as he did so, he saw the lights of a house glimmering steadily through the brush to his right. He came closer. There was no doubt about it. That was the house of Lawrence, from which he had departed not so many minutes before!

Somewhere in it, by this time, was doubtless that arch scoundrel, Dan Finch, telling his calm lies to the girl. Tirrel set his teeth and gripped the butt of his revolver. Then he went on a straight line, not for the house itself, but for the mare.

He found her safe, and his heart beat far more freely. She had finished grazing and lain down. She got up with a groan of straining cinches to nuzzle him in welcome.

He untethered her and let her follow behind him through the woods, for he had an odd feeling that he would not be safe, separated from her; and also, he wanted her to be present when he found Dan Finch and fought with him for the possession of her — and for that other, higher, unnamed stake.

Coming back toward the Lawrence house, he saw that the veranda was now dark. There were only three lights, two on the ground floor, and one on the floor above. The two lower ones were shuttered away so that the rooms could not be examined. The upper light, however, could be easily explored by means of a big tree which grew not far off.

Quick and soft as a cat, Tirrel climbed to the upper branches and looking through the window he saw Kate Lawrence in a chair that faced the window. She was in a position of the most utter surrender and exhaustion. Her face looked very pale. Her hair straggled into unkempt wisps. Her lips were wearily parted. One hand lay in her lap; one fell down toward the floor, and her head sagged toward one shoulder.

She might have sat for the picture of a dead woman, or certainly of a woman asleep. But he suddenly knew that she was neither dead nor sleeping but utterly exhausted.

Finch was not there, then! And where would Finch be? Had he not returned to the house, according to his boast, to let the girl know all that had happened — supposedly — to the false Tirrel?

It was inconceivable that he had failed to do this, and so right himself if he could. And perhaps it was because the girl had been able to look through his lie that now she sat overwhelmed with weariness and shame in her room.

Whatever his reasons, Tirrel formed on the instant a most rash and unwise resolution. It caused him to slip down the trunk of the tree and go straight to the wall of the house. He went up to the top of a window on the first floor with perfect ease. From the casing which topped this, he was able to stand on tiptoe and reach with his fingers the sill of the window of the girl's room above. Fixing his grip there, he drew himself up bodily, for his arms were very powerful. In an instant, he sat in the open window; the girl sat opposite him, her eyes wide now, looking at him with the most unspeakable horror.

Chapter Twenty-Two

"Get back! Get back!" whispered the girl.

Tirrel blinked at her, uncertainly.

"Has Finch come back here with lies about me?" he asked.

"Dan Finch hasn't come. And how have you managed it? Get out of the window — they've surrounded the house."

That statement was enough to bring Tirrel out of the window with a leap, and he landed on the floor, well to the side, and sheltered from view from without.

"I didn't meet a soul!" said he.

"They let you come through, then, so they could bag you in the house. Oh, haven't you eyes to see? They're all round. A dozen of them! They've searched the house from top to bottom. Sam Lowell is here!"

"Do they know that I'm not Finch, by this time?"

"They do."

"Do they still want me?"

"They want you both. Lowell's in a fury.

What did you do in Los Cavallos?"

And a little glint which was more interest than fear appeared in her eyes.

"I had to sashay out of Los Cavallos pretty pronto. That was all."

"Hush! What was that?"

"I didn't hear anything."

"I thought there was a creak of the stairs."

They were close together, whispering.

"I'll go back through the window."

"You'll be dropping straight into their arms."

"I can't be found here."

"What made you come back?"

"To tell you what I know about Finch."

"I learned enough tonight from you, already."

"Tell me this: Are you through with him?"

"Yes. Forever! I watched his face when you were talking. I never saw more guilt."

"That's all that I want. Goodby!"

"You mustn't go."

"I have to."

"Through the window?"

"It's the way that I came."

"Wait!"

She blew out the lamp and stepped to the window. Instantly she stepped back again.

"Two of 'em are waiting there beyond the hedge. You can see them for yourself!"

He stepped beside her and she pointed. He could see clearly enough, by the starlight. Behind the ragged top of the hedge were the faintly star-lit silhouettes of two watching men, and the glitter, very pale, of their rifles.

"I'll go down and make a break from one of the doors."

"Every one will be watched."

"I'll try a window, then."

"They'll ride you down! Sam Lowell means business. He says that he's been shamed in front of the whole world!"

"I've risked Lowell before; I'll have to chance him again."

"You can't win twice in one day against such a man."

"How did he guess that I'd be here?"

"He thought you were Finch, and he knew that Finch and I were engaged."

"I'm a fool! I should have guessed at that!"

"Will you tell me one thing?"

"Anything I know."

"Tirrel, you're a square shooter?"

"I think I'm reasonable straight."

"They've got a horrible story about murder. They say that if you're not Finch, you're worse — that you've killed your own brother!"

Even in her whisper there was a full measure of the horror which she felt.

"Jimmy and me," said Tirrel, "were as

close as any two brothers in the world. That's all I got to say."

"I believe you. I'm only telling you what they say."

"You believe me?"

"I do."

"Then I don't care what the rest of them say. Hold on — is there a cellarway out of this house?"

"Yes."

"Can you tell me how to get at it?"

"I'll take you there."

"I won't have you leave your room."

"You can't keep me here. It's my duty."

"You've got no duty to me."

"You've come back here to warn me about Dan Finch. I've got to get you loose again."

"Are they in the house as well as outside it?"

"I think so."

"Where does that door lead?"

"To the hall."

"And the other door?"

"Into an empty room."

"Can I get through that to the hall in turn?"

"Yes."

"I'll go that way. You keep behind me."

"I'd better go first. They won't harm me."

"And you suppose that I'll shelter myself behind a woman? Stay behind me!"

He pushed forward cautiously across the darkness of the room and when his hand touched the handle of the door, there he paused a moment, listening intently. It was very odd that so many fighting men could have surrounded the house, perhaps entered it, and yet made no sound whatever. He could have called it all a hoax, but he remembered the gleam of the rifles behind the hedge; that glimmer was potently convincing.

Softly he turned the knob of the door and felt it give in silence before him. The gap widened, he stepped through.

"Hands up, Tirrel!" said a loud voice suddenly.

He leaped back; a gun boomed; there was the sound of splintering wood as the bullet clove through the panel of the door. And then a voice in the next room shouted: "Mind the other door! He'll try to break out that way! Steady, boys, and we got him bagged!"

"It's Lowell!" gasped the girl.

But Tirrel was already convinced as to what he must do. There was only one exit where he would not be expected, the next instant, and that was the one he had just tried. So he wrenched open the door and sprang through, gun in hand.

It was a thoroughly sound maneuver. Dimly illumined against the stars beyond the open window, he saw the form of the deputy sheriff, his back turned, hurrying across the room. At the sound of Tirrel's entrance, he spun around on his heel, a curse half formed on his lips. But the long arm of Tirrel struck and the heavy barrel of the Colt cracked with sickening force along the bandaged head of Sam Lowell. He went down with a crash, and Tirrel, leaping over him, went on, reached the door beyond, and tore it open upon the noisy confusion of the upper hall of the house.

The Lawrence place was filled with sound, now, as filled as it had been by ominous silence the moment before. Feet pounded up and down the stairs; voices called loud orders and answers. There was a whisper of skirts behind him; he reached out and thrust the girl back. Then he stepped into the hall, shutting the door behind him.

"Who's that? What was that smash where Lowell was?"

"Him and me just slung a couch agin the door. Tirrel won't try to get out that way."

"Is it Tirrel or Finch?"

"It's Tirrel," answered Tirrel calmly.

They poured around him, four panting, eager men, sweating with excitement, the smell of horses about them. They had ridden fast from Los Cavallos. They wanted action, now.

"Who are you?"

193

"I'm Judson Beeman," said Tirrel.

"Beeman? I dunno that I ever heard — "

"Gloster, where's the sawed-off shotgun?"

"I left it down with the — "

"Throw a light here on this Beeman, will you?"

"Lowell wants Gloster and me to go down and shut up old Lawrence and tell him everything is all right," said Tirrel.

"Who are you?"

"Name of Beeman."

"I dunno you."

"Keep your eyes open, you fool!" bellowed Tirrel in pretended wrath, "and maybe you'll have better luck recognizin' me the next time! Lowell knew me good enough to ask me along! Are you gunna go down to the old man's room with me, Gloster?"

"All right. I'll go."

Tirrel led the way down the stairs, hardly able to believe that he was through that dusky tangle of forms. Someone had at last brought up or kindled a lantern on the landing above them, and now the broad shaft of the light pursued him down the stairs. But he did not turn his head. The broad brim of his sombrero would shield him from recognition from above.

They were guided to the room of Lawrence by a sudden outburst on the first floor and Lawrence shouting: "What in damnation is all this about? Who's in my house?"

With Gloster at his side, Tirrel marched up to the old man. A double barreled gun was in his hand; the pale lamplight flowed through the open door of the bedroom behind him and made him seem a black and towering figure. Tirrel marched up to him, saying: "Get back into your room. I got the order of the sheriff for the searching of your house."

"The sheriff!" gasped Lawrence, and gave weakly back through the open door. "The sheriff!" he exclaimed.

"Watch this here door," said Tirrel to Gloster, "and see that he don't come out!"

Gloster took a position before the door but exclaimed angrily: "Who the hell are you to give me orders?"

And, at that moment, a confused clamor roared above them: "Lowell's been dropped. He's gone below — he's busted loose — "

"By God — " exclaimed Gloster, as sudden light dawned on him, and he jerked his revolver from its holster.

A bare hand is faster than a weighted one, however. A straight arm right clipped Gloster upon the chin and sent him stumbling back; Tirrel jerked the door shut and turned the key in the lock. Then he turned to flee. He had gained three seconds, perhaps, if only he could use them properly.

Chapter Twenty-Three

Behind him, as he turned, Gloster was shouting wildly, and smashing his weight against the locked door, which shuddered and creaked violently with the heavy impacts. From above, came the thunder of descending footfalls.

He darted through the house and, snatching open a window, he fairly dived forth, as though at a surface of water. A strong-armed bush received him. He rolled out of it to his feet, running with all his might, and he saw the flash of a rifle spitting at him, cat-like, from the nearest trees. He swerved to the right. Straight before him, another form stepped out; a gun belched before him and the hiss of the bullet kissed the face of the fugitive. He could not dodge again. He snatched his revolver breast high and fired, half blindly. The other groaned and threw his hands high; Tirrel was past him before the wounded man had fallen.

Wounded, or dead?

He darted to the left again, running like the wind, dodging through the stiff black trunks of the trees, until he reached the spot where the mare was waiting. As he ran, he dropped the revolver into his holster and snatched out a knife. There was no time, now, to unravel knots. A slash of the knife sent the reins dangling and flying, and Tirrel, leaping for the saddle, let Molly Malone have her head.

He could not have trusted better. So confused was he by the noise, and the speed of his escape, that he would have driven her, of his own volition, in the wrong direction; she herself quickly caught him away from the angry voices, and the sound of the guns, for still they were firing near the house — at chance shadows, perhaps.

He found himself clear of the trees at last, in a valley pointing toward the northwest, as he made sure by looking up to the stars that streamed above him to the south and east, like sparks upon a wind; and as he galloped, he turned again in the saddle and looked back. There was no danger from the rear, but now, out of the edge of the woods just south of him, came half a dozen riders. They cantered their horses easily; then with a sudden impulse they darted ahead at full speed, and straight for him.

They had the advantage of the downslope in their charge, but he called to the mare only once, and that was enough. She bounded up the valley like an antelope. For two grim minutes the roar of hoofs rang and echoed behind her; then the sound a little decreased. The first rush of sprinting had ended, and immediately her superiority was telling. Rifles began to ring. The slower members of the pursuit pulled up, left or right, and, drawing their guns from the long holsters, they poured in a steady fire.

Three still rode on hotly enough, but Tirrel was rid of all at once by entering a region of great rocks and big brush which shielded him first from the bullets and then from the eyes of his enemies. He kept on at a vigorous gait for another five or ten minutes, but when he had put this time behind him, he halted. There was no sound to the rear. The mountains slept, and not an echo was disturbed.

So Tirrel knew either that the pursuit had been abandoned, or else that the pursuers came on with a more leisurely calm now, hoping to surprise him.

He was vastly relieved. But instead of pushing ahead, he turned in at the first cañon mouth and there made a camp in a nest of trees where there was water and grass for the mare and some shelter for himself. Here, in five minutes, he was asleep.

He was wakened once by the breath of the mare, snorted into his face, and looking up, he saw that she was standing over him, her great eyes shining with the starlight, her head pointed toward the trees. He called out; instantly there were stealthy sounds of some wild animal withdrawing at bounding speed through the brush.

Then he slept again until the morning and awakened in the rose of the dawn quite refreshed, with a cheerful mind and a courageous heart.

He did not use his rifle to get a good breakfast, however, and afterward he was heartily glad of this forbearance, for as he rode fasting over the crest of the next low range of hills, Molly Malone pricked her ears and halted as suddenly as a wolf halts in the presence of danger. Then, standing on tiptoes, he looked down into the next hollow and saw that half a dozen men were riding in a close body through the valley.

He reined Molly back instantly, and it seemed as though she understood beforehand that peril was there. For his part, it well might be that these were perfectly harmless travelers. But there were six, which was exactly the number which had ridden after him the night before, and they were armed to the teeth with revolvers and rifles — the latter a weapon which a cowpuncher would not normally be carrying.

He watched them out of sight, presently, and then he considered gravely what this could all mean. For, in the first place, if they were hunting for him they were going about it in a strange manner, grouping as they were in a single lot; they looked rather as though they were bound for a definite destination that had nothing to do with him.

In the meantime, there seemed little chance that they would be returning down the valley, and therefore he rode down into it, for he saw a small hut in it, standing south of a hill's slope, with a stream running before it, and a little grove at its back, as pleasant a spot as a man could wish to find.

Numbers of sheep were beginning to stream out from corrals near the house, the gray currents of them widening as they proceeded; and the sharp, shrill yelpings of the dogs were stabbing at the ears of Tirrel. Two boys, helped by the activity of the dogs, were sending the flocks afield, and this looked such a scene of prosperity that he promised himself a hearty meal when he came to the house.

He was disappointed. These Mexicans were rich, but they lived like the most starved peons. In fact, they were of that class, and they had not allowed themselves to forget it. Housed in one not over spacious room lived the whole family, consisting of two boys, a mother, a father, and a young baby. They had a thatched roof above them, heavy adobe walls around them, and a packed dirt floor beneath their bare feet. The woman was sprinkling this floor with water. The baby crawled bare-headed in the pleasant morning sun, trying to catch the tail feathers of a strutting rooster. The father of the family, his face dignified by a great, black patriarchal beard which signified more Spanish than Indian blood in him, smoked a cigarette beside the door and worked with rapid fingers on the construction of a bridle.

When he saw the stranger approaching closely he apparently called to his wife, who now brought out a rifle and leaned it against the wall beside him. So prepared, he went on busily with his work until Tirrel rode up. Then he got to his feet as the other dismounted. If Tirrel was hungry, he was welcome, he was told, but they had nothing delicate to put before him — only the regular daily food.

The woman then gave him cold tortillas, very thin and white, and beans, boiled with red peppers and very hot. There was not even coffee. There was only a bit of extremely bad wine, mixed liberally with water. Tirrel, after the first taste, preferred the river water undiluted. He finished that meal and he praised it.

He said that he never had eaten better tortillas and that he could tell that the peppers had been chosen by a master cook. This he said, while his throat was burned to the quick, as though by cold fire. He said it looking down, so that the telltale tears in his eyes might not be seen.

The housewife was very pleased. If he came to them on Saturday nights, he would enjoy a feast of roast kid; otherwise they did not taste meat during the week, unless the boys managed to trap squirrels or rabbits; but fish they got in quantities out of the creek.

The grass was very good near the house — the sheep always were grazed at some distance — and while Molly Malone cropped it busily, Tirrel sat on his heels beside the door and talked to the shepherd. His black beard gave him a formidable appearance, from a little distance; also, he was very brawny, with a high-arched chest and capable shoulders; but at close hand, one saw a brown eye, as open and harmless as the eye of a calf.

"How long have you lived here, *amigo?*"

"I was born here."

"And your father?"

"He was born here, too. He died last year, poor man."

"We must come to that."

"So the priest says."

"How many sheep have you?"

"Enough for mutton, and enough for shearing."

"That is a good thing," said Tirrel, wondering at the simplicity of this life, and also at the bank account which this simple life must allow the shepherd to pile up.

He added: "You send your boys to school in winter?"

"They will learn what I learned, and what my father learned before them. It is enough!"

"Yes, it should be enough. You live very pleasantly here."

"Well, we have the tiger to watch us."

"What tiger is that?"

"Yonder," said the shepherd.

He pointed to a mountain which lifted high above the foothills, an imposing mass.

"Why is it called that?"

"You'll see when you look at it. It's like the face of the woman in the moon. You have to look for a long time. But those two points on top are the ears, and that dark gulch is the mouth —"

"I can see the head, now. It might be called a tiger's head, at that."

"If you look further down you see the two big folds of rock, like the paws crossed over."

"Now it's so clear that I wonder I failed to see it before!"

"You have quick eyes. My oldest son has not yet seen it! Whenever a child of ours sees the tiger, it must have a pony to ride."

"And until then it walks?"

"Yes. Of course."

"What lies across the ridge, there? A big valley, I suppose?"

For he could not see any mountains beyond the Tiger.

"We can tell, but not by what we have seen; we never pass the Tiger."

"Why not?"

"He doesn't like to have people behind his back. But he is kind, they say, to those who live before his face. That is why we and the flocks are safe."

Tirrel smiled a little. He never had met with such imposing simplicity.

"But what are you told lies behind the Tiger?"

"Behind El Tigre is La Cabeza."

"La Cabeza. What is that?"

"La Cabeza is an even greater mountain, but we are so close to El Tigre that one cannot look past him to the other except from a very great distance."

"How does it get that name?"

"It has a bald head of shining rocks, but it has a white beard of snow — strings of snow that lie in the cañons until September. When

204

La Cabeza loses its beard, then we expect the rains."

"The Tiger and The Head!" mused Tirrel, and suddenly he opened his eyes.

"I've heard of them before!" said he.

"Most people who come into this country have," said the shepherd. "They are famous. There is a story about them, you know."

"What is the story?"

"El Tigre went hunting, a long time ago. He was very hungry. But he couldn't catch an antelope, and he couldn't find any buffalo. But at last he found a man. The man was not strong enough to fight him, and not fleet enough to run away. So El Tigre ate him. He was finishing his meal, and had come to the head, when the great spirit, Tirawa, happened to blow the clouds aside and look down to the earth. There he saw what was happening, and he was very angry. He turned the tiger to stone and he put him on top of a mountain, and he turned the head to stone and put it on top of a higher mountain, which he heaped up with his hands, and he forced the tiger to lie there forever, watching the head. That is why we never go past the Tiger. It would be dangerous to come at his back!"

"Has anything happened to people who go past him?"

The shepherd frowned, as though the

thought were painful.

Then he said: "Señor, six men rode up the valley toward El Tigre this same morning!"

"That is true. I saw them."

"Señor, not one of those six ever will come back again!"

"Hello! What makes you say that?"

"We have seen a few others ride up that pass. They never have come back."

"Perhaps they've ridden on through the mountains?"

The shepherd spread out his hands with a most eloquent gesture, and looked once up toward the sky.

"Perhaps!" said he.

Tirrel was on his feet.

"How, then, would one get across the mountains without passing the Tiger?"

"That is easy. The best way is to ride west and take the next valley. It is much easier than this one. It brings one to La Cabeza without passing the Tiger."

"Thank you," said Tirrel. "Because this is a thing worth knowing. I must go. This is something for your sons, to buy them whatever they want."

The shepherd put back the hand that offered the money.

"God forgive me," said he, "if I ever sell

anything but mutton and wool! God gives us our food so that others may share it if they will. Farewell!"

Chapter Twenty-Four

Slowly enough, Tirrel sent the mare up the slope down which he had just come, but as soon as he was fairly across the crest of it, he turned her up the valley as the shepherd had directed for all those who wished to reach La Cabeza without turning the back of El Tigre — which would have such disastrous results! But what made him hurry so fast was the sentence he had read, those days before — how long a time it seemed! — from the red wallet.

"It is under the head, in line with the tiger!"

That had seemed mysterious enough when he had first looked at it and never since had he been able to make out its meaning, but now chance, his own idle questioning, and the amiable answers of the shepherd offered him a solution. The head and the tiger were the two mountains of Indian lore — La Cabeza and El Tigre. Therefore he must find a place on The Head, in line with The Tiger, and there would be an old spruce, and beneath it he would find "it."

What made him hasten so fast and avoid the direct line past El Tigre's shoulder was not the warning of the shepherd but the remembered sight of the six horsemen who had been journeying in the same direction. He was starting well behind them, but they had not ridden with any great speed, and he trusted that the mare would enable him to outflank them and get to the strategic position before them. So he gave her her head.

It was no more necessary to spur her than it would have been to spur a willing human runner. She accommodated her pace to the ground, cantering up and down gentle slopes; racing with long, bounding strides over every approach to a level, and the rest of the time undertaking everything with a brisk trot. There was no need, either, to check her in direction, for, once she was put at a point, she kept at it steadily, never varying from her course except as the terrain forced her to swerve aside. And her ears were pricked and her head always high.

The sun slipped higher into the sky. It was nearly prime before the mare reached the crest of the first mountain barrier, and then Tirrel found himself looking down into a valley ten or twelve miles wide, and utterly dominated, from the other side, by La Cabeza. It was perfectly easy to understand its name, now that the features had been pointed out. There was the bare poll of rocks, kept naked by the polish and sweep of the winds which blew forever, there in the heart of the sky. And beneath this bald head, there was a tangle of white, where the snows of the spring still were clotted among the shadows of the ravines.

The heart of Tirrel rose, like the heart of a boy, confronted by some inexplicable mystery, and he laughed aloud, so that the echo came oddly back to him from the rocks around and startled him into a suspicious silence, again.

To the right, staring with the eyes of a hawk, he saw a cloud of dust whirled thinly up into the air, and as it blew away, he made out a train of six horsemen, moving slowly, two miles or more distant.

With all his detour, the speed of the mare had held them even. What could she gain in the ten or twelve miles across the valley, and in the additional miles up the rugged breast of the mountain? He would try her now!

She went down the slope in fine fettle, and, steadying to a long stroke as she got toward the more level going, she sailed splendidly away — like a hawk dropping from a height and then shooting on swift, steady wing across a level stretch of air.

So Molly Malone devoured that valley's width in less than an hour and began to clamber up the mountainside beyond, aimed only once at La Cabeza, and thereafter staying true to her mark like the wise-headed horse that she was!

Her rider helped her greatly, now. Looking back, through clefts in the brush, and around the corners of the great boulders which had tumbled down the mountain's breast from above, he had glimpses of the six riders and their slower progress. They had not forced their horses; they had not such horses to force! And he already was a goodly distance up the mountain while they were still in the middle of the valley.

He had gained well upon them, but still he was anxiously on the alert, clambering and running and panting at the side of the mare, so as to ease her saddle of his weight in this uphill pull. For he must save her as much as possible. Who could tell what work would lie ahead of her later in this day, or how much of her vital force had been drained away by this forced march through the mountains?

It was still not noon. The air was windless. The sun bucketed down its white heat from the center of the sky, and the trees cast little shade against its perpendicular force. With sweat streaming down his forehead, stinging his eyes, Tirrel ranged his glance from side to side, while he wove an irregular, looping course up the mountain, partly to ease the mare, and partly to cover more ground, for he must find that particular tree under the head, and in line with the tiger!

It might have several meanings. It might be anywhere along the side or the bottom of the big mountain, and again, it might be high up, just under the edge of the beard of the head proper. So, eagerly watching, he let the mare work herself into a lather, while he himself, half blinded with sweat, struggled on at her side, only clinging to a stirrup leather to help him in the race.

Near the top, he looked back; the six riders had disappeared from view under the edge of the trees which fringed the lower part of the slope. That meant danger. It was as though murder had entered the front door of a house; sooner or later it was apt to find him!

He paused, nevertheless, and, mopping his forehead with a handkerchief already soaked, he turned again, with teeth set, to face the slope — and saw before him a dead tree, one side of it splintered by a thunder bolt, a ruined branch now moldering on the ground beside it.

He passed that tree and turned back. It lay

exactly in line with the head of the Tiger, across the valley, and at its base, two great roots elbowed out in a capacious fork.

Instantly he was at work. A large stone lay against the fork, and this he rolled away with a little difficulty. He stared at the bark against which the upper edge of the stone had rested and noted that it had cut in through the bark, and that the tree had not given to it, as would have been the case had the growing trunk rubbed against such an impediment.

The rock, therefore, had been comparatively recently leaned against that tree; and under the rock, as he could have sworn, was "it!"

With the rock removed, he saw a rubble of small stones. These, hastily, he scraped away and found hard-compacted earth beneath.

This made him pause, and he was about to commence his digging again, when the mare whinnied behind him — no louder than a whisper, but a sound which he felt to be a warning.

He straightened himself upon his knees, and then, distinctly, he heard noises coming up from below on the mountainside — ringing above all else, the sharp crack of a shod hoof against a rock. This was enough warning to him to hurry. He fell to work with a passionate zeal, and soon he had uncovered a surface more than a foot square and fully as deep between the forking roots of the trees.

So, scratching with both hands like a cat, he felt a fingernail catch in leather. He stopped. A thrill of icy excitement benumbed him and made him tremble. Then, savagely, he dug again, uncovering the mouth of a bag made of strong buckskin, puckered together by the pressure of a heavy buckskin thong. He pulled at the bag. Its swelling belly and its own weight foiled him. He tugged with all his might, and straightway the bag gave way with a jerk.

He cast it down on the ground and tried to untie the thong which bound it, but the thong stuck tight. Distinctly, up the hillside, he heard the coming of the six riders.

Patience, patience! More haste, less speed.

Snatching out his knife, he slashed the bag wide open and through the wound, with a soft clinking, flowed a little torrent of gold pieces. He picked up three or four. They were heavy and looked as though they had been clumsily molded. In a moment he had recognized them as ancient coins of Spain. He groaned, despairing and yet avaricious, for he saw that he could not transport much treasure, bulky as this. And suddenly he wanted it all, with a vivid, burning thirst for wealth consuming him.

He reached into the hole again; his exertions were widening it, and excitement made his hands very strong, so that he was able to drag out in swift succession three other bags. Two of them were of equal dimensions with the first and filled with the same heavy golden coins. The third was not a tithe of the other three in weight.

This too he opened, cutting the thong, and he saw beneath a wad of paper, jammed together, damp, spotted with mold. He stared for a long instant at that unsightly lump, in spite of the noise of horses coming up the hillside. He was fascinated, for he knew that these were greenbacks from the United States Treasury, promising to pay the bearer, in gold, the dollars stamped upon the face of the note.

No matter how near the riders came, he could not hurry too much. He lifted the lump of the moldering paper currency, and beneath it he saw a mass of glowing color, all heaped together in a sea of dull fire. There were streaks of green and red and yellow, and bits as of moon-brightness dropped within, and all these glowing colors heaped carelessly together.

Tirrel sprang back and his throat was so suddenly packed with joy that he shouted aloud, and his wild, ringing laughter rushed and rang down the mountainside.

Gathering the top of the bag together, he leaped on the mare and drove her to the side into the screen of rocks and of trees, and as he did so, he saw coming up toward the tree images of men and horses, distorted through the screen of leafage. One man broke through before the rest, and it was the man of the cloudy blue eyes, riding up in the lead. At sight of him, Tirrel's heart sank a little. He was beginning to feel a strange certainty that this man was intimately connected with his destiny.

However, there was only one glance, and then he sent the mare away as fast as she could go.

Chapter Twenty-Five

Of course the best speed was downhill, but he checked that impulse. Behind him, men were yelling like devils, as though fury fairly transported them. It was a temptation to take the shortest course, but he remembered that these horses, though they had not traveled as fast as his own mare, had gone as far. Moreover, they had not enjoyed the breathing spell which recently had freshened her. So he took her on a course winding up like the thread of a corkscrew, until a streak of snow showed through the trees before him. He dipped below this, and then he came over the shoulder of the mountain and saw the plain stretched out beneath him, the hills tumbling down into it with their forests turning pale gray and growing ghostlike as they marched into the hotter, dustier air of the lower level.

He could see three roads coming at different places out of the hills and pointing toward one spot. Smaller trails, too, ran in a meager pattern of tributaries into the larger roads, and he told himself that where the three ways joined, beneath the dust films of the valley, there must be a town. That was what he wanted. These six gentlemen would not be apt to stay in striking distance of Molly Malone all the way to the distant city.

He could hear them now; they had given up all pretense of subtle silence in their hunting; they raged and cursed one another and all living things as they stormed through the trees. Grimly looking over his shoulder, he patted the stock of his rifle; it would have been a game to tag some of the leaders of this pursuit. He wanted, above all, to make sure whether or not Deputy Sheriff Sam Lowell was riding with this crew. However, he was too sensible to take any further chances. He loosed Molly and she went down the slope like water down the bed of a cataract.

To go uphill is hard enough. To go downhill is the most difficult of all tasks for a horse. It grows weary in the shoulders from the constant pounding, all the weight of every step thrown forward. It is confused with fatigue; the pebbles and the rocks bound and strike around it, dangerously; and in such circumstances a stumble may bring death to horse and rider.

But Molly Malone went down that slope like a beautiful mountain sheep, regardless of long drops, coasting with braced legs, squatted low, over inclines that caught away the breath of her rider. Nothing could have been more plain than that she loved her work. Her pricked ears said so, and her dainty, tossing head.

The six riders came out of the woods above in time to see the fugitive skidding around a boulder, jumping a creek, and flashing out of sight in the lower belt of woods.

They came after as well as they could, opening a dropping fire in the general direction in which he had ridden, but there was not one of those good horses, not one of those reckless riders, who could hold the pace with Molly. In a brief half hour, Tirrel was in the beginning of the big foothills, and there was no noise of pounding hoofs behind him.

He halted there and examined the feet of the mare to see if they had suffered damage from that wild descent, but they were as sound as when she started that morning. So he mounted and went on again, more leisurely, the mountains growing bigger behind him, the hills smaller before his face, until at last he came down into the valley road.

The vegetation was different, now. Those upper slopes bagged many a goodly rainstorm when the winds blew over them, and therefore the growth of trees was noble in size; but here he was again with the Spanish bayonet, the ocatilla, greasewood, and other pale gray shrubs, holding the edges of their leaves to the sun. He passed a colony of prairie dogs, yapping at him furiously from a distance, disappearing in a wave before him, reappearing in an equal wave behind. Here and there stood a grave little owl; and yonder was the bright coil of a rattler, sleeping in the sun. And suddenly Tirrel realized that all living things have peril for a close neighbor; and, for his peril, he had a treasure in reward!

He was more comfortable in this open, flat country than he had been in the hills, for he was a man of the desert, there bred and there raised. Even the heat did not trouble him; his lean body had grown accustomed to oven temperatures by the labor and the endurance of many years.

The town which he had suspected must be here in the flat now began to loom before him. He could tell it first by the manner in which the dust clouds of the travelers and wagons along the converging roads dissolved at the meeting point.

More than that, he now made out broad, swelling outlines which appeared gradually as houses, rising distinctly through the desert haze; and finally he was riding into the town. It was exactly like a hundred other places of some thousand or fifteen hundred people, scattered through the West. Sun and wind had worked the paint from its houses and it never was replaced. The thin unseasoned boards had warped away. Sometimes five years would wreck a shack utterly, leaving only a few skeleton uprights, with a tumble of dried boards scattered at their knees. But there was life in this city. The more flimsy the town, the more powerful the blood which flowed through it, seemed to be an old Western rule. There were cowpunchers from the flourishing cattle range; there were miners here from the hills; there were teamsters, freighting with twelve and sixteen mule teams to great distances, for the railroad was far, far away. Over those roads, too, stages were dashing, day and night, with swift relays of horses; and a constant procession of strangers poured through the hotels and the gaming halls and the saloons of Apache Crossing. Many a town like this had Tirrel known, and he smiled as he saw it unfolding before him.

He passed to the center of the place, which was laid out as a large, barren plaza. Some optimist had brought in a pair of palms, at great cost; but a drunken puncher had deliberately shot off the heads of both the trees. The bare stalks remained, dead and hopeless. But Tirrel smiled at this, too.

He had two reasons for taking to a town. The first was that it would probably never occur to the hunters who pursued him that he had sought refuge in an inhabited place — wanted as he was by Los Cavallos for murder. The second reason was that he wished to dispose of this treasure which had been miraculously placed in his hands.

Also, two or three days of graining would do much for Molly Malone.

He saw her stabled; then he went to the nearest hotel and took a back room.

"I gotta have quiet," said Tirrel belligerently, "and if any drunk comes in and makes noise after twelve, I'm gunna start an argument."

They gave him a back room, and after he had locked the door and made sure that no window overlooked his and that there was no tree in the branches of which a spy could be sheltered, he placed himself comfortably at the little deal table which stood in the center of the room and laid the contents of the buckskin bag upon it.

Before he looked at it, he shielded the rich heap with both his hands, as though he wanted to keep himself from being dazzled. And he turned his chances through his mind.

It was quite true that the police of Apache Crossing must have been warned by the authorities of Los Cavallos concerning the wanted man; it was true that the horse would be described as well as the rider. But he had put up the mare in a stable away from the hotel. He had approached that place on foot, and he flattered himself that it would take a very close-eyed person to be able to distinguish between him and a hundred other punchers off the range. Moreover, men in such a town were not used to examining strangers carefully. All that was demanded of anyone was that he should pay his bills and not ask too many questions.

Reassured by this train of thought, Tirrel spread the treasure before him and examined it in detail. He shut his eyes against the heap of the jewelry and counted the bills. It was a delicate process to disentangle them one by one from the wad into which they were almost melted. But patience accomplished it. One by one he worked them loose. After the outermost ones had been detached the core worked more easily, and he put pressure, at last, on the total pile, and pressed it as flat as he could.

The bills were of large denominations. There were only a few twenties, after that came fifties, hundreds, and five hundreds. Altogether there were two hundred and forty-nine bills, and when he had added up the long columns of figures, he found that before him on the table lay more than forty thousand dollars in hard cash!

He closed his eyes and said it over again to himself. Money was worth eight per cent at least, in those Western days. Eight times forty thousand made thirty-two hundred a year, and this was affluence!

Or, again, forty thousand dollars would buy a fine stretch of range and stock it with cows. All the world of opportunity was revealed here before him, under his very hand.

He pressed his lips together. A sort of mad joy was rising in him, bubbling like wine in his throat, and this he had to control sternly.

Then he went to work upon the jewels. He knew little or nothing about them, but he segregated the diamonds in a little pile by themselves, and he contrasted the stones with those of his stickpin. That pin must be worth more than a thousand. To judge by this, then the much larger stones of the buckskin bag would amount in themselves to more than the value of all the stack of greenbacks which he had just placed so tenderly inside the red wallet.

There were larger heaps of rubies and emeralds than of the diamonds, but the glory of the collection was undoubtedly the pearls, not only the unset ones, but, above all, a cross worked over with pearls in almost a solid mass, and with a jewel of great size at top, bottom, and at the end of each arm.

He simply could not estimate this whole mass of treasure, but he could see that there was enough of it to have justified the feeling of Dan Finch that he could buy off Tirrel with a moiety of it and still retain enough to leave himself rich for life.

He began to breathe hard.

All at once the duty of finding Nicholas Bramber, and the dread of the law, and the pursuit of that pale-eyed man called Chandos seemed to Tirrel nothing at all.

He was the victor, and the proof of his victory was spread there upon the table before him.

But what to do with his treasure?

Chapter Twenty-Six

There was, of course, the first obvious temptation — which was to hide it. And thinking of this plan, instantly there passed through his mind's eye all the best available places which he had seen in his journeyings. He thought of deserted shacks, of hollow trees, of mountain caves, of little mountain lakes where a leaden box could be sunk.

But no matter what care he used, he was reasonably sure that his trail might be followed to the hiding place; the cloudy eyes of Chandos haunted him; they never would give over the search. Perhaps even now Chandos was at the desk of this very hotel, inquiring.

Sweat burst out upon Tirrel.

Or, again, he might use a different name and simply place his treasure in a safe-deposit vault of the Apache Crossing Bank. But to this, again, Chandos might trace him. Or, failing that, might not some clever yegg succeed in cracking the safe, or in bribing a bank clerk?

He could, of course, keep the stuff with

him. It was not too bulky to be safely lodged in a saddle bag. Yet if he were taken, of course the treasure would instantly be lost to him, even if he saved his life.

In spite of his anxieties, there was a thread of golden joy woven through.

He not only had the money and the jewels, but also he could rejoice in the manner in which he had gotten them. Dan Finch and the rest, entangled in a skein of enmities and hatreds which he could not pretend to understand, had fought with one another, as nearly as he could make out, for this prize. Finch had won, only to be trailed down to the hiding place — no doubt by him of the agate, clouded eyes — and these victors, in turn hiding the loot, had been plundered by Tirrel himself as they were about to reclaim their wealth.

That was the story as he saw it, with many and vital chapters missing from the narrative, of course; he would know more before the end, he hoped!

In the meantime, he was keen with anxiety to learn more about the sum of his wealth. For that purpose, and also to reduce the bulk of the treasure, he set to work loosening the pearls from the cross on which they were set. Through the late afternoon and almost to sunset he worked, and by that time he had succeeded in stripping the wood. There remained only a little chasing in silver and in gold. He broke up the antique and shied it out the window and into a junk heap which was just in view in the back yard of the hotel.

Then he went down to the street.

Apache Crossing, resting from the dust, the heat, the labors of the day, was beginning to relax. Up and down the street strolled gentlemen in careful black clothes, with pale faces, and tapered, delicate hands. These were the professional gamblers. Girls for the dance halls were sauntering to their places of work, brilliantly painted, always laughing with that peculiar grimace of the professional entertainer.

And Tirrel, with the flow of laborers, miners, punchers, mere adventurers, thieves, cheats, crooked promoters, drunkards, wastrels, fools, investors, went up one street and down another until he found what he wanted — a pawnbroker's shop. Better still, he found two of them. They were exactly opposite one another, looking out, as it were, with an air of confident rivalry from beneath their golden moons.

"How come," asked Tirrel of a lounger, "that they got their pawn shops so close together in Apache Crossing?"

"I'll tell you why. The old man, yonder, made his son sore. His son left and fixed up a

228

rival business. They try to cut each other's throats, and the result is that we get a fairer price for our junk now than we ever got before."

"Who's the best of the pair?"

"The son gives you a shade the best of it. Try for yourself, if that's what you're aimin' at. The old man has the shop over across the street, there!"

The old man was a patriarch with a silken white beard — yellow white, carefully combed into two flowing masses. It was of the most beautiful texture, but so thin that the black of his coat showed through it, in most places. His old hands, too, were the hands of a patrician, being very slender, dead white, with heavy blue veins showing like streaks of lapis lazuli against the skin. He wore spectacles with glasses so very round and big that he looked the part of a wise old owl.

His voice was low, rather broken and earnest, so that he gave an impression of speaking in a tone shaken with emotion. He seemed continually protesting against the avarice, the cruelty, the harshness of his clients, who wrung the money from his weak, helpless hands.

This manner was the rock upon which he had raised his fortune. He was very rich, cold-hearted, and cruel, and Tirrel guessed at all of these facts with almost the first glance he gave the pawnbroker. He took from his pocket the smallest of the big pearls from the cross — the one which had formed the top of it. This he laid upon the counter.

"Do you want a loan?"

"I have to sell it."

"You name a price, then."

"I don't know much about these here things," said Tirrel honestly. "I'd like to have you tell me about what I should get for it."

"And then," said the other, "when I tell you about it, you'll ask double what I offer!"

"Maybe," admitted Tirrel.

The old man shook his head at this confession of iniquity, but he raised the pearl between thumb and forefinger and examined it close to a small, intense light. In the ray, the pearl glowed throughout, suffused with wonderful translucence.

"This is a good thing," said the pawnbroker, still shaking his head a little.

He put down the pearl on the counter again and veiled the light. Then he peered inquiringly at Tirrel.

"You've brought me a very fine pearl," said he.

"I'm glad to know that."

"I know all about pearls," said he. "I collect them. I love to look at them, for my own pleasure. That's why I'll give you a good price for this one — because it's worthy of going into my own collection!"

He smiled a little.

It was as though he saw that he should not exhibit such enthusiasm if he wished to beat down the price — but his frank emotion had carried him away from himself.

"And what's the price, then?"

"I've got to pay you three hundred dollars for this fine pearl," said the pawnbroker.

"Hold on! That ain't up to your talk!"

"Young man, young man," said the old fellow sadly, "there is a great deal of grasping greed in this world! There was a time, when I was younger and had more strength, when I used to juggle the prices, also, and try to revise them downward to suit myself. But as I grow old, I no longer have the energy. Sharp bargains appear to me just another game of cheating!"

Greatly impressed, Tirrel listened to this speech, nodding his head; but he could not help thinking that pearls, according to size, were strangely cheaper than other jewels.

"I suppose that I'd better take it, then," said he. "I don't want to beat you down. I just want to get at a fair price for it. *I* don't know what the thing is worth, and I suppose that you do?"

"I've spent my life in the love of pearls,"

said the pawnbroker. "In the open market you might get two hundred and fifty dollars for this. But from me — well, that is a different matter. I need it. It appeals to me. So I offer you a higher price at once!"

As he spoke, he opened a cash drawer and, keeping his eyes fixed all the while upon his client, as though watchful in case of an attack, he fumbled until he found the bills and counted them out in a little stack before Tirrel. Then he held out a hand, palm up, to receive the jewel.

Tirrel extended the pearl, but then he hesitated. There was as he thought, the slightest quiver in the hand of the ancient. It might be mere weakness of age, but it might also be eagerness. He dropped the pearl into his pocket and said calmly: "No, I don't think I can sell at that figger. It's worth more than that to me, just to have it and look at it!"

The pawnbroker shrugged his shoulders, snatched up the money and thrust it back into the drawer.

"Young man, you disappoint me," he said gravely.

"Goodby," answered Tirrel, and turned to the door, rather shame-faced.

"One moment. Ah, I'm a weak-minded old man! I'd offer you another fifty dollars for that! We'll call it three hundred and fifty dollars and I'll take the pearl. I'll be a beggar, if I keep up at this rate!"

Tirrel turned at the door. He was frowning a little, and beginning to suspect.

"Suppose that I said five hundred and not a penny less?"

"Are you mad?" cried the old man. "Five hundred dollars! For that?"

"I'll see if I can get it across the street," said Tirrel.

He had his hand upon the knob of the door again when the pawnbroker cried out in mingled anger and anxiety:

"Not to him! Not to that ingrate and traitor, that unnatural son! Leave it with me. Yes, I'll rob myself rather than that he should put a price on it. Yes! Five hundred, then!"

But Tirrel shook his head.

"I'm going to get some more prices," said he. "Three hundred looked big at first, but now my ideas are getting bigger. Goodby!"

He heard an outcry from the old man, but he resolutely crossed the street and entered the other shop where a tall, pale, calm young man with a mist of yellow-red hair above a high bald forehead took the pearl and examined it by the same sort of a light as his father had used.

He placed it back upon the counter.

"I can pay you eleven hundred dollars," said he.

Chapter Twenty-Seven

Tirrel smiled. He was not thinking of the price now offered, but of the pathetic attitude of the old robber across the street when he had offered three hundred. Compared with him, this youngster was a pillar of honor and honesty. But still, his generosity might be merely a comparative thing. Tirrel allowed his smile to widen into a broad and ugly sneer.

"I'll tell you what," said he, "you take me for a fool!"

The youth looked at him gently, patiently. He sighed.

"One makes mistakes, now and then," he said.

He examined the pearl again, and now he lifted his brows and exclaimed suddenly: "Yes, yes, yes! I understand now!"

He put the pearl back on the counter.

"Frankly, you are right. It's more valuable than I thought. I could even pay fifteen hundred dollars for it."

"Or three thousand, maybe?" asked Tirrel,

suddenly flushing with excitement.

"Three thousand?"

The pawnbroker shrugged his shoulders and spread out his hands in a gesture of surrender.

"Perhaps that is a joke," he suggested.

"No joke at all, but something I mean. I'll try your father, and see what he'll offer."

"He never paid that much in his life for a pearl. But — one minute! Three thousand? Wait! I'll pay it!"

"You damned robbers!" said Tirrel, with an honest wrath, and he strode from the shop.

The old man was at the door of the place across the street, beckoning to him; Tirrel approached.

"You couldn't sell it?"

"I've refused three thousand for it," said Tirrel angrily. "You started the bidding at three hundred, a little while ago!"

The old fellow laughed, musically, shamelessly.

"One has to be amused," said he. "I shall always laugh when I think that I was able to offer three hundred for that pearl, and almost to get it. But now I'm ready to talk serious business with you. You've refused three thousand for it. You were quite right. That pearl is worth in the market about forty-five hundred dollars. Now, when I make my commission, pay for insurance, wait for a sale, etc., you may be sure that I could not make a profit by paying you more than four thousand dollars."

"I'm not at all sure of that."

"Tush, tush," said the pawnbroker. "You must not think that I'm still trying to cheat you!"

"Six thousand hits my mind, now," said Tirrel.

"Six thousand? That's a great deal of money."

"Of course it is. And a great deal of money is what you have, and you'll sell this again for a great deal more than I get from you. Suppose that I say six thousand?"

The other looked narrowly at him. Then he began to nod his head.

"Where did you learn jewel prices?" he asked.

"From you, right here, this evening!"

The old man smiled, a little sickly.

"I'll tell you what. You have an eye. You could be in this business yourself. You see what's in the mind of a man!"

Then he added: "Six thousand is it? Come into the shop, my young friend, and — "

But Tirrel said calmly: "I'll not come in. I've learned what the pearl is *half* worth, at least, and it'll have to go at that. Good-night to you!"

He went off down the street, and behind him he left a pawnbroker at the door of either shop, staring gloomily after him, and then wickedly at each other.

In all this little controversy about the value of the pearl, his heart constantly had risen. The first price had made him feel that his treasure, after all, could not be so extravagantly rich as he at first had thought. The last price convinced him that it was a dozen times more valuable than his fondest hopes. If six thousand were the price of the one pearl, then what of the prices for the other great pearls upon the cross, and above all for the great beauty which had ornamented the base of it? But the whole double-handful of stones was magnified and set off by that bargaining with the dealers. He had his head high, now. The consciousness of the value of his prize made him increase his estimate of his own worth. He had become a man of the greatest importance. He was as rich as any mine owner of the town. He felt as though already he were looking over a fine sweep of country, from hills to hills, and all within the skyline his, and all the stamping herds of beef, and the white wandering sheep, and the black ploughed lands by the river, and the smoke of forests which hung upon the mountainsides.

He loved wealth. He loved wealth with the

thirst of long poverty. He never had known that riches were of such blood-red importance to him until the opportunity to possess them had been given into his hands. Now he rejoiced in his holdings. He grew as keenly timorous as any antelope; he was as dangerously alert as any wolf.

It was full night. The streets were well filled with the crowds, but not as they had been. Now the center of circulation was more contracted, for everyone with money to spend was at the places of amusement, and merely poured continually from one brightly lighted entrance to another. Strongly burning oil lamps, backed with great reflectors, showed the way into these spiderwebs of entertainment, and ordinarily Tirrel would have been among the first to enter.

Now, he shuddered at the mere thought and walked on. If a bee can smell honey, the human wolves in those places would be sure to sense the loot which he carried.

Passing through the weaving crowd filling the sidewalks was in itself dangerous enough to such loaded pockets as his! He sweated with fear and with exasperation because he had not contrived a safer method of conveying his wealth. No sooner did he return to the hotel than he would be sure to construct a wide and strong belt, worn next to his body, and filled with secure pouches, so that no pick-pocket could annoy him!

Of course, he made himself most keenly aware of every man who came near him, and it was not long before his sharpened senses told him that he was being followed. He turned the next corner, but still he was conscious of that weight in the small of his back, a cold weight, gradually chilling his blood.

So, passing through a tangled group in front of a gambling hall, he turned suddenly into the next doorway and waited there, pressed deeply back into the steep shadow.

In another moment a big shouldered man went by and the heart of Tirrel leaped into his throat. It was he of the clouded agate eyes — it was Chandos!

Tirrel was worse frightened than ever he had been in his life before, because, in the rest of that life, he had had only his own person to place in danger; but now he carried something more than his very life, as it seemed to him.

He told himself that everything he had done since leaving the mountains with the jewels and the money had been folly of the first water. Madness, above all, to come to this town. Like a magnet, as it attracted him, so had it attracted the men of iron who followed him.

His obvious course should have been to trust the matchless speed and the endurance of the mare across the open spaces of the mountains or of the desert. He wanted nothing, except to be free from this great mantrap, for so Apache Crossing now appeared to him.

But how should he get away?

If he returned to the hotel for his pack, he would probably be waited for there. If he went straight for the mare in the stable, she, too, doubtless had been spotted and was also watched.

Furthermore, he could not tell what policy the others would follow. He was only reasonably sure that Lowell or any other officer of the law was not apt to be joined in the hunt with such men as these who had ridden behind him through the mountains. Whatever they did, they would not care to let the law place its hands upon the money!

Then, driven by his sense of danger, it occurred to him that perhaps the safest thing would be for him to follow Chandos, even as the latter had followed him. He hurried out into the street, but there was no Chandos in sight, and, crossing the street, he started back for the hotel.

Under the light at the entrance to the hotel he found a small group of men, chatting quietly together; and suddenly he realized that he dare not pass among them. Lowell might be within, or Chandos, or one of the emissaries of Chandos.

So he turned to the side and crossed to the rear of the hotel. His room looked out in that direction. Near by there was a shed, whose roof prolonged itself beneath his window, only four or five feet below, and it seemed to Tirrel that the only sensible thing would be to climb to his room in this fashion, and then to make up his pack and retreat.

He was strong and active as a cat. It was nothing for him to gain the top of the shed, and, passing cautiously along its sharply sloped roof, he was soon beneath his window.

He stood up and looked inside with the greatest precaution, for what more likely, as he now thought, than that they should have planted a man or two inside his room to wait for his return? And what better pistol target than a man climbing through a window, helpless with his hands, and framed against the stars of the sky?

He probed the darkness with the greatest care, but he could make out very little — the bed, the table, the chair were separate mounds of darkness.

At last he forced himself to go forward. He drew himself into the window and climbed inside. There he actually dropped upon his knees, crouched against the wall, and waited, gun in hand, for assailants to begin shooting. He had to tell himself that he was a fool. Then he stood up and went to light the lamp.

The most foolish thing he could do, it seemed!

He dropped the match from his suddenly numbed fingers. For why kindle the beacon that might tell half a dozen watchers that the rat was safely in the trap?

In the darkness, then, he got together his things, and, having made up the pack, he paused for an instant to remember, for he did not want to forget any item. In that pause, he saw the dark silhouette of a man's head and shoulders appear at the window!

Chapter Twenty-Eight

Only by the greatest effort of the will was he able to keep himself from snatching out a gun and firing. The head of the stranger was turned straight toward him for a long moment. He could actually hear the man's breathing, labored a little after the climb.

"I'll tell you what," said a second, coming into view, "you better climb in and make sure of things."

"What things?"

"I dunno. It might be safer for us to tackle him there."

"It ain't our job," said the first man in equally low tones, which now Tirrel thought that he recognized. "We're to see that he don't get out this way."

"I'd rather be inside to take a whack at him."

"You're a fool, Dutch."

"Fool yourself, Ormond!"

So, in a breath, he had them placed. One was the kindly host of his brother — Dutch Methuen. The other was Lefty Ormond, the yegg.

And, knowing them, the fear of Tirrel grew suddenly more stringent. Each of them had seemed to fill the part of a cool and deadly fighting man.

"Well, we'll stay here."

"All right. You're the boss. Bramber gave the orders to you!"

Bramber!

That name aroused in Tirrel latent ferocity, and suddenly he was hotly glad that Bramber was included among his immediate enemies. Better to face out the whole crowd and, somewhere among them, find and pay off the murderer of Jimmy Tirrel.

He sat on his heel, low against the wall, secure in the darkness. The two at the window had moved aside so that they were no longer visible against the star-freckled sky; but though their voices were low pitched, he could hear every word they spoke except when occasional bursts of noise rushed from the streets and drowned lesser sounds.

"Where did Bramber find him?"

"The jackass was down at the pawn shops right away. If he'd laid low for a while, we'd of been on through the town. But Bramber, he don't throw away no chances!"

"Him? I reckon not. Have they spotted the mare?"

"Nope. They're looking for her now,

though. When they've got her located, they'll likely come back here."

"Bramber?"

"I dunno. Him or Finch, maybe!"

"Funny to have Finch back with us."

"Yep. I dunno though. He's as good a fighting man as you'd want."

"What we need with more guns than we got?"

"Because this Tirrel is a fightin' fool."

"I never heard of him."

"Neither did I. But there's many a common puncher that'll raise hell if he gets half of a chance to stir him up. There's many a house-dog that'll eat the hearts out of wolves, if ever he gets the taste for the game. Beside, look what Tirrel has done already to us!"

"He's had luck.

"Nobody has no luck against Bramber. It's only brains and guts that counts when you're up against a — "

Here the noise of several riders galloping through the street shut out the sense of the following words and when Tirrel was able to hear again, the other speaker was in the midst of a sentence.

" — to make a split."

"You gotta leave that to Bramber."

"He'll hog about half himself. He's that kind of a gent!"

"I suppose that he is. Would you like this game without him?"

"There's only one agin us all!"

"That one has slipped through our fingers in the woods at Los Cavallos, and has walked out of the hotel and laughed at our guns. Poor Jess Creamer will never laugh again, God help his unlucky heart!"

"No, Tirrel salted him good and plenty."

"He salted Chuck, too."

"Chuck'll get well, I hope."

"I hope. Hopes ain't the facts, though."

"Look at the hell of it! Seems that we never scratched him, even!"

"Lowell got him in his hands. That's one thing."

"Lowell couldn't keep him. He faded through Lowell like a ray of light through a window pane."

"He'll wish to God that he never got Lowell on his track. Sam is a bulldog. He'll never stop!"

"Sam'll find this here Tirrel dead on the trail. You mind what I'm tellin' you."

"I hope to have help alongside of me if ever I back into Tirrel."

"And me, too. Finch says he's lightning on the draw."

"Me taking him for Finch! That was a rum play on my part!"

"They got the same lines."

"That's why Finch played him, too!"

"Sure. Where's Bramber now?"

"He's either busy spotting the mare, or else he's working to get the boys ready for raidin' the room."

"He won't do that till Tirrel comes in, will he?"

"I dunno. He might take it into his head to occupy the room first and wait for Tirrel in *there!*"

"Yes, he might."

A burst of laughter, singing voices roared up from the street and for a minute or two there was no chance to hear further. What he next made out was simply:

" . . . talked too much."

"You're right. We'd better shut up."

And they were silent. Only, after a moment, one said: "Damn me if I wouldn't like to roll a cigarette."

The other answered curtly: "Make a go of to-night and you'll be smokin' cigars, tomorrow!"

"I'm takin' mine to Denver."

"Wait till you get it before you spend it, will you?"

Again there was silence, and Tirrel smiled grimly. He had been at the meeting of the wolves in which they planned to eat him, as it were.

In the meantime, he had gathered items of much importance — that in the organization of which Bramber appeared to be the formidable head, Dutch Methuen and Lefty Ormond both were members, and Dan Finch himself had come back to the crew. They feared Tirrel, but they would not flinch from a meeting with him. They respected their leader and the resources of his mind. And Tirrel himself grimly acknowledged that Bramber had picked up the trail with speed.

He cursed himself for his eager folly in going at once with the pearl to the pawn shops. He could have guessed, if he had possessed keener wits, that the pursuit might make inquiries at just such places.

He wondered what he could do, now. The window as a means of exit was blocked. The front door of the hotel, also, surely was watched. He might, however, go down a story and then find an empty room and so climb through a window to the street in front, or the yard to the rear.

Precarious business, to be sure, but when a man's back is to the wall, what is there for him to do?

Again, he might defend himself in his room and keep them off, but, in that case, he would simply be surrendering himself into the hands of Lowell who was sure to be in Apache

Crossing before long.

He stood up with his pack, ready to start, when the floor in the hall creaked stealthily, and then the door sagged softly open.

Tirrel waited, frozen, pistol in hand. He pressed himself close against the wall. First, through the doorway, as at the hotel in Los Cavallos, came a ray of light which flicked around the room like the tongue of a snake of fire. The ray disappeared. There was a faint metallic click.

"No, he ain't here yet," muttered the man at the door.

"I tol' Bramber he wouldn't be. He ain't got wings."

"Bramber wanted to make double sure, that's all. We better go in here and wait."

"I don't like it."

"Why not?"

"Shootin' in the dark. I hate it like hell. It's murder!"

"Murder! That's too strong for your stomach, is it? The split that we're gunna get out of this is gunna be medicine that'll make you feel better, agin!"

He added:

"C'mon in!"

And the two passed through the doorway at the same time that a stealthy murmur came from the window: "Hello, boys!"

There were stifled, excited exclamations, and then the two newcomers stole straight across the room toward the window. A rapid, whispered conversation began, and Tirrel slipped sidewise for the door.

He gained the threshold. He crossed it, slowly and softly he drew the door shut.

"What's that?" said a sharply muttering voice.

Tirrel closed the door and turned the key. Instantly a heavy hand turned and wrenched at the knob and there was a deeply stifled curse.

Tirrel went down the hallway with long strides. His whole body was burning as with a fever in the sense of relief. There was a window at the end of the corridor. Through it he climbed, dropped the pack to the ground beneath, and lowered himself after it. The fall was not far. He landed with the pack itself to break the jar, and, picking himself up, he hurried out into the street through the side alley.

There he paused to look back. He could see the side of the hotel, and hurrying along the side of it, where the roof of the shed ran, were four stumbling, shadowy forms.

An impulse of savage vengeance caused him to grip the handle of his Colt, but he changed his mind instantly.

Silence and speed were the laws by which he must live and act until he was clear of the dangers that waited for him in Apache Crossing. He turned again and went forward as quickly as possible toward the stable where he had left the mare.

His troubles were not ended.

Chapter Twenty-Nine

The stable had one advantage, from the eyes of Tirrel; it was tucked out of the way so as hardly to be noticeable, particularly at night. One had to turn a distance down a dark and narrow alley to come to the barn. But the stable had one great disadvantage; there was only one apparent way to get to it or from it, and that was down the alley. A single man on guard could survey every soul who came back and forth!

But down the alley Tirrel went, stepping swiftly. He would have been glad to run, but he feared that he would simply be drawing greater attention to himself. It was necessary for him to get to the stable before possible pursuit from the hotel; it was no less necessary for him to slip from the town unnoticed.

He came to the foot of the little alley, where the way was dimly illumined by the light cast from the lamp that hung in front of the stable, and by this light he saw the black silhouette of a man passing up on the far side of the alley.

By instinct, then, rather than observation, Tirrel knew that the fellow had stopped and turned to look at him — and instantly the cold wave of terror came over him, benumbingly.

He caught his breath and looked back. The other had disappeared by sheer magic! No, yonder he was close to the shadow of the wall, and running like a frightened rabbit for the mouth of the alley.

Beyond doubt he had recognized Tirrel and now bolted off to give warning.

What was there now to do? To flee on foot would only give him safety for a moment. To attempt to wait until the mare was saddled, would be fatal, no doubt. And yet again there grew up in Tirrel the feeling that without Molly Malone he could not win through. She was his luck and when a man feels that his luck lies in a horse, he cannot get on without it.

So Tirrel whirled and raced for the stable. He went through the door with a speed that made the old man on watch there gasp and swear. He reached the stall, jerked the halter from Molly, and snatched the heavy saddle from the peg behind her. The cinches creaked as he dragged them home to the buckle. The bits rattled against the teeth of Molly as she opened her mouth willingly to it. And he was in the saddle and sweeping through the doorway, Molly's smooth-shod feet skidding on the boards, and the rattle of a couple of heavy silver dollars, dropped down by Tirrel in passing the stableman.

One plunge brought Tirrel to the foot of the alley; one glance showed him that it was plugged securely against him. A squad of five or six men, with the glitter of guns in their hands, barred his way. They came slowly on, as people who know that their game is in their hands.

And was it not?

He gritted his teeth as he pulled Molly around. The stable was a perfect trap, it appeared. Its own face filled all the foot of the trap. To the front appeared a four-foot timber wall, with three feet of barbed wire stretched along the top. The same sort of fence guarded all exits at the farther side.

No horse could clear such a barrier, he felt, and, even if cleared, there was no surety of escape. Houses rose beyond; clothes lines and the poles which supported them and the racks on which berry vines grew appeared in a tangle.

But if he left Molly to escape on foot, what would follow was fairly clear. Apparently Bramber had quite limitless supplies of assistants whom he could place to spot the fugitive. Tirrel was known to them; but most of them were strangers to him. He would be hunted down at leisure!

Now, these thoughts went through his mind at full length, but with the speed of a rushing express train — a whir of lights, then darkness again. And then he saw one faintest chance.

Just before him, one of the sticks which supported the strands of barbed wire leaned out, and, running the mare to it, he grasped it with both hands and wrenched at it. It gave way instantly, and, with a screeching of drawn nails, the two nearest sticks also failed. The whole section of the wire now leaned out and sagged down a foot or more, making still a perilous leap of six feet or thereabouts.

Molly could jump, but could she jump such an obstacle as this? He whirled her back into the entrance of the stable to give her a proper run at the fence, and as he turned her again, he heard the sudden and noisy clamoring of voices as men hurried down the alleyway. They had heard the tearing at the fence, of course, and perhaps they rightly guessed what it meant.

He called to Molly. She sprang from the door of the stable with a bound. She started to swerve toward the mouth of the alley, but when he pulled her straight for the fence she faltered a little, head high, as though she recognized the purpose in his mind but doubted her ability. Then, before he could call to her again, she lengthened her stride and drove straight at the obstacle. As she came nearer, it seemed to lift higher before them. It was old wire, rusted, dim. It showed forth with no glitter but as three dim lines of shadow across the stars. But spiderweb though it looked, Tirrel knew that those strands were strong as lariats, that they were armed with cruel barbs capable of gripping the ankles of a horse, tangling about the legs, and bringing horse and rider down to a fall which would be ruin for Molly, perhaps, and death for Tirrel himself.

But he had committed himself to the attempt, and Molly cantered bravely at the risk. Rounding on the run from the alley's foot, shadowy forms of men sped into view at the corner of Tirrel's eye; then he lifted the brave mare at the jump.

She had shortened at the last moment almost to a halt. Then she reared and leaped upward. Straight up, too straight she went. There was no doubt of clearing it, in height; but to Tirrel it seemed certain that she would drop straight down into the horrible entanglement.

He, shooting upward with her, saw before him on the farther side of the fence the jumble of the vegetable garden of the house beyond, the lofty berry racks, a wheelbarrow close to the right — then he jerked his weight violently forward to help Molly complete the jump.

They seemed dropping sheer down, but he felt behind him the twitch and jerk of muscles as the wise mare tucked her heels far up under her belly. That final effort pulled her clear, and they dropped down to the soft garden soil within the fence, while a rifle clanged on the farther side, and a bullet clipped open the shoulder tip of Tirrel's coat.

One bound placed them beyond the berry racks, however, and now he saw before him a low gate which shut off the back yard of the house from the path that curved around the side of it.

He had no time to pause and open it; behind him, the pursuit was clambering over the fence with curses. So he steadied Molly at the gate and she flew it with ridiculous, flaunting ease. What was this to her, after the peril of the wire fence?

She skidded, landing on the gravel beyond, but recovered in her own cat-footed way and sprang on. Her hoofs plunged deep in the soft soil of the grass plot in front of the building; she vaulted over the hedge, and, whizzing past the face of a startled pedestrian on the sidewalk, she landed in the roadway, the dust puffing beneath her feet.

Tirrel turned her head down the street, not at a racing pace but at an easy canter. Her strength was not needed at the moment, and he felt her ribs heaving with the strain and the excitement of her great jump. So he leaned from the saddle and stroked her damp neck, and Molly canted her head a little to one side, looking back at him with one eye, plainly rejoicing in herself and in such a rider.

Suddenly he wondered what choice there was between all the treasure with which his pockets were loaded and the possession of such a horse as Molly. And how would he exchange them, one for the other?

He laughed softly, fiercely to himself. There was no need to make a choice. Both were his! And yet he knew in his heart that he would have paid down all the diamonds and the rubies and the pearls, all the banknotes for the sake of Molly. Money could not buy her gallant and cheerful heart!

So he swung out of the town. He went down the valley on the side where the desert opened before him. All the stars were out. The night was his, and the desert was his country. Let them pursue him here, if they could!

He was in no haste. They surely would have little idea of the direction he had taken, if he left the road. So he parted from the trail and jogged Molly forward through a surface of soft sand which swished like water about her hoofs. For a scant hour he moved on until he reached a water hole, draped about by willows. There he halted for the night's rest. By earliest dawn he would resume the journey toward ultimate safety.

In the meantime, here was grass for Molly, safety for him, peace in his mind, cheer in his heart, and the treasure in his pockets. And all the danger through which he had passed, and all the rush of wild events since that first meeting at another water hole with Dan Finch seemed to give seasoning and pleasure to Tirrel's thoughts. Back in his mind there was one vague regret. He could not place it. It was merely a feeling that something of vast importance, of vast value, had been near him, and that he had lost it again. But he could not locate the fact.

Sleep came upon him and sleep, after a single instant, as it seemed, departed. He looked up at a pale morning sky, tinged with red from the desert atmosphere and knew that he must ride on. For breakfast he tightened his belt two whole notches, with the grim reflection that a hungry dog fights best. Then he saddled and mounted the mare and turned her east over the widening desert.

To either side, the hills were drawn far back,

in mists of rolling blue. Only directly behind him, beyond Apache Crossing, the heights looked near; he would be happier when they were well lost beneath the horizon line!

He kept his glance busy, trying to locate in the distance some upward arm of smoke which would mean a house and a chance for food, and so it was that he saw, very far off, three small dots, which grew into three horsemen. And he noted in them one great peculiarity — that they were all at a great distance, one from the other. They were, in fact, fully half a mile apart, but as they drew nearer to him, they began slowly to draw to a focus.

He halted Molly Malone and frowned in sudden doubt.

Chapter Thirty

If he had had any sort of a field glass with him, of course he could have made his determination much earlier. But if they really knew him, he would soon test them. He swung Molly to the right and rode due south, at right angles to his first course. Narrowly he watched, and presently he saw that the three riders had swung to the same direction. He jogged Molly, and they trotted their horses. He galloped Molly, and they all cantered.

At this, he was both alarmed and scornful — alarmed naturally at the thought that either the law or Bramber had come so quickly upon his traces, and scornful of all horses which dared to challenge Molly Malone.

He took her straight out at a hard gallop which sent the ground flowing back beneath her as if beneath a train; but he was worried to notice that she did not shift away from the others as rapidly as he had hoped. However, what better than a real test? He sat down to ride her with care, and presently he could see that she was gaining. Not that he had her at full speed, but, well inside that speed, she still continued to pull off from the three. He determined to ride around them on the right and so win well away from the hills and head out into the broad face of the desert again. Yet they maintained a hard gallop, and when he began to swing across their heads, curving slowly in, the leader abandoned his reins and started firing with his Winchester.

Now Tirrel was quite close enough to the men to see that all three were mounted upon blood horses, long-legged speedsters which must have been specially chosen for this work; and, as they spurred ahead, he pulled Molly back to a straighter line for the hills, flattening the curve. For there was no use in running her into danger of being struck by a chance ball.

She had, at length, what seemed to him a sufficient start, and he had pulled her head about and sent her due east when, from under the shadow of a hill, with the bright rose of the morning flooding the eastern sky, three horsemen came out like three bright arrows and let drive at him, full speed.

It was well for him that Molly was a cow horse. He stopped her on braced, skidding hoofs, put her about, and shot off across the valley again. Behind him the three came like the wind, and he gritted his teeth as he thought out the trap.

Bramber, or whoever was the controlling genius in this man-hunt, must have sent down groups of fighting men mounted on the best horses he could find. They had stretched themselves here and there, in different spots down the desert, hoping that one group might be able to drive the fugitive into the arms of another set of the same people.

It seemed that the trap was about to close. No horse can run forever without losing the edge of its speed. For a solid mile, Tirrel could not gain a whit; and, looking back at the jerking heads of the horses and the bowed forms of the riders, he knew that they were riding for his life.

From the right, the first trio were pushing on not in a straight line for him, but off at an angle, keeping their horses at a moderate gallop, as though they hoped to come in at a later time in the race, should the quarry try to double.

He had Molly headed straight up the desert, in line with the southern hills, and pointed more or less toward Apache Crossing now, but he was liking the game less and less. The three most recent pursuers were already falling back a little, to be sure, but Molly Malone had paid bitterly for this last challenge. She dripped with sweat; he could see the bulge and quiver of her straining nostrils and the standing veins along her wet neck. And Tirrel carefully reduced her pace.

If only he could rate her at an easier gallop, if only he could bring the gallop to a canter, then he could be confident that she would outlast both sets of her pursuers, but these riders would not let her relax. They pushed their own mounts on, first one and then another spurring ahead and opening a plunging, distant rifle fire.

There was little danger that one of these bullets might strike him; there was hardly more that Molly would be hurt, but now and again the hornet sound of the flying lead purred at his ear and annoyed him.

He wasted no time in replying to the fire. His business was to keep himself constantly in harmony with the laboring mare, but he decided that he had his work cut out before him. It was hardly probable that he could win his way back down the desert. He would have to edge in toward those southern hills, an unknown country, except for his last flight across them, but a region where Molly could show off her hill-climbing ability to a rare advantage. Then let these long-limbed racers handle her if they could!

He had another cause for worry. It seemed

to him that the firing of the guns behind him made a pattern of sound, and it was perhaps likely that they shot the rifles to send a flying signal ahead of them. Was there still another party of hunters before him?

At this thought, fairly desperate, he strained his eyes toward a scattering wood which lay before him just at the base of the hills, and it seemed to Tirrel that he saw among the trees a movement of other forms. It was only vaguest guess-work — the trees were still a good half mile before him — but he knew that Molly Malone could not stand another hard challenge. The veriest cowpony would be able to catch her in a sprint, now. Her stride was still as long and free as ever, but he knew that she was running on her nerve.

He swung her toward the left and urged her toward the hills, and, as he did so, he looked back over his nearest pursuers. They were working frantically with whip and spur, edging in to cut him off, but he had a safe lead, and he pointed Molly at the mouth of a narrow draw between two hills. That should give him a smooth passage into the uplands.

He looked back toward the woods and started violently in the saddle, for out of the shelter had poured four riders who were driving straight down toward the same ravine mouth which was his goal!

Sweat poured down the face of Tirrel, and then a sort of desperate disbelief arose in him that the desert could be made to pour forth enemies in this manner. Armed men on fleet horses seemed to start up out of the ground. It was like a dream, a nightmare of the ugliest sort.

He could judge that he had a six or seven hundred yard start on that last group, but they were cutting down the interval, and he dared not ask Molly for more speed. She was ready to give it. She had seen the newcomers and seemed to know what it meant, but he kept her in with a tight rein; she could kill herself, but that would not save him. He would have to depend on the long stroke of her gallop holding off even this new challenge, after the first rush of the sprinting horses died away.

Then, before him, the shadowy mouth of the ravine loomed like a gate. A gate to either life or death it was to Tirrel. Perhaps here, too, enemies were lodged. And, instinctively, he put down his hand to the stock of his Winchester as he thought of what would have to follow!

Through those narrow gates he rode and gave a last glance behind him. He saw the latest quartet drawing in toward the same goal; he saw the second trio in the distance, laboring in the same direction; and far away were three other specks. They were the riders who had first started him off in this relayed chase. And he felt, even then, an amount of grim satisfaction in knowing how thoroughly the good mare had beaten two sets of her opponents in that morning's run.

At that moment, the sun was up, the purple and rose left the sky, and he saw the brown faces of the hills swelling up before him, with little cover and few patches of rocks. He could hardly hide in such a landscape; only the legs of Molly Malone could save him.

The cañon spread a little; it gave him assurance that it was no box into which he had taken the mare; and then he heard behind him the deep roar of echoing hoofs as the pursuit thronged into the throat of the pass.

He turned an elbow corner of the valley; the sounds died a little behind him, and in front he saw the walls of the ravine give way to gradually rising ground.

His hopes increased. He put Molly at the gentlest section of the rise, bringing her down to a walk. He was almost at the top of the first small rise when he heard the clatter of the riders lunging around the ravine's corner. They were not a furlong off, coming hard, with every man's head down, and every horse a straining beauty. Yet he let the mare walk on to the crest of the rise. He knew the dreadful strain of fast motion uphill for a spent horse. So, walking her on, he set his teeth and listened to the depth and the harshness of her breathing. She stumbled a little on a small stone, and that meant almost more than the heaving of her tired sides.

From those four riders a single deep shout went up. They had him. That was their thought.

He felt that he could identify two — the rangy fellow on the right was surely Dan Finch, now with his fortunes thrown in with old enemies, as it appeared. Next to him was another known figure. The broad shoulders and something about the air of this man, even on horseback, seemed to Tirrel to identify Chandos, the man of the dim, agate eyes. And that chill which he always felt when he thought of the man came to him again.

Perhaps the great Bramber was one of the other two.

But now the mare gained the top of the low hill and before her there spread a fairly long stretch, almost level or only slightly tipping up.

Over this he let Molly gallop, telling himself that even the brief breathing spell uphill had lightened her stride. Beyond the slope was another upgrade, and here again he let the mare not walk, but jog. He dared not walk her, now. Turning in the saddle, rifle in hand, he watched the four riders, their sweating horses flashing in the sun like creatures made of metal. Tireless as metal, too, they streamed on toward him.

A hundred and fifty yards, if he knew distance as a marksman, lay between him and those four nodding heads. And every stride made it less.

He gained the top of the next slope and here he saw before him, with a heart of joy, a goodly downward sweep. Other high ground rose beyond, but he dared not think of that. He loosed the reins and the gallant mare struggled into a gallop again.

Chapter Thirty-One

To Tirrel it was a double horror — the sense that he was killing the mare, while she gave her honest heart so willingly to the labor and the dread of the pursuers which forced him on. But down that easy slope she gained on them, actually, no matter how much fresher their horses might be. He knew it as, gaining the foot of the short, steep slope behind, he glanced back to them and saw another priceless seventy-five yards added to the interval between.

He flung himself out of the saddle and scrambled with all his might up the steep slant of the ground, with the mare trotting like a dog beside him. He expected every moment that they would open fire upon him, but they seemed too sure of their game. He gained the crest unharmed. He looked back, and saw the four just at the foot of the hill. A wave of his arm sent the mare on a few strides out of danger. Then he fell on his stomach and opened fire. He of the wide shoulders — he of the clouded pale blue eyes — he was the man to down, Tirrel felt, and his first bullet jerked the hat from the head of that rider. The others scattered to either side. He fired right and left, but two were already in cover beneath the trees; two more had divided, and, riding on either hand disappeared under the outer arms of the hill. They would undoubtedly strive to rush up the slope and take him from the sides.

He remounted. It had been only an instant's pause, but he felt it might be a priceless gain for the mare, as he stretched her into a gallop again.

In fact, he was a quarter of a mile in the lead when he gained the foot of the next slope, and the enemy appeared over the last ridge. That had been a famous check for them. With a grim heart, in which hope was just beginning to appear, he jumped from the saddle again and toiled up the broken ground. It was not high but very much steeper, and when he was half way to the top, a bullet hummed past his ear and splashed to water on the face of a rock just before him.

Looking back, he saw that three of the riders were pushing in to close with him; but one man, his horse halted, was taking careful aim and placing his shots. The range was easy. Only fortune could save him, but save him it did.

He came to the top of the slope, and he saw that before him all the country was a duplication of that over which he had just ridden. There were endless narrow plateaus, and behind them abrupt rises of ground; it was like a huge, irregular stairway, roughly chopped out of the lower mountains.

He made another pause and opened fire on the quartet; and again he knew that he had failed to reach them, as they swerved out of sight in the increasing masses of trees. Again he turned to Molly Malone, and, looking carefully at her as he mounted, he saw that her front knees were trembling a little, her head hung, and though she pricked her ears at him, her eyes were dull.

A lump swelled in the throat of Tirrel, but he made his voice cheery as he called to the good horse again and sent her forward over the level.

Still they pressed hard after him, shooting when there was a fair opportunity, but always missing him by the grace of luck; and still he worked ahead of them, leaving the saddle to rush up the steep slopes springing again on Molly's back when there was easier going. So he eased her and then used her, and in this way staved off the repeated challenges of the enemy.

They climbed higher and higher. The sun

rode high and blazing hot. There was not a single cloud of merciful shadow in the sky. But twice, crossing brooks, he allowed the mare to scoop up a priceless mouthful of water. He himself leaned from the saddle and dashed the water into his face.

He was hot and half exhausted. Those sprints up the mountainside had taken a vast deal from him, and the enemy were now beginning to adopt his example, keeping to the saddle only over country where it was obvious that a horse could make much better time than an active man on foot.

They could not gain. Sometimes they were a furlong back. Sometimes there was a half mile interval. But it was hard for them to place their rifle shots with any exactness, for the country was much more broken with rocks and trees, now, and with tall brush, though there never was a region so broken that he could afford to attempt to dodge to one side or to the other; neither was there any natural little fortress into which he could turn and give battle, his one rifle against their four.

The odds, really, were far greater than that, if he attempted a stand; for as he climbed higher and higher, looking back toward the foot of the steps, he could see a group of three riders, several miles away, sadly distanced but still clinging to the chase with an admirable persistence. And still farther behind them, he had no doubt, the first set of three, who had taken the edge of Molly's speed and endurance, must be jogging doggedly at the trail.

Only a short halt would pool all those trained fighting men about him, and the cause would be lost forever. He had to stick to his course, only turning a little from time to time as peculiarly rough passages forced him to zigzag up a slope.

And so, at the last, he came to the top of the ridge and saw before him a great and easy sided valley with a bright streak of water down its center and a surface over which any horse would have enjoyed a race. If there were half her strength remaining to the mare, she would laugh at the pursuit, now!

He let her jog forward, bending low and leaning to listen to her breathing. It was very harsh, hurried, and deep. There was a sort of flutter, he thought, in the heaving of her ribs. And again he turned cold with grief and with pain. At that dog trot he kept her until the four riders scrambled into view three hundred yards behind her. Then he angled her down the valley's side at a gallop, and well and truly she ran, with no sagging of the knees.

He looked back. The four came furiously behind. Every man of them was well mounted on horses so evenly matched that not one of them could gain greatly upon any of the other three, except that now always in the front was that man of the wide shoulders — Chandos. He came like fate, steadily, his bare head distinguishing him from the rest. Six separate times Tirrel tried shots at him, and six separate times he missed, and knew as he pressed the trigger that he would miss.

There was a sort of hypnosis about the thing. He could not understand it, and it filled him with a ghostly apprehension. When a man's last day has come, all luck turns against him. This, then, might be the end for him!

It seemed to Tirrel that the rhythm of the flying hoofs of the horses continually beat out the phrase: "The last day! The last day!"

He fell into a sort of semi-delirium. Sometimes he actually forgot that he was in danger, riding for his life. The struggle of climbing up the slopes, the horrible continuance of the peril had sapped his strength. His hand shook on the reins. Perhaps that was why he missed so many attempts with the rifle.

And then again he felt the superior calm of Chandos like that of a man sure of himself and the success of all of his purposes. Chandos alone, of all the band in the rear, had never laid hand upon rifle or revolver to take a shot at the fugitive, as though he scorned to do with a rifle at long range what he was so confident of accomplishing hand to hand!

Desperately the fugitive glared back over his shoulder. He felt that he was growing unnerved.

Or again, it appeared to Tirrel that the horse was drifting in a straight line, slowly, while the brown earth heaved up and down and fled beneath the belly of the mare.

They reached the bottom of the valley, and, striking the level, Molly Malone staggered and almost went down.

Tirrel looked back. He actually had gained upon the four in that swift descent, which had lengthened and strengthened the stride of the mare; but, flying down as she had done, she had weakened herself terribly in the pounding forelegs. She could hardly stand, now. Her gallop was a broken, unrhythmic thing. Her ears were flattened against her neck. Her mouth pulled wide, and the thick white foam flew back, spotting her throat and her shoulders.

It was the end of that ride for Molly Malone, and Tirrel looked wildly about him for the spot where he could make his last stand when, swinging with deadly slowness around a corner of the road, he came upon a buckboard drawn by a span. A girl was in the driver's seat, letting the mustangs jog slowly on.

Tirrel jerked up his face to the heavens, in praise of the mercy of Providence. Still, the thing was not done. If the girl heard him in time, of course she would give the horses the whip, and poor Molly never could catch them. But the road was deep and soft in muffling dust, there was the pounding of the hoofs of her own horses, the rattling of the wheels, the jingling of some ironware in the rear of the wagon that filled the ears of the girl.

Now as he swung down close to her, she jerked her head around, and he looked into the face of Kate Lawrence. Of course it was she, and this was the long valley through which he had ridden Molly Malone on the night when he had escaped from her house.

Her first impulse made her lash the horses to a gallop, but instantly she mastered them again and brought them down to an excited, high-stepping trot. Tirrel swung himself out of the saddle and crashed into the wagon.

He saw Molly swerve instantly aside from the road and there stand with braced legs, hanging head, utterly spent. But nobly, nobly she had served him that day!

He turned to Kate Lawrence.

She, wide of eyes, and with a pale face, looked tensely at him; he wondered with all his might how she had found the courage to wait thus for a stranger.

She merely said: "Who is it?"

"Bramber's devils are after me. Your friend Finch is part of 'em."

Her eyes closed, then opened brighter than before.

"Can these horses hold them?"

Already he was in the seat beside her.

"I don't know."

"Take the reins," said she. "I'll use the whip."

He took the reins, and around the bend behind them came the pounding of the pursuit.

Chapter Thirty-Two

The whip sang in the hand of Kate Lawrence, and the mustangs leaped into their collars. The light buckboard, jerked suddenly forward, bounded and danced wildly over the road. There was no attempt to keep the team at a trot. A gallop was what was wanted, and as fast a gallop as the mustangs could raise.

It could be seen, now, how much Molly Malone had accomplished even in her exhaustion, with the long stroke of her stride. For the quartet, riding solidly together, certainly held their own even against the furious pace of the pair of mustangs.

They had before them a straight stretch, a mile long, and down it they flew. Kate Lawrence, looking back cried sharply: "We're lost!"

"We're holding them still!" declared Tirrel, glancing back over his shoulder.

"It's Bramber! It's Nick Bramber!" said the girl. "Oh, God help us!"

"Which one is Bramber?" asked Tirrel.

"The one without a hat."

"That's Chandos. That's not Bramber!"

"Nick Bramber! Oh, I'd know him as I'd know the devil! It's Bramber, I tell you! There's Dan Finch beside him, but Bramber in the lead!"

Tirrel freshened his grip on the reins.

"The whip!" he said hoarsely.

"They're doing their best," answered the girl. "The whip would do no good. The whip's not what you want. Only if they had a scrap more foot! How far have they ridden after you?"

"Nearly from Apache Crossing."

"Then they still have some running in them. Bramber keeps the best horses in the world, next to Molly Malone!"

In the distance, they heard the whinny of the mare, almost as though she were answering her name. She had not moved. She had only thrown up her head and now called after her last master, as though appealing against such a desertion.

And Tirrel said through his teeth:

"I'll have her back. I'll have her back!"

"Think of your own life and not of her," answered the girl, overhearing him. "Bramber usually rides alone. If he's taken help with him, it means that he wants you with all his might!"

"You want to know why?"

"Yes. Of course."

"Reach your hand into the coat pocket nearest to you."

She hesitated, and then, doing as she was told, she brought out a small handful of stones — all rubies and emeralds, which glowed and flashed past belief in the naked sunshine.

She held them for an instant in her hand. There was no need of the whip. The mustangs, ears flattened, flew down the straight road.

"What's this?"

"*They* used to have it. They want me for other reasons, but they'd sell their souls to get at me now — for the sake of this."

"I'd pawn my soul to help you," said the girl, with a ring in her voice. "I'd be Mrs. Dan Finch today, except for your coming."

He risked a glance aside at her. She was flushed, excited, fearless of the danger with which they took the next corner on two wheels and skidded over the brow of a sharp descent at the bottom of which was a bridge.

They struck the bridge with a crash that threatened to reduce the wheels to matchwood. Then they sped up the farther slope. And, glancing back again, they saw Chandos, alias Bramber, gallop first over the ridge, the other three strung out behind him.

The pursuers had gained on the buckboard, and they were still gaining. The rush of the buckboard down the slope could not compare with the free gallop of those hot-blooded horses which Bramber and his men bestrode.

Besides, the mustangs were not mated. The odd horse, an undersized pinto, galloped as best he could, but the collar always was dragged half way up his neck. It was the near one of the span which did the work, pulling the buckboard, its load, and half the weight of its running mate. This was a tough looking roan, ugly, but apparently full of speed and spirit.

They plunged up the farther rise and hurtled forward over a winding stretch, where the road wound sharply back and forth among a grove of trees.

Behind them, the four riders had disappeared from the road, and next Tirrel could see blurred glimpses of them, galloping beyond the trees. They had left the windings of the trail and were following an air line across the fields to save priceless distance.

The girl saw, too, and slashed at the lagging pinto with a savage whip. But he was doing his best. He merely shook his head at the pain and could not get greater speed from his short legs.

Then Tirrel said:

"It's the last trail for me. I never can shake them clear. I've known almost from the start that it was the finish of me!"

"It's not the finish," she argued. "They're burning up the last that's in their horses in one grand spurt. Hold them off now, and we'll make it clear."

He shook his head.

"I can see the way their horses are striding. Empty that pocket of everything in it. It's yours. If you don't need it, your father and your mother do."

"Are you offering to pay me?" she asked.

"Listen to me," said Tirrel, "I got no time for no damn nonsense. I never wasted my time making pretty talk to girls. I never seen a face among 'em that ever sank into my head, except your face. I wanted you to have everything that's on me. But I can't. If they found me cleaned, they'd search you. But you could take the fill of that one pocket and they'd never guess. They'd never dare to search you, then!"

"Bramber would dare anything."

"You'd better risk it."

"I can't!"

"You've got a reason. Your old man is about broke, I take it."

"We'll go to work with our hands to make a

living, then. We're not afraid of poverty!"

"I've got no time to argue. I say that I want you to have it."

"There'd be your blood on it," said the girl.

They spun wildly around a curve, but he dared a glance at her, and found her eyes fixed not on the road, but on his stern face.

And, in that flashing glance, they each saw more than they had dreamed to find. They became silent. But suddenly the fear left the heart of Tirrel and in it remained only an aching sorrow. He had lost on this day, of all living things, that which had meant the most to him — the beauty, the faith, the dauntless courage and speed of Molly Malone. And now he lost something else — or the hope of it, at least. More than hope, indeed, for he had looked very deep into the eyes of the girl the instant before.

They came to another straightaway. Behind them the four riders entered the road; they were dangerously close, and gaining with a terrible speed. So close, indeed, that now their wild yell of exultation went up from their throats like the voices of four savage Indians, closing upon the blood at the end of the trail.

That sound was shattered and driven far away as the buckboard dipped into another winding section of the road.

Then the girl gripped the arm of Tirrel.

"Two hundred yards off, close on the left, there's a break in the trees and a lane. You hear?"

"I hear you."

"If you can double into that, it may be that they'll over ride you."

"Not for more than half a minute."

"That's all the time you'll need. Have you a knife?"

"Yes."

"When we get there, pull up the span at once, as soon as you're around the first bend. Jump with your knife and cut the roan out of his harness. The one rein is enough to ride him by. He guides over the neck. Jump on him, then, and ride for your life!"

"And you?"

"Bramber will never offer to harm me."

"If I should run away from you — God forgive me!"

"Do you want to die, and me standing by looking on? Is that sense?" she cried angrily.

He did not answer. Close before him and on the left he saw the gap among the trees, and he pulled the span sharply into it — so sharply, indeed, that the buckboard skidded almost into the first tree on the right, slowly rocked back on all four wheels, and shot around the first turn of the narrow lane. There Tirrel, throwing back all his weight on the reins, and standing against them, managed to pull the buckboard to a halt.

He leaped for the ground, with a vague picture of the girl standing on the ground beside him, his rifle in her hands, as she faced back down the lane.

He, in the meantime, had slashed through traces, and collar straps. He tore the harness away and left the roan barebacked, shuddering with excitement and with terror, while across the mouth of the lane the four riders crashed, and sped up the main road.

At that, mutely, the eyes of Tirrel and the girl met again, and the next instant he was on the back of the roan; they heard a distant shouting. Already Bramber and his men were pouring back upon the true trail.

Tirrel caught the rifle from her. He remained for a single instant. Through the trees he could see Bramber's wild riders rushing down across the open field upon him, but for a single second he stared into her face, and she up to his. Then without a farewell, he jerked the roan about and drove it at a gallop down the lane in the direction from which they had come.

Pulling to the left at the junction with the main road, he could see the four burst into the narrow lane just where he had abandoned the wagon. The girl stood there. He saw one of the four, he could not distinguish which, slash at Kate Lawrence with his riding quirt, and then the whole quartet spurred furiously after him.

Chapter Thirty-Three

After the long stroke and the spring of Molly's gallop, it seemed as though the roan were pounding the earth furiously, running on a treadmill, but presently he saw that Bramber and his men were not gaining. They had entered upon the last stage of that famous chase of which they still talk through the cow country. Men today in Los Cavallos and Apache Crossing discuss every detail with the utmost seriousness, though it is generally considered almost more than mortal horse could attempt — that spurt from Apache Hills and over the mountain, after being thrice chased by fresh relays of blood horses. What had saved Tirrel had been his own willingness to leap from the saddle and work his own weight up the steepest, roughest slopes. This, too, was commented upon. But every man has, in some point, his own favorite theory and, particularly of the conclusion, there are many varied points of view. For some actually declare that the roan was a finer horse than the mare. And, as a matter of fact, the roan is to this day given pasturage without labor, and leads a spoiled and pampered life. But that will be explained in detail.

Then there are some who declare that the girl had expected the fugitive and had gone out to meet him, taking along her best horse. A sufficiently absurd doctrine! But others again will avow that at least she must have seen him coming from a distance and prepared herself to receive him.

But the facts are exactly as have been narrated.

Tirrel ran off on the roan with a dreadful pang of heart and the certainty that he would be accused of having deserted her, after she had rescued him. And Bramber and the rest pounded along after him for a full hour, but they were hopelessly out of it. The mare had used up their strength, to begin with, and the roan, though not a speedster, was a tough mountain horse which could gallop all day; and gallop it did, for fifteen miles, until Bramber and his crew were beaten off.

From a distance they saw Tirrel round back to the place where he had left Molly Malone. And she, with two hours of rest strengthening her, was able to jog off, albeit wearily, at the side of the roan.

That put the day's work of Mr. Bramber

and Company at exactly zero for accomplishment. Zero, that is to say, for themselves, but infinitely more for Tirrel, as he was to discover before he was many hours older.

As soon as he got back into the safe hills, in a spot where there was a sheltering grove of trees, grass and running water, he stopped. There he dressed Molly thoroughly, rubbing her down powerfully, and he saw life come back into her eyes and the arch appear gradually in her straightened neck. She drank, she nibbled at the grass, she drank deeply again. And then Tirrel lay down in the shade and closed his eyes. His brain ached and burned — ached with the weight of his labors, and burned with the long fear of death which had ridden in his shadow through the day.

He went to sleep and wakened not until the dusk.

He was so starved that merely drawing up his belt would in no measure serve, so he looked off his mountainside into the valleys on either hand. They looked like deep blue skies, with yellow stars twinkling out at him. There were not many stars as far as his eye could reach, he counted three on the one hand and four on the other. Those lights were houses. A bonfire would not have burned with so steady a light on such a windy evening. Tirrel determined that one of those

290

houses should give him his supper.

He chose the nearest of the lot, on the right hand side, and went down to it — nearly an hour of steady riding, in spite of the apparent nearness of the ray when he began the journey. He came up in front of a small cottage of which the front door was open. A gray and brown mongrel was lying there asleep, his head on his paws.

Tirrel dismounted at a little distance and reconnoitered. In the house there was a woman of middle age and a boy — her son, no doubt — of fifteen or sixteen. He did not hesitate. He went to the door and said: "I'm out of luck, but not out of money. Can you give me a feed here. I'm able to pay you, but I'll about starve before I get to a town."

The woman had started up in alarm. She took the lantern off the wall and stepped closer, holding the light high. The boy picked a shotgun off the wall.

"Hold on, Paul," said the woman. "I guess this gent is all right. Come along in. We've gotta be careful, living here, but you're all right, I guess."

Tirrel went in and sat down at the table. The two had finished a supper of boiled potatoes and the hostess began to get together the remnants until her son, looking at the door, muttered: "Look, ma!"

Tirrel glanced at the door, also. There appeared the head of Molly Malone, her eyes starry bright. She whinnied softly after her master.

"It's Molly Malone!" breathed Paul.

Then he clapped a hand over his mouth.

"Do you think that you know that mare?" asked Tirrel.

"I seen her once, sir, and I'd never forget her!"

"Where did you see her?"

"A long time ago. Maybe a year. Over at Apache Crossing. Finch owned her then."

"If you know the hoss," said Tirrel, "do you know me?"

The boy was silent. His bright, quick eyes earnestly examined the face of Tirrel, but he said not a word. His mother had left the room; outside there was a stifled squawk, and then the sound of wings beating rapidly against the ground.

"You're gunna have a pretty good supper," grinned the boy, nodding toward the noise, and his mother came in carrying the chicken whose neck she had just wrung.

"Look here," said the boy, "you're kind of surprised, ain't you?"

"I am," said Tirrel. "I don't make it out, except that you seem pretty interested in Molly Malone."

"I'll tell you what," began Paul.

"You shut up talkin'," warned his mother. "You ain't old enough to talk to this here gentleman. Anyways," she added to Tirrel, with a really warm smile, "we're mighty glad to have you here. We ain't rich, but we ain't the kind that'd charge up a bill against such as you, Mr. Tirrel!"

He started. Instinctively he looked toward the door, but only the bright eyes of the mare were still there.

"Don't be afraid none," said the hostess. "My God, man, you're as safe here as in your own house. *We* don't love murderin' Nick Bramber no more than you do!"

"But was it true," broke in the boy, fairly quivering with eagerness, "that they hunted you all the way up the mountain from Apache?"

"Ay, that's true."

"My — jimminy — Christmas!" breathed Paul with bewildered joy. "An' they killed three hosses doin' it?"

"I didn't see any of their hosses drop, son."

He could see that a great deal of his day's work was known to these good people; certainly they did not appear to disapprove of it.

"*I* seen with my own eyes — look here, what color hoss was Bramber himself ridin'?"

"It was a pale chestnut, a kind of a washy color."

"I seen that hoss sink down on the ground, and I seen Bramber draw out his gun. I heard Bramber say: 'The goddam worthless pup has played out on me. Well, here's your ticket to the land of no work.' That's what he out and said, and then he shot that there chestnut right through the head. After that, he looked around, and I saw the smoke curling up from the mouth of the gun, and there was a little smile on his mouth. He looked mighty like a wolf, as though he'd be pretty happy to get his teeth into somebody else that was standin' around!"

"He will! He will!" said the hostess. "Nothin' ever will stop him from man-eatin' until they've put him down under the ground, where he's belonged for all of these years!"

"Do most people around here feel your way about him?" asked Tirrel.

"Me and my man, we feel that way. You ask Paul how *he* feels about him."

Tears rushed into the eyes of the boy.

"When I get to be a man," said he, "I'm gunna have it out with him!"

There were tears in his eyes, a quaver in his throat, but deep, prayerful courage in his whole face and bearing.

"I'll tell you why," said the woman. "You ever hear of John Cracken?"

"Sure I have," lied Tirrel solemnly.

"What you hear about him?"

"Why, what you mean?" asked Tirrel, cautiously.

"Good or bad, you hear of him?"

"Everybody that I heard speak, said that John Cracken was a man," said Tirrel.

That was a generalization which could be altered, he felt, to suit the case either way.

"He was a man!" cried she. "Yes, sir, he was a man. And them that finished him well knew that he was a man, and that was why they shot him through the back!"

"That was a piece of cur's work," said Tirrel.

"It was a piece of work for a dog. Who sat and talked to my poor Johnnie darlin' while the murderers sneaked up behind? It was him! It was that sneak and devil, Nick Bramber. He sat there with his pale eyes starin' at my boy, and the others, they come up and killed him, and that you mighty well know, Tirrel!"

"That's what I've always heard," said Tirrel quietly.

"And I hear that you've trimmed him!" said she, eagerly. "I hear that you've taken more from him than he'll ever get again! Is that right?"

"I've taken something from him," agreed Tirrel.

"God bless you for it! I only wish it had been his heart, so that I could of taken that heart and cooked it to a smoke!"

The chicken, in the meantime, was hissing and steaming in the frying pan, and now Tirrel was invited to sit at the table, where a clean end of the oilcloth was offered to him by Paul.

Chapter Thirty-Four

The boy, as soon as he saw the guest fairly seated, at once picked up the shotgun again, and left the house.

"You can eat safe and sound here," said the housewife. "Paul has an ear as good as the ear of ary a rabbit in the mountains."

"Why," said Tirrel, "this is mighty kind of all of you. But look here! There's a mighty small chance of ever having any trouble with Bramber and his gang this evening. They'll not be riding again today, I figger. But if the boy would do a fine thing for me, let him take this here mare of mine and give her some hay and grain."

"Paul!" called the woman.

Paul appeared, panting with haste.

"Take Molly Malone into the barn and feed her. Give her that good grain hay from the corner of the barn, and there's that batch of clean oats for her to eat."

Paul grinned and was gone again; and after

that there was full occupation for Tirrel as he devoured that chicken from beak to feet, as fast as his hostess could fry it. After that, he finished off on a cup or two of strong black coffee.

His hostess watched him with a contented smile, and Paul, coming back, grinned with delight at the heap of bones which remained of that once big rooster.

"I'm going to pay you now and then drift along," said Tirrel.

She shrugged her shoulders.

"I couldn't be takin' a thing," said she.

"This is fine of you," answered Tirrel, "but I wouldn't rest easy without payin'." Then he added: "Besides, suppose that Bramber trails me here, he'd be pretty mean about you havin' put me up, wouldn't he?"

"Into this here house he'll never show his nose!" she replied darkly. "We'll have no sight of him here, Mr. Tirrel! But the sheriff might be sashaying down this way. However, we got no fear of him, either. He ain't a black-guard like Bramber."

"You won't take even a penny?" said Tirrel.

"Not even a penny. What would my man be sayin' to me when he come back and learned that I had taken money from you? Why, he'd break his own nose to do the smallest of harms to Bramber!"

"Hates Bramber?"

"Hates his heart, and his liver, too!"

"I've had small dealin's with him," said Tirrel. "My brother had more."

"He did?"

"Yes."

"And my man's brother had trouble with him, too. Poor Jerry is a dead man!"

"Murdered?"

"What else?"

"What trouble had he had with Bramber?"

"The trouble of once workin' with him. And those that once work with Bramber never can leave him."

"He tried to leave?"

"He went to Bramber and says to him: 'I'm through. I'm gunna go straight.' Because Jerry always had been lazier than bad. There was nothin' mean or revengeful or black about him, I'd tell you. So he wanted to go straight. He thought that he had special cause for that! Kate Lawrence, she smiled at him, or something, and that set him up!"

She laughed, bitterly.

"She's smiled at plenty," said she, "and I reckon that she's smiled at you, too, by the tale of what she done today."

"I want to hear no bad about her," said Tirrel coldly.

"Sure and you don't. I'll leave that out. I

like her fine, anyway. Well, poor Jerry, he got fixed up pretty proud, as I was tellin' to you. He wanted to go straight. He told Bramber. Bramber says: 'You're a fool. I'll give you ten days to think things over and get better sense.'

"Jerry come back and talked it over with us. My man says to him that he'd better use those eight or ten days in leavin' the country as fast as he could, unless he wanted the worst kind of trouble with Bramber. But Jerry, he wouldn't leave. Why would he turn his back on Kate Lawrence? That was what he had in his mind. Though of course he didn't talk much about her, poor boy!

"Well, the ten days come along to an end. I was standin' here at this door. Jerry was whittling at a piece of wood when up comes Dan Finch ridin' a hoss."

"Finch?"

"Ay, him. He says: 'Jerry, I wanta talk to you.'

"Jerry says: 'Talk it out loud, then. I got no secrets here in this house from nobody.'

"Finch says: 'You mean that you're through?'

"Jerry says that he was: 'Then God help you,' says Finch, just like that. And he turned the head of his mare — was riding Molly Malone, of course, in them days — and off he

300

went. Jerry was scared, but he was steady as could be. And nothin' happened to him until pretty near a week later when he was down in the woods cuttin' cord wood to sell in town. He never come home. My man went out and found him. He'd been shot through the back — "

"The back!" exclaimed Tirrel.

"Ay, Bramber and his kind don't take no chances. They're like the Injuns. They'd rather kill from behind than the front. The safe way is always the best way, from their manner of thinkin'! But Jerry, he lived long enough to say one word: 'Bramber!' Then he died.

"I thought that my man would of pretty near gone mad. He was gunna climb onto his horse and start off to find Bramber. I had to beg and pray him not to. He listened to me, finally. He come back into the house, and a black ten days I had with his face opposite me at table, and him never sayin' a word but eatin' his heart out with hate. Finally Dan Finch, he come along by and he stopped at the house here and he asked for a chance of a meal. My man says to him: 'Finch, I dunno if it was you that killed Jerry, but one of your damned crew it was that done it, and I'll tell you this: I ain't gunna go out of my way to make trouble for you. I can't afford to. I got

301

my family to look after. But if one of you comes sashaying even along past the door of my house agin, I'll salt him down. Go back and tell the rest of your tribe what I say, will you?'

"Finch is a stark enough man. He's never been knowed to back down, but that day, he didn't say nothin'. He just turned the head of his hoss and he rode off. And never a one of 'em has been back this way since. For which I'm thankin' God. But that's the reason that I'd never dare to take money from you nor from any enemy of the Bramber gang."

It was an explicit enough explanation.

"How long has Bramber carried on in this neck of the woods?" asked Tirrel.

"About nine or ten years. Before that, he was up Montana way and worked that part of the world. But he never done as well there as he's done here. He hadn't come to himself, yet. But when he come down here, he got a lot of reputation, such as him being with a charmed life — "

"Has he got that reputation?"

"Don't you know that much about him?"

"I know mighty little about him!" But he shuddered. He remembered the hopeless sense of weakness which had come over him when he pointed his gun at Bramber. "He usually goes by other names?"

"He's got all kind of names. He works himself up in different wigs and things, too, so's his own dog wouldn't know him. But under the skin there's always the same devil. That I know!"

Tirrel stood up.

"There's nothin' that I can do for you?" he said.

"Ay, ay," said the woman, "I right well think that there *is* something that you can do for me, and for the whole range. And if you can't do it, I doubt as there's another man that can now livin'! Kill this Bramber from off of the face of the earth! Ah, that'd be enough to be worth a statue; and you'd have more than a statue's worth here in this house, Tirrel!"

She said it with a passion of meaning, and he answered her: "They've all taken their crack at Bramber, I suppose. You want me to go out and shoot down a gent that has a charmed life?"

"You can do it. What is a charmed life to you? You got one yourself! Everybody says so! The whole mountains is talkin' about the man that rode into them at Los Cavallos and then rode out agin in spite of the sheriff and of Sam Lowell, and of Bramber, and Dan Finch and all of the rest of 'em! And then, to show that you scorned 'em, you rode down into Apache Crossing, and there while they was spreadin' out their nets for you, you walked through 'em agin, laughin'. Ah, they'll never get done talkin' about you, Tirrel, and mostly of all, they'd never get done talkin' about what you done this day, ridin' over the mountain from Apache!"

Her voice rose, her face lighted as she spoke, and Tirrel could see that he had ridden himself into a legend in the few brief days since he first came to Los Cavallos. This night he learned it. Indeed, looking back, it seemed to him that from the moment he had met with Daniel Finch at the water hole his life had been only a legendary thing, impossible of credence.

He said goodby to his hostess. He went to the stable and watched Molly finish her oats and begin on her hay. There he sat and watched her with a sleepless content, for every ounce of strength and rest that went into her body of wire and whalebone was so much more security for his own person. More than that, he had come to love her and her honest heart, and he yearned over her, like a parent watching a hungry child.

Paul came out and joined them, as Tirrel at last saddled the mare again.

"Ma says you won't want to stay here all night? She could fix you up a place, all right."

"I got to move," said Tirrel.

He took from his pocket a single stone. This he wrapped in a corner of paper and put into the boy's hand.

"What's this for?"

"You give it to your mother and you tell her that it's from Bramber — though he don't know nothin' about it!"

"I will, sir. Mr. Tirrel, I wisht that I could be ridin' off with you to find him. That's what you'll be doin', I reckon?"

"I'll be doin' that, if I can. So long."

"So long," sighed Paul.

And he went outside and held the stirrup for the fighter and watched him ride off to the battle.

Chapter Thirty-Five

We must leave Michael Tirrel and step suddenly to the side of Nicholas Bramber, who
rides through the woods on the southern
verge of the valley the next morning, mounted
on a strong half-bred gray. A thoroughbred
will hardly bear up, for long, the solid bulk of
Bramber, for he is one of those fellows who
outweigh their appearance by twenty or even
thirty pounds, and though his shoulders appear broad, the depth of his chest is unnoticed. He is dressed without ostentation. His
hat, for instance, is not a sombrero, today,
but an old time-stained felt, weathering from
black to green, and sweat-marked about the
band. He has on a checked flannel shirt, a
bandana knotted under one ear — since there
is little or no dust on this trail. He wears chaps
of brown leather, because of the brush which
one often has to ride through and which, otherwise, would soon slash straight through the
best and the toughest of trousers. His rig is in
no way remarkable; his horse is also plain, but

strong and with good lines.

Coming over the ridge of the hills, a man in blue jeans, with a rifle in his hands, looking like a hunter out to shoot his breakfast, steps from behind a big trunk of a tree and nods at Bramber, who waves back, curtly, and goes on.

Then half way down the hills another man, this time a puncher on a wiry, sweating mustang, comes suddenly out into the trail, and there are words.

"How is it?"

"Nothing wrong."

"Where is she?"

"You foller the next forking to the right."

"No news?"

"Of him?"

"Yes."

"No word of him, damn him!"

Bramber went on without further conversation. "Him" was now Tirrel to all the crew. He filled their minds. He was an obsession, and the long failure to capture this single enemy was breaking down the strength of Bramber himself. His men began to stir, restlessly. For the first time in his life, Bramber began to appear as a fool in the eyes of the world. They watched, amazed. They hardly could understand. It was as when the crowd goes to the championship fight, having bet its pennies upon the champion, and sees, bewildered, that the new man is about the old like a wasp about a dog, eluding every stroke, and tormenting the old master beyond endurance.

So the whole cow range felt as it observed the maneuvers of Tirrel and the failures of this man who *never* had failed before. But Bramber concealed his rage and his disappointments well enough. He kept a high head and an impassive face. Turning now down the trail which went to the right at the next forking of the road, he presently came on Kate Lawrence, sitting on a fallen log with a roan pony beside her.

"Good-morning, Kate," said he.

She waved carelessly to him.

"You got him back safe and sound, then?"

"There he is."

"A little tucked up, I'd say."

"Nothing to hurt him. He ran like a scared rabbit, Michael says."

"Is that his front name?"

"Michael Tirrel, yes."

"But you don't call him Mike, eh?"

"I don't know him well enough for that. What are you driving at around the corner, Nick?"

"Nothing."

"You are, though."

"I want to know how he got the roan back to you."

"Why, he brought him in, of course."

Bramber started.

"I don't believe that!"

She shrugged her shoulders.

"I mean," he said, "that it's hardly probable. I've had the place pretty closely watched."

"Yes, you have," she said bitterly. "But," she added with some venom, "it's not the first time that he's walked through a crowd of you, and walked away again, without a scratch on him!"

Bramber swung down from the saddle and sat down on the log beside her.

"This is a pleasant place," said he, looking up to the sun through the thick green field of the pine needles.

"Why did you send for me, Nick?"

"I wanted to talk. You know that I can't come near your place any more without sending your old man into a fit. He'll die of apoplexy if ever he sees you speak to me again."

"He doesn't seem to like you," agreed the girl.

He said suddenly, but in his usual quiet voice:

"D'you think that your friend Michael will win?"

"Over you?"

"Yes."

"I think that he'll beat you, Nick."

The other nodded, as though registering the thought in his mind and wondering over it.

"I don't understand," said he. "As though this were the first rub that I've ever had! As though I never had trouble with a man before this. People begin to say: 'Bramber is broken!' Even you, Kate. I'm surprised at that!"

"Of course you're surprised. It stands to reason that you would be. But though you've had trouble before, you've never had such things happen to you as have happened lately."

"You mean that he's slipped in and out of my hands, like a fish?"

"I mean that, in part. You, with the sheriff to help you!"

Bramber flushed a little.

"Besides that, of course he's dipped his hands into your pockets and filled them!"

Bramber grew still more red, and he turned his pale, strange blue eyes upon her.

"Men tell me," went on the girl, "that when Finch got him to come up here on Molly Malone, he hoped that you'd mix up the pair of them and kill him in the place of Dan. Is that true?"

"Does it sound true to you?"

"Anything is likely.

"Perhaps. I thought you were fond of Dan Finch."

"I was, sort of. Then I learned what he'd tried to do to Michael. Now I hear that you and Dan have buried the hatchet, and that he's with you."

"Perhaps. Why should we let old grudges come between us?"

"There was blood in those grudges, I believe."

He smiled oddly at her.

"You're writing me down pretty low, eh?"

"Pretty low, yes."

"You think Tirrel has me?"

"I do!"

"Kate," he answered, "Michael, as you call him, is as safely in the palm of my hand as I please."

"Is he?"

"Yes."

"Where is your trap for him now?"

"You are, Kate. He's sure to come back to you again. You're the bait that keeps him here. Otherwise, he ought to have broken out of the country."

"He tried to and had bad luck."

"At Apache Crossing?"

"Yes."

"He had some luck, there, and the greatest mare in the world, I think. But if he keeps rising here, I'll spear that fish, Kate."

"I think that I can stop that."

"I don't think that you can."

"That I can't dismiss him?"

"I don't think you could. You're pretty fond of that fellow, eh?"

She met his eye; suddenly she crimsoned and looked down.

"Of course I knew that was it," said he. "But now I have another solution for this."

"Solution?"

"Yes. A real one."

"What is it?"

"It's sealed up in this envelope."

She leaned and read the name of Tirrel on the paper.

"I want you to give this to him."

"What's in it?"

"Not poison, and not magic," he said, still smiling.

"I don't want anything to do with it," said the girl.

"If you refuse, you'll regret it."

"But why should I?"

"Because I tell you it's a remedy.

"For you, perhaps?"

"For everyone and everything. It brings things to a finish."

She took the envelope with an impulsive gesture.

"I shouldn't do this," she said. "Besides, I may never see him again."

"Oh, I'll take the chance of that!"

"What makes you think that he won't be out of the country before this?"

"Two good reasons. One is that, after her long run, he wants Molly in perfect shape before trying to break away. The stronger reason is that he wants to see you again, and still again. Of course he's bitten."

She stood up suddenly.

"I'll have to go back home," said she.

"Well, so long."

He held her stirrup and gave her a hand up. She gathered the reins and looked down to him, half resistant, and half bewildered.

"We'll be better friends one of these days," said he.

She laughed a little, bitterly.

"You take note," said Bramber, "that I generally get what I want. The others come and they go again. But I'm still on the job, Kate. That's worth thinking over."

She reined the roan suddenly away from him, partly as in fear, and partly as in disgust, and spurred off through the trees without a word.

313

Chapter Thirty-Six

Bramber watched her go with his head tipped a little to one side, as if in an impersonal curiosity. More of his thoughts had revolved around this girl than around any other person in the world. He would have been blind if he had not seen how powerfully she was drawn toward Tirrel, and this added the final poison sting to his emotion toward that venturesome man. He would have been still more blind if he had not interpreted correctly the movement of fear and horror with which she left him, but he also felt that there was something worthy of another interpretation. If he could fix himself strongly and long enough in her mind, then it was very possible that all her emotions toward him might eventually change.

And he was not one who was unable to wait. He had the patience, often, of a cat watching at a mouse hole. He would use that patience now, if need be!

So he turned back to his horse, mounted it, and rode back toward Los Cavallos. He kept up a steady gait, not furiously or recklessly fast, but a good twelve miles an hour, over rough and smooth. Beyond the first crest of the hill he found a man waiting with two saddled horses. One of these was a strongly built bay; the other was a mustang. Here Bramber halted, mounted the bay, and without a word rode on again, heedless of the snarl of discontent with which the man looked after him.

It was always a principle with Bramber that his inferiors need not be conciliated by pleasant manners if they could be imposed upon by the largeness of his accomplishments. He believed more in actions than in words and he had been heard to say that the reason he was yet allowed to live in peace by the law was that, although everyone knew that he existed by crime, yet no one ever had heard him talk about his achievements. So now he understood and accepted the snarl behind him and rode blithely on his way thinking only of the future.

He had before him, in contemplation, a plan which was the simplest he ever had conceived and yet he felt that it would achieve greater results than all he had ever done before. It was most perfect because, above all, it would use the power of the law. That law which should have attacked him with relentless venom he would now be able to use for his own purposes. And he was enchanted by the prospect.

He went over the ground carefully as he galloped on, working the bay at exactly the same rate as when he was riding the gray. He came into Los Cavallos in the middle of the afternoon. It was very hot. Siestas were not yet finished. Dogs and chickens, even, were sheltering themselves from the blast of the sun; only here and there a cat slipped cautiously across the open spaces of the streets. In fact, it was like a night scene, except for the power of the sun and its blaring brightness.

Bramber, looking over this field for endeavor, was amused. He had done most of his campaigning in great cities where the loot was more easily obtainable and where it lay in greater quantities, and yet never in Manhattan had he had access to such a quantity of treasure as he hoped to have in his hands before the close of the next day.

He went straight to the sheriff's office.

"Is the sheriff here?"

"No, but Sam Lowell is here."

"How is Lowell?"

At this, the man who answered the door, slouch-shouldered, fat, with an ugly fighting face, grinned broadly.

"He's been kinda upset, as you might say."

"Ask him if he'll see Chandos."

"Chandos? Sure, I'll ask him."

About one man in twenty knew the identity of Bramber in Los Cavallos. And to those who were in ignorance, Bramber was in no haste to advertise the real truth. It was again an exemplification of his theory that talk is more dangerous than deeds.

He was brought in presently to see a rather pale young man with a bandage around his head and a great purple stain descending beneath one eye. But the glance of the other eye was as fiery and straight as ever.

He looked fixedly at his guest.

"You're Chandos, are you?"

"That's right."

"You're Bramber too, I take it."

"Bramber? Perhaps I am."

"A damned lot of nerve you have coming into my office, then," said Sam Lowell with heat.

Bramber was not disturbed. He knew that Lowell would have fought a cage full of tigers in an effort to reestablish a reputation somewhat shattered by his adventures with Michael Tirrel.

"Why is it nerve?" asked Bramber.

"Being what you are!"

"You're an officer of the law."

"I'm sorta surprised that you know that."

"Are you? Of course I know that you're an

317

officer of the law and that's why I realize that you've nothing against me until there's a warrant out for me and a proved crime against me."

"Is that your line?" asked the deputy sheriff.

"That's my line. I think it's a pretty good one."

"What you think makes no difference to me. I'm here to tell you, Bramber, that I know that you're a — "

He paused. Bramber had slowly lifted a hand, and there was a smile in his pale eyes.

"Of course you know enough about me," said Bramber. "But that's not the point, just now. I've come here to offer you my help."

"In what? In arresting you?"

Bramber overlooked the savage sneer.

"You want one man a pile more than you want me."

"What man?"

"You can name him yourself, I think."

"You mean Tirrel?"

"That's what I mean."

"Do I want him more than you do?"

"Not a bit more," admitted Bramber. "The fact is that we've both got to admit that he's made a fool of us. I'll admit it; I take it that you will, too!"

Sam Lowell actually closed his eyes and

groaned in the depth of his shame and his fury.

"He's made a fool of me," he declared. "He's made a ragin' fool out of me. But maybe the dance ain't been danced to an end, just yet."

"Have you any plan up your sleeve?"

"I have the plan of never resting until I get another chance at him."

"Your time is pretty short. He's about due to drift East. He's got the fastest horse on foot under him; and as soon as he gets into the desert, he's at home. We'll never see or hear of him again."

Sam Lowell sighed.

"You think that, Bramber?"

"I know that. I say that here's a job too big for either of us."

"I'm damned if it's as big as all that! He's had luck —"

"Luck can't explain it all. He's been in your hand and out. He's been practically in my hand a couple of times. Every time he gets away. Finch has a still wilder yarn to tell me about him. Well, I won't go into that. The fact is that he's a straight-shooting, hard-riding, quick-thinking devil. The law wants him. I want him. Now I ask you what could be more sensible than for you and me to throw in together in the trailing of him?"

"A fine thing for the law to throw in with such as you!"

"You're using hard talk, but it's straight talk. All right. Suppose that I'm the worst man in the world. Ain't the main thing that you should get rid of Tirrel?"

"God knows that it is, just now!"

"How can you get rid of him? You don't know. I offer you a chance. Will you turn it down?"

"Go on, then, and tell me what's the chance?"

"I'm willing to. First we have to make our bargain. I'm not doing this for nothing."

"Well, then, what will you want out of him? His blood?"

"I'll leave that for the law. It's what the law always wants. After he's caught, what I want is everything that's in his pockets, down to the skin. Is that fair? I'll take the trimmings, and leave you the rest of the roast!"

The other chuckled.

"He's trimmed you, they say!"

"He has," said Bramber frankly.

"And how are you going to get hold of him? Haven't you chased him already through the mountains and back and forth?"

"I've chased him — I've nearly had him — and I've lost him again. But this time it'll be a different story. I'm not going to chase him.

He's going to chase me."

Sam Lowell whistled.

"Are you sure of that?"

"I'm pretty sure."

"Where will he come chasing you?"

"Suppose that I invited him into Los Cavallos?

The other started.

"Are you crazy man?"

"I hope I'm not!"

"As though he'd come here!"

"What would you depend on keeping him out?"

"He wouldn't dare! Come here again?"

"This town is where he'll come. And when the time comes, I can point it out to you!"

"I'll — I'll have him or die trying," said Lowell eagerly.

"Try with straight-shooting guns," said Bramber. "That young devil leads a charmed life, it seems to me!"

"I'll undo the charm for him!"

"And our bargain?"

"Well, why not? Why shouldn't I? I will! If you can put me in touch with him, you have the trimmings and I get the roast."

Bramber's eyes shone with pale fire.

"Will you shake on that?"

"I will!"

And their hands closed.

Chapter Thirty-Seven

In the golden time of the later afternoon, when the shadows of the trees stretched grotesquely far and the sun looked deeply through every grove, finding its way between the brown trunks, Kate Lawrence cantered her horse straight up the valley, then left the central trail and pushed to the left, suddenly doubling up a rocky slope, twisting back and forth among big boulders. At last she paused, and stood up in her stirrups to look over the brow of a big stone and listen keenly.

Presently she had sight of a horseman who broke out of the grove and plunged down the valley, his eyes glued to the trail — reading it like an Indian, at a gallop. But when he came to the point where she had diverged from it and turned up hill, he did not pause but continued. He was lost in the next grove and after him came two more scampering riders who did not seem to have any regard except for keeping their leader in view.

These, also, being swallowed from sight

among the evergreens, were lost to her. The girl shivered a little. However, she had a good Winchester stuffed into the holster down the side of her saddle, and she could use the gun as well as most men. She gave the stock of it a nervous pat; then she rode her mustang from the rocks and doubled back through the valley in the direction from which she had come, but keeping to the higher ground until she came to a point where the waters of a creek worked with a twist and a writhing through the broken ground.

Up this she turned, but had not gone fifty yards before it opened into a little dale, with great trees looming on either side of it. Tirrel, rifle in hand, stepped suddenly into the trail before her. He looked her quietly in the eye as she appeared.

"You've had trouble," he told her.

"I've just shaken off three of 'em," replied the girl.

She swung down to the ground.

"You've got to get out of here, Michael. They buzz like bees every time that I start out for a ride; they have an idea that I may show the way to you. And perhaps I will. I never know. Some time I may think that I've fooled 'em, and they may come back and pick up my trail again. They're as smart as they're hard, and they can't be turned into fools forever!"

He listened and agreed with a nod.

"I've got to get out of this," consented Tirrel. "I've given Molly her rest."

"Where is she?"

He whistled. Out of the woods, like a deer bounding, appeared the mare, and came frolicking to them.

"She's sleek as a pig," said Kate Lawrence. "I never saw her looking so well!"

"If they run her now," agreed Tirrel, "they'll have to use more horses than they had the last time."

Molly, leaving her master, advanced cautiously on the girl. She was as playful as a great puppy, nipping at the brim of Kate's hat, and the girl pushed her away, and threatened her in vain with a lifted hand.

"Look," said she, "No one ever has been cruel to her. Not even Dan Finch, I suppose! There's no fear in her! She's famous, now. She's famous all through the range. The newspaper in Apache ran a long account of the story of the hunt."

"I'd like to see that," commented Tirrel. "If they tell the straight of it?"

"They added in a little. They gave about five relays chasing you instead of three, and they about doubled the distance. That's all. No, they said that you fell off your horse exhausted when you got to me, and I got you up

324

and dragged you into the back of the buck-board."

They smiled at each other.

"They've copied the story East and West," said Kate. "They've made you into a famous outlaw, Michael, a terrible man, that killed your own brother and breaks through the hands of sheriffs and mobs, and outrides a whole army. You're as big and bad a man as Bramber himself, right now!"

They laughed together.

She had brought him up some provisions — coffee, bacon, flour, plum jam. These things he looked upon with great relish. This quiet corner in the hills was the best sort of a home to him, he declared.

She criticized that suggestion sharply.

"Let one of them come wriggling along through the trees like a snake and find you out — there'll be no Michael Tirrel at the end of the ride for me, that day!"

At this, he began with a sudden emotion: "And suppose that I was scratched off the book, Kate, would it make you — "

"Well?" said she.

"I'm getting kind of sentimental about you," confessed Tirrel.

"I believe you are," said Kate. "You look sort of worked up, just now."

"I always suspected that you'd laugh at

me," he declared, instantly resigned.

"You did? Am I laughing?"

"Why — " began Tirrel, and stepping a little closer, he reached out his hand and laid it on her arm.

She did not step back or brush the hand away, though the touch of it was as light as thistledown.

"You'd better not," she said.

"No," he agreed instantly. "But — if I talked, would you listen, Kate?"

"I'd ride a thousand miles to hear you, Michael." Then she added, as his eyes widened: "I'd ride a thousand miles to follow you, too. But there's no good in that. I've got to stay home and see how things will turn out, there."

He said not a word more. Molly came in between them, and when she had passed on, Kate Lawrence was saying: "I've seen a friend of yours, today."

"Who?"

"Bramber."

Tirrel raised his head.

"You saw Bramber!"

"Yes. I know him pretty well. And he knows me — not quite so well, I think."

"Why did he come to you?"

"He came to talk about Michael Tirrel."

"And what did he say?"

"He brought me a letter to give to you."

She produced it, and Tirrel opened the envelope and spread out the single sheet of paper which it contained.

That sheet was covered with a fine, almost feminine hand, and Tirrel read it slowly, aloud, for he had to spend a little time in spelling out every word, so closely and rapidly did the syllables run together. He read:

Dear Tirrel,

Our trails have crossed so many times, lately, that you'll hardly be surprised that I'm writing you a letter. Since you came to Los Cavallos, you've done a great many very clever and very brave things, and you've established yourself with such a grand reputation that it really appears to me that you deserve extra consideration from me.

It was my purpose, at first, simply to get rid of you with the simplest possible means. I was tempted, when you visited your brother at the shack of Dutch Methuen, to wait until you came back inside from the stable, and then to kill you out of hand, so that your two ghosts could keep each other company in the most brotherly fashion.

I changed my mind at the last moment. As I see it now, it appears to me definite that fate kept me from wiping you out so casually. It was to appear, afterward, that you are a fellow worthy of a man's death rather than a dog's.

The chase you led me across the hills really was enough to give you the reputation which you enjoy at the present time. The range is worshiping you as a brand new and very capable hero. Well, old fellow, why shouldn't you have a hero's good chance?

I am going to give you an open chance at me. I can't say that I'll actually offer you the first hold, but I'll agree to be in Los Cavallos, in the plaza, near the hotel patio entrance every evening after sundown, for one hour — which is as long as good shooting light lasts, as I think that you'll agree.

Of course this will sound to you like a trap, but, as a matter of fact, I'll give you my word that neither I nor any man of mine ever will attempt to lay a hand on you during your trip into Los Cavallos. Besides this, we'll let the town know that we've invited you in. And although I have the reputation of being a rather hard fellow, I have another sort of reputation as well that I wouldn't be apt to throw out the window.

If you don't come, every dog on the range will howl at you. If you do come — good luck to you!

Adios until we meet next in Los Cavallos.

But I must explain one thing.

You may wonder why I set the place in Los Cavallos. Because only in a crowd would you trust me to play fair. Otherwise, you'd think that I'd be too apt to simply trap you. But how can I trap you in a place like Los Cavallos?

I'm letting the contents of this letter be spread around. Everyone will know it inside of a few days. And we'll grow more and more expectant in the town.

Adios again.

NICHOLAS BRAMBER.

When he had finished reading the letter aloud, Tirrel looked with a frown at the girl, and she with a frown at him.

"Let me see the letter."

He passed it to her.

"It's his own handwriting," she murmured. "I don't suppose there are ten men in the world who have seen specimens of it. How much he wants to get rid of you, Michael!"

"He does," said the other, "down to the point of offering a fair fight to me!"

"Fair fight?"

She puckered her brows in gloomy consideration.

"I can't understand everything in this letter," she said. "But I'll tell you this: The fight wouldn't be fair, and no matter what he says, Bramber *is* laying a trap. If only we can see through it!"

Chapter Thirty-Eight

She was so filled with confidence that Tirrel listened to her as to a prophet.

He said at last: "Bramber is a cold proposition."

"Chilled steel."

"What people think don't make much difference to him?"

"Not a bit."

"Really?"

"Oh, a little, of course."

"What *you* think, for instance?"

She shook her head.

"Are you sure?" pressed Tirrel.

"No," she admitted. "I'm not. I suppose that Nick does care a little what I think."

"Up and down the range, besides, he's looked at as a great man, isn't he?"

"Yes, that's true."

"Suppose that Bramber invites me to Los Cavallos, what do you think he'll do?"

"Have twenty men ready to blow you off the earth, Michael, and give you a flying start for another life!"

Tirrel nodded.

"But if he had me mobbed after promising me a fair fight, what would the people up and down the range think of him?"

"He's done cold-blooded murders before this."

"People say that he has, but nobody knows. They suspect that he's bumped off a lot of people, but nobody can put his finger exactly on the sore place and say this is the spot."

"That's true. No one knows much about Nick."

"But if he had me mobbed in Los Cavallos, after letting everybody know that he'd invited me there on a fair and square challenge?"

"That would be pretty black."

"Would even the crooks stay with him?"

"I don't think so. Not the Westerners, anyway."

"I work it out that way, Kate. He wants to snag me, right enough. But he wants to keep his reputation pretty well in hand, don't he?"

"Yes, I suppose so. He would have a hard time here in the West if his gang murdered you under those conditions, Michael. But you have to remember that it isn't cut and dried, yet. We don't know that he's sent out any public challenge to you. And — there's one thing that looks very queer to me!"

"Well? You mean he confesses that he killed Jimmy?"

"That's it, of course."

"It does look queer. But still, it isn't a clue that the law could use to hang him by."

"*Could* he have killed your brother?"

"I should have thought that Jimmy couldn't have been killed, that way, except by a fellow he took to be a friend."

"Was Bramber a friend?"

"Of course not. It was he who shot Jimmy at the crooked card game."

"How much has Nick Bramber to win by downing you?"

"This much!"

He put his hat on the ground, bottom up, and, unbuckling a money belt, he emptied chamber after chamber into the hat. It was more than half filled with treasure.

"And this besides," said Tirrel.

He took out the red wallet and opened the flap of it to show the thick and hard compacted sheaf of bills.

She was filled with awe.

"What can it be worth?"

"I don't know. I don't hardly dare to guess. I should say more'n half a million, anyway."

"Will you let me see the wallet a little closer?"

"Here it is."

She took it and turned it in curious fingers. It was not at the money, but at the leather itself that she stared.

"You're a friend of Bob Smalley's, are you?"

"Why do you ask that?"

"But are you?"

"I never heard that name before."

"This wallet was Bob's. I've seen it a hundred times."

"This red wallet?"

"Yes."

"I tell you, Kate, I never knew any Smalley. That red wallet is what my brother picked up, and it had in it the message that finally took me to all the loot."

She shook her head.

"I don't understand!" said she. "Smalley's in prison, now. How could his wallet have gotten here?"

"I don't know," admitted Tirrel. "Who was Smalley?"

"Smalley was a cheerful sort of a fellow. A natural liar. Never did any work. Always had lots of money."

"Gambler?"

"Yes. And a lot more than that. It was Scrope and Smalley, you understand, that robbed the First National at Elm City."

"When?"

"A month and more ago."

"What did they get out of it?"

"More than fifty thousand in bank notes, I think."

Tirrel looked at her again.

"That's about what's in this wallet," said he.

She stared.

"What in the world does it mean, Michael?"

"I don't know!" he said. "But for the first time, I think that maybe we're coming close to something. Scrope and Smalley robbed a bank and got fifty thousand dollars. My brother picks up Smalley's pocketbook, not with the money in it, but with a paper that has the direction where to find the loot! That's a queer combination!"

He picked out the narrow slip of paper and showed it to her.

Dear old man,

It is under the head in line with the tiger at the forking of the dead spruce.

Yours by the old sign.

This she stared at.

And suddenly she said: "That's Smalley's writing. I know that it is! That's Bob Smalley's writing! And he's still in prison — and

335

isn't this a frightfully hard thing to understand?"

"I been breaking my heart over it for a long time."

"Of course he might send out a message from prison."

"He might."

"And in his own red wallet. But he was mighty proud of that wallet. He said his money was always well dressed when it was inside that red leather!"

"Did Finch have anything to do with that bank robbery at Elm City?" asked Tirrel suddenly.

"Not that I know of."

"What became of the man you called Scrope?"

"Scrope was killed."

"When?"

"Four days after the robbery, or about that long a time. They hunted the robbers hard."

"There were only the two?"

"No, there were three that they hunted. Then they lost the trail of one of the three."

"Where did they lose it?"

"In that badland of rocks right up the valley from here."

"By the Lord!" groaned Tirrel. "Am I beginning to understand, at last?"

"Understand what?"

"It's as twisted as a snake's trail, but this is what I make of it."

"Go on with your guessing, no matter how wild it is."

"The three who robbed the bank were Scrope, Smalley, and Dan Finch. They're closely hunted. Finch has the money in his hands. That often happens, I believe, and one man keeps the swag until the gang gets to a safe place to divide it. On the way, he takes a chance to give the others the slip. It wouldn't be so very hard, seeing that he has Molly Malone under his saddle! He slips away from the rest and heads into the rocky land. But he doesn't want to carry all that coin about with him. He and the others have been hunted too closely to make him feel very happy. The result is that he makes up his mind that he'll cache that bunch of greenbacks. He turns up a stone in what looks to him like a good place. And it *is* a good place. He couldn't hardly have found a better. As a matter of fact, he runs into the place where some Spanish land pirate had sunk his plunder in the rich old days. And there's where he leaves the greenbacks, along with all the rest of the swag that has been lying there so long in the cave. He's sure that his money will be dead safe there, because the Spanish loot remained there so long, undisturbed by anyone.

337

"But he makes one great mistake. The Spaniards had covered up their tracks fine. But he hadn't had the time, probably, to wipe out his own sign. Was Smalley a good trailer?"

"Yes, and Tom Scrope was one of the best in the range. He was half Indian and he had the Indian eyes!"

"Then Tom Scrope was the fellow who worked out the trail when him and Smalley found that Finch had given them the slip. They'd much rather die than let him get away with that!

"So they find the place by the fresh made sign, they take the recovered coin, and the old jewels too, and they cart it across country and bury it under the spruce. That's simple. Now, Scrope is killed, and Smalley's caught and jammed in prison. He sends word from prison to a friend giving him the information about where the stuff is hidden. He sends that message in the red wallet. Everybody knows the red wallet. It'll be proof that his messenger is not a fake. The messenger loses that wallet, and Jimmy Tirrel picks it up. That's one part of the story. D'you follow it?"

"Like a book!"

"It tails together! They try to kill Jimmy. They shoot him up but they don't kill him. He figures that the wallet is something terribly important. Maybe he works out the whole problem, some way. That's why he tells me about the great things he's gunna do.

"In the meantime, there's Finch waiting in the desert. Finally he decides that things have quieted down enough for him to come back. He wants to get you and he wants to get the money. He starts back. He meets me. He hears from me that Bramber is in Los Cavallos. That means a good deal to him. Probably the three of them were working under Bramber's orders when they robbed that bank. Bramber has come out to make trouble, and Finch is scared almost to death. He was going back with a free hand to pick up the loot and you and start away for a happy life ever after."

"Go on!" said the girl. "It sounds like the fact. I believe that it *is* the fact."

"I begin to think so, too! Of course, when he learned that the terrible Bramber was on the spot, and probably looking for his scalp, Dan Finch changed his mind at once. He didn't want to go any closer. But then he had his great idea. He was pretty well known on the range, but not in Los Cavallos. In fact, he'd been there only once. There was only one thing about him that was famous, and that was his mare, Molly Malone. So he got into that poker game with me and deliberately he chucked everything that he had — his money, his clothes, his horse! He lost it all. And he gave me the horse by throwing away the seven of diamonds. You see? He knew that I was riding on toward Los Cavallos. I'd arrive there, he hoped. Since Bramber personally didn't know me, it was very likely that he'd start out to get me murdered and then forget all about such a person as Dan Finch, thinking him under the sod. Dan, quietly, would pick up the money, pick up you, and be off, unnoticed. I was to be the scapegoat. But luck stood by me. I got the thing that Finch was after. When I came here to the house and listened to him talking to you, he decided that it would be worth while to buy me off. So he tried to do it but found that his supplies were gone. And there you are, Kate, except that Finch has joined up with Bramber, at last, and all that any of them want is my head!"

Chapter Thirty-Nine

They agreed that there would be no purpose in Tirrel accepting the strange invitation to Los Cavallos unless it became certain that the whole of the range had been made aware of the challenge. Even then, Kate Lawrence was against any such risk, though she grew silent when Tirrel said quietly:

"Someone killed my brother, Jim. Bramber claims the honor of having done that. If he did, I'm going to have my chance at him."

"But suppose he's simply telling you that to get you into a trap?"

"Then I'll have to trust to my luck. That's all!"

She left him, and he resumed his vigil in the little valley, with Molly Malone for a companion. The mare was in the finest fettle. Always beautiful, with good living and much rest she now glistened like a polished jewel; she was like a colt, frolicking on the grass.

The next afternoon there was a grating of shod hoofs coming up the rocks of the ravine, and Tirrel, looking out, rifle in hand, saw not the girl's graceful figure in the saddle but the form of a man, broad shouldered, narrow hipped, his face lost in the steep, inky shadow of a great sombrero, leather chaps over his legs. There was something not quite ordinary about the appearance of this man, but he could not put his finger at once on the unusual feature.

Throwing his rifle over the crook of his left arm, he stepped into the open.

"You got business up this way, partner?" he asked.

The stranger rode straight on.

"Are you deaf?" shouted Tirrel. "Rein up!"

But the other did not stir in the saddle, and Tirrel jerked the butt of his rifle into the hollow of his shoulder.

Only then it seemed to him that the features beneath the hat and its shadow seemed oddly youthful — a moment more, and as he sighted for his bead, he saw that the stranger was smiling, a familiar smile, and then behold! It was Kate Lawrence!

She took off her hat. A bright shower of hair fell to her shoulders, and then slipped down in a long coil.

"What sort of a game?" asked Tirrel, as she swung down to the ground. "And are you wearing stilts?"

She was almost as tall as he, and she stood

awkwardly, in long riding boots many sizes too large for her.

Still she laughed and would not explain.

It was not until she had hobbled to a rock and sat down in the shade of a tree that she would enlarge on her disguise.

"You see how the thing goes, Michael?"

"I see that you're dressed up like a pretty poor imitation of a man, honey."

"You didn't know me till I was right on top of you."

"Who'd be expecting such foolishness, Kate?"

"Suppose it was dusk, Michael?"

"I don't want to suppose, honey," said he, "because I might easy of planted a bullet between your eyes, if you'd rode right on at me, that way, in the dusk!"

She nodded at him.

"I thought it would turn out that way," said she.

"You have something in mind," said Tirrel. "What's the little old game, Kate? You must be hot in all that man-wear and padding around the shoulders."

She peeled off the coat and, looking oddly small and childish, leaned back against a rock, beneath the tree.

"This is the idea, big boy. You follow me?"

"I'll try to."

"Suppose that friend Bramber has you framed?"

"Well, supposing. What good does it do to have you dressed like a man?"

"Look here — you come sashaying up to Los Cavallos in the dusk of the day. What's the first thing that they'd spot you by?"

"Why, by the mare, of course. They'd spot Molly. What of it?"

"There's a lot of it! Suppose that you start to meet Mr. Bramber in the plaza, just where he's been so brave and invited you to come. Well, you start off on my mustang, there, and cut across country, and come in the East gate of the town just after sunset, when nobody would be expecting *you* from that direction or on that sort of a horse. I've brought along a set of false mustaches for you, if you want them. They look pretty ropey, all right, but they might do."

"Go on with the story," said Tirrel. "I'm full of interest."

"Sure you are. It runs along this way. You slip from the back, so to speak, and in the meantime, through the western gate of the town, where you'd be expected to come, I ride up on Molly. I come along with the sunset light at my back and the sombrero low over my face. All that will be noticed will be that I'm riding Molly Malone. And if Bramber has

344

any trap planned, he'll spring it, and get me, and Molly, but not what he's after!"

"Suppose that he doesn't set a trap for me, but gets ready to tag me with a bullet when I come in through the gates?"

She shook her head.

"I've thought of that," she said. "But there's no chance of that. He's tried tagging you with bullets long before this. He's posted his thugs to get you, and you've melted through their hands. He's been on deck himself, and still he couldn't handle you. Now he won't leave it to any chance. He'll want to get you into their hands — and *then* finish you off."

"It would improve it a lot to have him finish off you instead of me!"

"Of course you won't see things straight, Michael. The real way of it will be that he'll spot me as soon as he's touched me. He will have showed his game. *You* won't have to carry through the duel. And Bramber will have the name of a yellow dog all over the range. Isn't that right?"

He smiled at her, wonderingly, pityingly, and with infinite love. She was as eager as a child, leaning forward to question him.

"Did you think that I'd let you go?" he asked her.

"Of course I did!" said the girl. "And you

345

will, too! And it's time for me to start, now, if I want to get to the town by dusk."

"It's too late for the ride to Los Cavallos, now," said he.

"Not if you hurry."

"I'll wait till tomorrow, anyway. There's no such hurry."

"You have her saddled?"

"Yes, for luck, I suppose. I feel a little safer when I get the saddle on her for a while each day."

"Let me get into the saddle on her."

"So that you can ride to Los Cavallos? Kate, you're wild! What kind of a man d'you think that I may be?"

"A wise man, Michael. You'll play the game the way I suggest, because it's a pretty good way!"

"It's the way that a low hound and coward would want you to play it!"

"I know that you're brave, Michael, but bravery and straight shooting can't always win. Not against odds of ten to one, such as you've always been playing around here. It's got you famous, but it'll also get you dead, Michael. D'you hear me?"

"I hear you."

"What are you looking so dreamy about?"

"I was thinkin' what a fine little girl you are, honey, and I was also thinkin' what an idea it was, for you to go riding off in the lead — and get yourself dropped in my place!"

"There'll be no dropping, Michael! I promise you that. I just know! Don't I, Molly?"

She got up and went to the mare, and Molly met her halfway and stretched out her head to the hand of the girl. She struggled into her big-shouldered, padded coat again.

"But," said Tirrel, "your idea for me to go in through the Eastern gate isn't at all bad. They won't expect me from that direction, will they? They're not apt to, at any rate!"

He did not receive an answer, and only heard, in reply, a little grunt of effort. Then he saw that Kate Lawrence had climbed into the saddle upon the mare. The long and awkward man's boots, like stilts upon her, were being fitted into the stirrups.

"Kate!" he shouted in a sudden fear, and plunged for the head of Molly.

But cat-footed Molly was not easy to reach. It was a mere game of tag, she thought, and bounded sidewise, and then ahead.

"Kate — for God's sake!" screamed Tirrel, rushing blindly after her down the ravine.

Her voice floated back to him:

"You can follow along on the mustang!"

Chapter Forty

There was no more restless spirit in all Los Cavallos than Deputy Sheriff Sam Lowell. He had relished neither food nor sleep since the unlucky day when his trail crossed with that of the presumed Dan Finch now known to be Michael Tirrel, for up to the moment of that crossing of the trails, the way of Sam Lowell had been constantly up. He had loved glory; he had loved the man-trail; he actually had loved law and clean keepers of the law for their own sake. There could hardly have been found a better young man for the difficult post he filled, for the actual sheriff was rather elderly, losing his activity, a deadly fighter and a willing one, to be sure, but less able to get to the place where the fighting was apt to be done.

Sam Lowell, honest, straightforward, and of a burning energy, was suddenly bumped from the tracks of ambition. Tirrel had done it! His pursuit of Tirrel had been a grand effort, with a ridiculous result! His very heart burned at the thought! Men on the street smiled when they told the story!

It was some small consolation to know that even Bramber, the great and mysterious Bramber, had failed still more lamentably to hold this wild man from the desert. It was a salve for the hurt spirit of Lowell to remember this. But still, Bramber had never been tapped upon the head, while his prisoner walked out of the room and away from his custody. That thought used to waken Sam Lowell in the middle of the night, a stabbing pain through his head and through his heart.

But now he was tormented in a new manner. This great encumbrance to his fame, this hated enemy, Tirrel, might possibly be removed from his path, but it would be through the agency of Bramber himself, who now sat opposite the deputy sheriff and smoked a long black cigar with care and with great relish.

The deputy broke off his pacing up and down.

"I'll tell you what," said he. "Tirrel never would come here. He never would be the fool to come here! Of course he wouldn't!"

"What makes you think that?"

"He'll suspect a trap."

"Of course he will. Every sane man in the world will suspect a trap."

"And there *will* be one."

349

"Not one that I had anything to do with. And besides, we're not so sure that Tirrel will come at once. We can't count the chickens before they're hatched."

"I say we can't. Oh, Bramber, I'm in hell! I can't tell what's the right thing to do. I only hope to God that he don't come at all, up to Los Cavallos!"

"He's gotta come some time. Look at the lay of the land. Everybody on the range knows about the challenge. No matter where Tirrel goes, no matter how many brave things he's done, people are going to shake their heads at him unless he comes up here to meet me. They're going to suggest that perhaps he had a yellow streak in him, somewhere!"

"They are! That's nacheral!" agreed Sam Lowell. "But oh, Bramber, to set a trap, this way, appealing to a man's sense of honor! To bait him with that, and when he comes up here like an honorable man, then to snag him — "

"It's an ugly job. It's a damn ugly job, I know, but it has to be done!"

"Stand out and fight him fairly, as you've fairly challenged him, then."

"I'm not one of these romantic fools," declared Bramber. "I don't intend to take a chance with my hide — not when it could be punctured by a slug from that fellow's guns.

350

If the worst comes to the worst, then I'll tackle him single-handed. I only hope that the worst won't come. I'm trying to provide against that worst right now."

"By getting me to do the dirty work, eh? No, no, Bramber! *I'll* be in the plaza at the right moment, and there I'll stand up to him and fight him!"

"You're as brave as they come," said Bramber in his quiet, unemotional way. "But where does courage take you, at this rate? Where does it bring you, Lowell? You could stand up and face him. You could fall down full of lead, too! That would be a big advancement for law and order, wouldn't it? And — "

"A bullet will kill any man!" said the deputy sheriff. "Suppose that I get in the first shot?"

"You won't. You wouldn't take advantage of him, in a fair fight. And if you give him an even start at his guns, he's a faster and a surer man than you are, Lowell."

"He is!" groaned the deputy sheriff. "But am I letting fear run me, in this business? God forgive me if I am!"

"No, you're playing the part of a man of sense."

"You'd say that."

Bramber removed the cigar from his mouth and blew forth a pale cone of strong smoke.

"Look here, Sam," said he. "I like to see the workings of an honest man, like you. I'm not honest myself, and you know it. But I appreciate honesty in the other fellow. However, you don't want to let it make a damn fool of you. Here's the hard-boiled facts about Tirrel. He's broken away from the law; he's tapped a sheriff over the head to get loose, and thereby made the law and its officers look pretty sick, around here; he's stolen the horse from Dan Finch, and in that alone there's enough to hang him!"

"It's never been proved that he stole the horse from Finch."

"Is it likely, I ask you, that Danny would have gambled away the mare, as Tirrel swears?"

"No, it's not likely. But it might have happened."

"But chuck all of that to one side. Tirrel murdered his own brother. He deserves to die like a dog."

"There's no proof of that, either."

"Proof? Millions! Who else was anywhere near the shack?"

"Old Dutch Methuen, for instance."

"Dutch Methuen! Man, man, you're not suggesting that that old fellow could have done it!"

"He's not too old to ride with you, if what I hear is true."

"He's a friend of mine. I've loaned him money, from time to time. He'd do what he could to please me. But murder Jimmy Tirrel? What in the name of God could have induced him to do that?"

"I don't know. I'm only giving you the possibilities."

"Of course you are."

Lowell dropped into a chair.

"You want me to deliberately post men and murder Tirrel when he comes into the town?"

"Of course I do. Murder him and be sure that he drops dead!"

"That's kind advice, Bramber! It's — it's what I'd expect from you, after all!"

Bramber said slowly, his deliberation giving his words sudden weight and effect:

"Lowell, you talk like a fool. You want to eat your cake; also you want to have it. Do you want Tirrel alive, a regular question mark against your reputation? Or do you want him dead?"

"Not dead by murder!"

"Is it murder for a sheriff to kill a murderer, an outlaw, a fugitive?"

Sam Lowell was stilled in the midst of his arguments. He could only groan: "I want to do the right thing. I don't want to let jealousy or fear run me!"

"There's no danger of that. Everything will be arranged for you. You have your own men, I hope?"

"I have eight men."

"I wish you had more. No, eight will be enough. Put four at the Eastern entrance to the plaza, and four at the Western. They'll handle him."

"But suppose he rushes through?"

"Then he'll reach me."

"You intend to be in the plaza, then?"

"Of course I do. I'm not going to play the part of a yellow dog in this show. Not a bit of it. I'm simply going to be waiting for my man to come, but before he can get to me, the deputy sheriff, Sam Lowell, who doesn't want duels and insists on the execution of the law, steps in and takes his fugitive man!"

He waved an eloquent hand which seemed to erase all the objections which had been written in the air by the voice of Lowell.

"Do you think that other people would approve of this idea?" asked Lowell.

"You have a mind to make up for yourself, I take it. Do your own judging."

"I can do my own judging, but I've been brooding about this job until I'm more than half mad!"

"Not a bit of it. Your course is as straight as the trigger finger of Tirrel's right hand."

"He's wanted by the law!" the deputy reassured himself.

"Come, come! Make up your mind. Rule out all the doubts. That's the only thing for you to do! There's this fellow who's robbed, stolen horses, committed the most horrible kind of murders — and you're the deputy sheriff. You're letting a bit of pride blind you worse than dark glasses. And that's the fact of the matter!"

"Ah, I suppose that it may be!" sighed Sam Lowell.

"You've got to set your teeth and dig in your toes. Get your men together. Talk the thing over with them. Tell them that you've made up your mind that you're not going to be disgraced by allowing a duel to take place in this town publicly, while you're here. You'll enforce the law. You're sworn to do it! Duel to you is simply murder!

"Now, then, they can't answer back to that. You post them before sundown. In the meantime, I'll have watchers all around the town, so that a black crow couldn't get into Los Cavallos without being seen by me. I'll send on the signal as soon as Molly Malone is sighted."

"Do that, then. I'll be prepared. God help Tirrel today. Or tomorrow. Or whenever he comes. But, Bramber, you really think that he *will* come?"

"He will. He wants to be the hero. He wants to do the impossible things. Of course he'll come. He's in love with Kate Lawrence."

"Ha?"

"Why, that's old news, by this time. And what's more, she's in love with him!"

"Great God!" breathed Sam Lowell. "That lovely girl? I'll kill that scoundrel, Bramber, with all the pleasure I'd feel in shootin' down a lobo wolf!"

Chapter Forty-One

When Tirrel saw Molly Malone swinging down the ravine, he stood helplessly. His brain and body were chained up. Then he leaped for his rifle and raised it. There was no way of stopping this mad girl before she got to Los Cavallos except by killing or crippling the mare. But when he strove to steady the rifle for the shot, his hand shook, and the sight wobbled crazily from the mare to the rider. He dared not pull the trigger; and at the last moment, Kate Lawrence turned in the saddle and waved cheerfully back to him. Tirrel dropped the rifle and covered his eyes with his hands.

So, stunned, sick at heart, with the icy sweat dripping down his face, he prayed for knowledge of what could be done, and at last a dim hope burned up in him.

The trail to Los Cavallos lay over easy country, swinging, from the point where they were situated, in a broadly looping arc. The chord was a far shorter line. And if he rode it, he might, conceivably, reach the town before Molly Malone. There was only one trouble. In the way of the straight line, driving every traveler to one side or the other, was a rough ascent, with a precipitous slope facing toward Los Cavallos from the north.

But at least there was a hope that he could push on and get to the Northern gate before the girl reached the Western. It depended much upon the speed at which she cared to take Molly along.

That part of the question was very largely answered before he had ridden three miles in the pursuit. He laid the first part of his course straight behind the mare, and along the usual trail, and he had, at the end of that time, a view of Molly — a bright flash in the far distance — swinging over the top of a hill, almost like the flashing flight of a bird.

Tirrel, at that, ground his teeth together and looked to his mount.

It was nothing like Molly Malone. It was that same sturdy roan which once before had saved his life and beaten off the last challenge of Bramber and Bramber's men. Perhaps, thought Tirrel, that was an omen of good luck, and, having served greatly once, the roan would be able to serve again.

He turned the head of the gelding straight toward distant Los Cavallos, and drove him forward through the heavy air and the flooding, intolerable sunshine.

They were quickly in broken ground, and here the gelding showed himself an excellent mountaineer, taking the ups and downs, not with the goatlike skill and deftness of Molly Malone, but with a sure foot and a fearless heart. The hopes of Tirrel increased. They began to climb, the roan sticking stoutly to the labor. He had no wings to lift and float him up great ascents, as Molly had, but he was a patient and courageous plodder, and rapidly he gained the summit.

Before them, the white walls of Los Cavallos were turning blue with the northern shadow. The westering sun poured slant floods of golden light over the hills. Windows in the town flashed like great signal lights burning. And from the valley road puffs of dust rose and dissolved in the colorful mist of the lower air.

Beneath Tirrel and the gelding dropped a sheer slope — often so smooth that not even grass had clung to it, but broken here and there where a wretched tree, taking desperate fingerhold, clung against the sharp face of the ground. It was a far ride to the bottom — rather a slide than a ride.

The roan sniffed at the descent, laid back his ears, and had to be thrust over the rim with a savage jab of the spurs. Tirrel sat back in the saddle, kept a good grip with his knees, and trusted the rest to luck and the sure-footedness of the gelding.

And never did a horse answer better, for they had barely started when the ground beneath them gave way with a sudden lurch that spilled the roan sidewise and hurled them, like a stone, broadside at a boulder that rose from the mountainside like a shark's dorsal fin from the sea.

It looked like the end to Tirrel, but the gallant roan, scrambling like a dog on bad footing, righted himself and passed the edge of the boulder like a shot, only grazing the leather of Tirrel's chaps against the stone.

The speed increased. They dodged trees again. Rocks leaped up before them, reached at them, disappeared behind. Dust and gravel flew up behind them, and larger stones, loosened as they began the slide, now overtook them. A hundred pound monster leaped past the ear of Tirrel with a roar and split itself with a crash like the explosion of a cannon on the face of a larger boulder beneath.

And then they struck the level ground. It knocked the feet from beneath the mustang. He toppled and spun over and over, casting Tirrel like a top rolling before him.

But horse and rider were whalebone. They

rose, staggering. Tirrel dragged himself into the saddle and cantered the good mustang on toward the Northern gate of Los Cavallos, with a great outpouring of hope in his heart and of gratitude toward that gallant mustang. He felt that he had more than a good chance, now. It was true that Molly Malone was swift indeed, but long, vital miles had been clipped from the course by the way Tirrel had ridden. And perhaps he still would win the race.

His heart leaped before him. It seemed to him that the grunting, flying little horse was standing still, as it galloped up the last slope.

A hay wagon, as he approached the gate, drew into it from the inside, and he drew rein, cursing. The few seconds wasted as the big, awkward wagon lumbered through might prove life or death to Kate!

A peon at the roadside came closer and raised his straw sombrero with a grimy hand. He wanted a few pennies, he said, because he was an unlucky devil who had not had work for a month. The señor had a kind face, and if he would —

Tirrel threw him a coin and a curse, and, as the wagon at last lumbered through the narrow passage, he drove the spurs into the roan and leaped on. Something, as he reached the dark of the arch, made him look back, and he saw the late beggar waving his hands toward the tops of the wall — singular motions, with an apparent reason behind them.

He set his teeth, well guessing what this would mean to him, but he drove the gelding on.

"The plaza!" he bellowed.

"The cobbled street, señor!"

The cobbles rang like smitten anvils beneath the hoof strokes of the roan.

He reached a dark twist, a blind alley.

"The plaza?"

"Back two squares, and then the first to your left — "

"Oh, devils and damnation!"

He jerked the roan around with a hand of iron, and plunged him back, crossed the two squares, took the first on his left, and raced down a rather broad, winding way.

"The plaza?"

"No, no! Back, and the first on your right — the little alley, señor!"

"The devil made this town!" groaned Tirrel. "And the devil still owns it and lives in it!"

He gained the alley's mouth and went through it, cursing with every stride that the horse made. People stared at him. A white sow rounded a corner and blinked uneasily at him; he made the gelding leap it and on he went. He dodged a mother with a child in her arms, by inches. He drove madly through a close cluster of children and set his teeth against the screams he expected, but only heard shouts and angry cries behind him.

"The plaza?"

"There, there, señor! The first street upon your left, and then straightaway!"

He swung the gelding about, and before him, at the end of the street, he had a bright flash of a picture as from a brilliant book. It was well past sundown. Towering western clouds received the sun and raised two great arms of fire into the sky, blinding bright. But all the earth was growing dark, and the city squatted flatter to the ground, and the glory in the sky made it seem more sordid, and the humans who walked the streets were bodiless, soulless silhouettes of blackness.

So it was through Los Cavallos, but yonder Tirrel saw a form of shining brightness, and he knew that it was Molly Malone, and the masculine figure which sat in the saddle was the girl.

So good was her imitation that, at first, he told himself it could not be she.

But it was the girl, and indeed he had arrived in time. In ten seconds he would be beside her!

Molly and her rider disappeared behind the corner building and Tirrel went for the same spot like a bolt. And a weakness of joy rose in his heart, and a savagery of hard work well accomplished possessed him, also, as he sprang forward on the roan to reach the girl. It seemed to him, as he rode, that he was gathering Kate Lawrence in close to his heart, and making her his own, and surrounding her with his love, and making her a part of him forever.

He rounded the corner with a skid that sent the roan staggering, halfway across the street, and then, beyond the dust cloud which his own horse had knocked up, he heard the rapid clanging of rifles, and after them the cry of agony from the lips of a woman. And the scream dwelt and rang in his ears and knocked at his heart, and the iron echoing of the guns beat into his brain.

He knew, then, what had happened, and, bursting forward, he sent the gathering crowd scattering with his shout.

He saw Deputy Sheriff Sam Lowell standing up, with the fallen form in his arms, and heard the white-faced sheriff saying with a stammer: "A woman! Kate Lawrence!"

Tirrel leaned and stared. Molly Malone was already nosing at his shoulder; and now he saw that Kate Lawrence lay without stir in the arms of Sam Lowell. Her head hung far back over the crook of Lowell's arm, and so her throat was exposed, and fast running blood dripped down it.

Chapter Forty-Two

He vaulted into the saddle on Molly. No man had noted him. No man had heeded his coming. But the crowd, packing in closer and closer, took note of the sunset light on the beautiful, still face of Kate Lawrence, and on the tragic face of Sam Lowell. A whisper had run everywhere, answering the heads that thrust out from doors and windows.

There had been a joke, it appeared; and now there was a death!

Tirrel worked his way with difficulty through the narrow street. It had not occurred to him that Sam Lowell could be to blame for the thing that had happened. Sam Lowell was an honest man and a good man, he could have sworn, and beneath this work of the devil was Bramber.

There was no hysterical passion in Tirrel, but a sort of coldness, even in the sweat that formed on his face; so iron is cold with sweat upon the hottest day!

He came to the plaza, and here there was a

greater crowd than he had dreamed it possible that Los Cavallos could furnish, as though thousands had come here to wait for a spectacle. He could guess what that spectacle was to be — the stand-off fight of two famous gunmen, well advertised. But treachery had stepped in between. Now, disappointed, hungry and sniffing for blood, the crowd flowed toward the street from which the scream and the sound of the rifles had flung out at them.

Already the news had rippled over the heads of the mob. It was not Tirrel who had fallen, but a woman, Kate Lawrence, beautiful Kate Lawrence, of all creatures upon the earth!

He probed at the faces of the crowd. His eyes were as clear as the eyes of an eagle. There was not a twitch of nerves in him, but he felt like some precise and dreadful machine, sent for one purpose into the world. He never had known what that purpose was before; he knew now. He must kill Bramber. God had designed him, body and soul, and God had equipped him with experience, and placed him upon the back of a matchless horse, and tempered his soul to steel with hot grief and cold agony, and all to give him the necessary quality for the destruction of Bramber.

Before him he saw the crowd thinning. All were running toward the scene of the shooting, but yonder, at the appointed place, he saw a tall man, with broad, powerful shoulders. He thought he should have known that man if he had seen him only by the dark of the night. There was something in his very soul, made to sensitively perceive the other.

And he called out in a great voice:

"Bramber! Bramber! Nicholas Bramber!"

Nicholas Bramber lurched forward and a gun flashed upward in his hand; Tirrel shot from the hip!

The flash of the gun in the hand of Bramber turned into a long gleam as the weapon was knocked spinning to the ground. Bramber, with an oath, turned and ran for the entrance to the patio. Tirrel laughed and raised his gun to shoot him through the back, but another weapon cracked and he received a shrewd blow across the side of his head.

It flung him out of the saddle, but the very shock of his fall restored his wits.

Looking aside, through the cloud of dust which had puffed up about him, he saw a short, thick-made man, running toward him — Dutch Methuen, the kindly trapper and hunter, the befriender of Jimmy Tirrel. What mattered that? He was the ally of Bramber, and therefore —

Tirrel fired and saw the hunter fall. Then he himself arose, regardless of the blood that

367

poured down the side of his face, and over his clothes. He felt neither haste nor grief nor impatience, so great was the settled surety which had fallen upon him and the utter confidence that this day he would reach Bramber and slay him.

He reached the entrance to the patio. Behind his back was wild shouting as the crowd turned and flowed back to see the great battle, but before him, men shrank to either side.

Only from the corner of the hotel patio, where the twisted trunk of the great wisteria vine formed a nest among the shadows, a rifle glinted and spat fire at Tirrel. He, striding on calmly, turned without haste and fired as the gun darted red at him the second time.

He had no doubt of his aim. A peculiar prescience was on him and a sort of vast foreknowledge. So he fired, and lowered his hand to await results, and he saw the marksman from the shadows lurch forward a reeling step or two, then come to his knees, grasping at his breast with both hands, while the fallen rifle rang on the stones.

Tirrel stepped to him. It was Daniel Finch, with red blood running out between the fingers of his hands, and the fear of death twisting and jerking at his face.

There was in Tirrel no more mercy, then, than Achilles had shown before the walls of

Troy. He raised his revolver a second time and laid it against the forehead of Finch. And poor Dan Finch, with one hand still gripping the wound in his breast, reached up with the other and laid it upon the arm of Tirrel.

"Gimme a chance, for the sake of God, Tirrel! Lemme live. I ain't right to die. I done too much hell. Gimme my last chance to live — and to go straight, man, will you? Tirrel, you ain't gunna step on a worm?"

These words he gasped out, writhing himself closer to the conqueror on his knees.

"Where's Bramber?" asked Tirrel.

"I'll tell you," panted Finch, his eyes hungrily fixed upon the shadowy face of Tirrel. "He's gone up to the rear of the stable, and there he's gunna saddle himself a hoss and try to make a break through the patio and across into the plaza and so out of town."

"Will he stand and fight?"

"No, no! Not him. He sees that it's your day!"

"You've been a dog, Finch. You sent me up here with your horse to die. Is that right?"

"I did! I confess everything. Tirrel, will you gimme leave to live till I write it all down? It'll be something worth while for you to hear and read! I'll pull them all down! I'll show the truth about 'em all!"

But Tirrel already had turned away toward

the stable. There was nothing that he wanted from this crushed and broken man. Whether he lived or died, now, Dan Finch would never be a real man again. It was Bramber, Bramber that he wanted, and now he saw a rider on a tall horse swerve suddenly out from the stable passage. In one leap the pair were past Tirrel. He whirled and sent a shot after the fugitive, but he knew as he fired that he had missed Bramber. Half incredulous, groaning with unsatisfied blood-thirst, he threw himself on the back of the mare and sped in pursuit. He dashed recklessly through the crowd. One man, struck by the working shoulder of the mare, was knocked spinning away and fell upon his face. The others scattered, shouting. The narrow avenue which had opened behind Bramber had not time to close before Tirrel was through it.

He had the better and the more nimble horse, but Bramber had far the greater knowledge of the town, and he used it now to double here and there until he worked out to the Eastern gate of the town.

Tirrel dashed through behind him and saw the form of the fugitive in the dusk of the day, not a furlong before him, and Tirrel laughed, for it seemed to him an irony of nature that the man should have ridden out toward the desert from which Tirrel came, in order to die. For escape he could not. Of that a cruel, mortal certainty was in the heart of Michael Tirrel.

He galloped with a smile upon his lips; his eyes were calmly observant; there was not a nerve in his body that quailed or trembled. And the mare flew beneath him, not with pricking ears, but with them flattened to her back, as though she understood that this was a thunderbolt of vengeance which she carried upon her back.

It was a tall horse and a strong one that Bramber bestrode, but the mare flew up behind like the wind over running water. Twice Bramber turned, and twice he fired. Each time the bullet jerked past the head of Tirrel; and each time he laughed loudly, throwing back his head in the fullness of his unconcern.

He would not have called himself a messenger of God, but he felt armored in the righteousness of his anger.

He came still closer. The dust of the other's horse was in his face, and acrid with alkali in his nostrils. He swooped through it like a stooping bird on its quarry. And then Bramber turned.

For all Tirrel's confidence, he was almost surprised fatally by the speed and the skill with which the tall horse was spun about and driven toward him. A gun flared in his very face. He pulled the trigger of his own Colt, and it jammed!

He flung out his arms, therefore, and grappled Bramber about the body. There was a mighty wrench as though his arms would be torn from their sockets, and that shock ripped each from his saddle. They fell heavily to the ground with Bramber beneath. Something snapped with a dull sharp sound, and Bramber lay still.

Then Tirrel got up from the motionless body. He lighted a match and held it close to the face and saw that the skin of Bramber was darkly suffused but rapidly turning pale. His eyes were partly open. He lay flat on his back, his big arms thrown wide; a slight smile touched the corners of his lips with mockery; and the cloud of mysterious knowledge of man and nature still appeared to be glimmering in his eyes.

But Tirrel knew that he was dead.

He felt no pride in that achievement but a strange satisfaction, and it seemed to him that two-thirds of his strength left him the instant he was sure that Bramber was dead.

He was not a religious man, but Tirrel glanced upward toward the sky where the last of the sunset lights were falling away and where the stars were beginning to come out, pale and small. Antares was a red ghost in the southern horizon, and Saturn burned more bright and big above him. And into Tirrel came a conviction which he never could have confessed to any other man — that the power he had felt in him had been given to him from above, and that it was not his work which had been accomplished that day.

He closed the eyes and composed the body of Bramber decently. Then he remounted the mare and went back to the town.

Chapter Forty-Three

When he came through the gate of the town again, he found the place oddly quiet. There were men and women gathered everywhere, but the groups were only murmuring together. They seemed to know Tirrel instinctively in the dim light. A murmur ran before him, and behind. So he rode straight up to one of those nests of whisperers and demanded:

"Where have they put her?"

"They have carried her into that house, Señor Tirrel."

He went to the place, riding the mare through the arched way into the inner patio. There were half a hundred people gathered there.

As he checked Molly, he heard someone murmur: "He is back. He has killed Bramber! He has killed Bramber!"

So they had known, too, the surety with which he rode forth from that town.

Before a doorway and stairs they fell back before him, so he went that way to a big upper chamber. People whispered softly in the hall.

Tirrel laid his hand on the knob of the door.

"You'd better wait a minute," said a man near him, laying a hand on his sleeve.

"Being dead," said Tirrel coldly, "are there other men claiming her than me?"

"If she dies, I was the death of her," said the other.

"You're Sam Lowell?"

"I'm Lowell."

"You've got a warrant for me, I suppose?"

"God knows I haven't. Dutch Methuen is lyin' pretty sick. He's confessed to save his soul that he murdered Jimmy Tirrel. But don't go into this room until the doctor says that you may."

There was only one part of this speech that was important to Tirrel, at that moment. He clutched the shoulder of the sheriff and said in a trembling voice:

"Not that there's a chance, Lowell!"

"Ah, God knows! There's three bullets went through her. But I — I don't know!"

The door opened softly. A quiet and authoritative voice said:

"Can Tirrel be found?"

"Yes."

"She's whispering his name. He'd better come in."

"I've come," said Tirrel.

He advanced to the doorway.

"Mind you," said the doctor in the same stern, cool voice, "no loud talking. No emotion."

"No," said Tirrel.

"You're shaking like a leaf!" said the doctor suddenly. "You're not Tirrel at all."

"I'm his ghost, then," said Michael Tirrel. "Let me through to her!"

He stepped across the threshold. A lamp burned dimly in a corner. The last of the sunset light was still issuing from the west and it entered through the deep window like a palpable mist of rosy gold. By that light he saw the bed like a heap of snow, and on the bed lay the girl. A woman stood back in the shadows of the corner ready in case of need.

Tirrel tried to cross the room on tiptoes, but his knees failed beneath his weight. Upon those knees he slumped at the side of the bed.

"Doctor!" said a weak voice.

It seemed to Tirrel to come from an infinite distance, as of one departing and calling back half indistinguishable words.

"I'm here," said the doctor.

"Have you found Michael Tirrel? I asked news of him — days and days ago — nobody will tell me! Is he dead?"

The doctor answered: "He's alive and well.

He's here beside your bed."

A cold hand stirred and touched the face of Tirrel.

"Michael!"

"I'm here," said Tirrel.

"Was Molly hurt?"

"Never a hair of her."

"And you, darlin'?"

"Not a touch on me."

"Seems like I blotted up most of the trouble, then," said Kate Lawrence. "Hold fast to my hand, Michael. I want to sleep, now! How many days I've lain here already — how many — "

Her voice went out, and her hand relaxed in his; and there he sat beside her for the whole of the night, and sometimes her grip failed, and again life re-entered her hand.

The doctor never left them.

"Suppose that she's hanging by a life-line and the end of that line is in your hand. Use your will on her, Tirrel. You're a fighting man. They tell me you're the greatest that ever rode a horse into Los Cavallos. Now fight for her life. I've done all that I can!"

So Michael Tirrel fought for her, silently, till his brain reeled and his lip trembled with weakness, but he won.

The stolen greenbacks went to the bank

from which they had been stolen, with the full consent of Michael Tirrel. But there was no human being in the world to challenge his right to the rest of the treasure which he had found under the head, in line with the tiger. It was not such a vast fortune as he had imagined, but it ran to more than four hundred thousand dollars. As Charlie Lawrence said: "It was enough for Kate and Mike. It was enough for us, too!"

They lived at the ranch of her father and mother, they and Molly Malone, who was given a special pasture and a special stall and special care from the loving hands of her mistress and her master. And the rifle rusted on the wall, for danger never again came to Tirrel.

One might say that danger had been frightened away, for men had heard too much about those exploits which had scattered history from Los Cavallos to Apache Crossing and back again. The worst of the badmen never tried to add to his reputation by taking the scalp of Tirrel.

As for the mystery, it was cleared up to the last scrap.

Those deductions which Tirrel himself had drawn seemed accurate enough, and the confessions of Dutch Methuen and Finch cleared up the rest. Neither of them died from their wounds. Methuen, convicted of murder on his own confession, broke jail and escaped. Dan Finch, however, went to prison for fifteen years for the bank robbery.

It was learned that Methuen had taken in Jimmy Tirrel simply because it was feared that Jimmy had the red wallet and the message which the imprisoned convict had sent out in it — the wallet itself being the surety that the message actually was from Smalley. It had been intended for delivery to Bramber himself, who was to come into Los Cavallos to receive the message. But the messenger having lost the wallet on the road, Jimmy Tirrel unluckily was associated with the finding of it.

So he was taken to Dutch Methuen's house, but he managed to secrete the wallet up the creek and give the secret to his brother as he died. Methuen had provided for his death after the arrival of a stranger on whose shoulders the guilt could be placed.

As for those early dangers which Tirrel had run into after his coming to Los Cavallos, they had been, of course, the attempts of Bramber to get rid of a man whom he thought to be Finch; for of the men to whom he had entrusted his plan for the bank robbery, Bramber had known Scrope alone, in person.

It was old Charlie Lawrence who used to relate the long and complicated tale; Tirrel himself would never talk much about it. And often, as the narrative drew toward an end, a listener would say:

"There must have been a sort of a Providence behind this whole thing, Lawrence."

To which the old rancher would usually return:

"That's what some says, but not Michael."

"He doesn't lay it much to Providence?"

"Not a mite."

"What does he lay it to?"

"To the thing that sent him here. To the thing that was chucked away so's he could be delivered up here. To the seven of diamonds!"

THE END